The Jolly Roger

The Jolly Roger

A Story of Sea Heroes and Pirates

Hume Nisbet

MINT EDITIONS

The Jolly Roger: A Story of Sea Heroes and Pirates was first published in 1892.

This edition published by Mint Editions 2021.

ISBN 9781513290232 | E-ISBN 9781513293080

Published by Mint Editions®

MINT
EDITIONS

minteditionbooks.com

Publishing Director: Jennifer Newens
Design & Production: Rachel Lopez Metzger
Project Manager: Micaela Clark
Typesetting: Westchester Publishing Services

Contents

BOOK FIRST

THE WIZARD'S VENTURE

I

How the Ship *Vigo* Came to Witestaple

One morning in the spring of the year 1605 the honest dredgers of Witestaple were startled out of the calm and repose of their customary occupations by the somewhat unusual sight of a stately carrack, which swung round the Isle of Sheppey, and made directly towards their own town front, as if their little harbour was its destination.

It was a handsomely built ship, freshly painted and gilt, with new cordage and sails upon her, as if she had just come out of dock, as indeed she had. A gallant sight she presented to the staring eyes of these watchers on the shore, as she bore in before that easterly breeze—all sails set and bulging, with ensigns and pennons flying gaily, the morning sun gilding the sea under her, and herself like a purple haze against that golden glory.

The dredgers of Witestaple were an independent and a chartered body of men, who took life remarkably easy, and made the most of their royal privileges. They were rather conservative also in their ideas about strangers, and did not welcome them very graciously unless they considered something worth while could be made out of them. But a newly-bedecked carrack, fitted out for a sea-voyage as this one was, looked like something worth while, and therefore not to be regarded in the light of an ordinary stranger. She must have wanted something special from Witestaple, else she would never have turned out of her way down the Channel; and that something flavoured of profit to these hardy burghers of the waters; therefore with one accord they set down their morning mugs of beer, so that they might the better use their hands for the shading of their eyes; and rose from their seats, so that they might be ready to stroll down to the pier head, and lend a help with the ropes, by the time the carrack got there.

"Whoever is at the wheel o' that ship knows his way in," remarked one of the loungers as they stood waiting and watching.

"Ay, and they seem mighty short-handed by the way they handle her," observed another.

"A fine, fast craft, but curiously emblazoned," said a third.

"Lord a mussy! if she ain't a flying the wizard's ensign! Look, Aaron, the queer signs all over it done in silver, same as he shows up on the hill—stars and snakes, and sich-like devilish devices; and, by all the powers, yonder the old 'un comes with his witch sister to meet them. This is a curious sight, honest lads, and something that our good king might like to know about, if anyone could be found bold enough to tell it."

"Perchance, William, only the less one meddles with sich-like cattle the better for himself. I, for one, feel like going back to my beer."

"Right you are, uncle, so will we with you." Thus, as with one accord the dredgers had left their work and come to the jetty to see the ship, they all went back again and left the harbour clear, for that was their habit and how they were wont to receive unwelcome strangers.

Ancient families have always peculiar habits of their own to distinguish them from the people of yesterday. The Honourable Company of Royal Dredgers had pedigrees reaching as far back as any noble in the land—from the time when William the Conqueror granted to them exclusive fishing and dredging rights to the present day. And they had taken means to retain these rights, and transmit them jealously from father to son. From generation to generation the eldest son inherited the rights and drew the dues, and so never lost his interest in his native land. The younger sons, as is the case with the aristocracy, could go off and better their conditions as they liked best; so they mostly became either servants to their eldest brother, or else went off as sailors, while the heirs remained ashore on duty, and looked after the family privileges as eldest sons and heirs generally do.

While the industrious dredgermen were regaling themselves in the sea-facing yard of The Neptune, and showing their independence by ostentatiously neglecting the strangers, the bulky carrack was slowly and majestically advancing towards the deserted pier, the tide being at the time high enough to carry it safely into the harbour.

It was a picturesque sight, with its lofty and richly decorated forecastles, towering stern, and bulging sides. The anchors hung at the bows ready for dropping, while the men were hard at work taking in sail. They worked leisurely in those days, and seemed to be rather short-handed from the way they laboured; but as the wind was light, and their progress easy, that did not seem to matter much in the present instance.

Onward she glided, slowing off as the sails were furled one by one, and throwing her shadow in front of her until it reached nearly to that all but deserted quay.

HUME NISBET

A carrack of about five hundred tons, very lofty in the bows and stern, with the main deck low and exposed, and with but little bulwark to protect it, at present; in time of war or during a storm, however, they used nettings to keep off boarders and guard the passengers.

She was coming on, and showing more of her bows, with the sides fore-shortened; curved, rounded upper bows plentifully ribbed and barred, with her four anchors hanging over, and the figure-head, a female half-length, protruding under the bowsprit, picturesque and clumsy-looking as a Thames barge of the present day, only more so, with her gun-holes and guns sticking out at every available space, from the top line right down to almost the water edge.

An old ship, and of Spanish build, which had been recently thoroughly overhauled, patched, and fresh painted, so that she glowed upon the waters in all the glory of her new coat. All the sails were at last reefed, so that she was crawling in with the tide, and the impetus of the wind which had lately bellied out her sails.

A four-master, with two yards on the fore and mainmasts, and lateen sails on the small stern poles. Heavy masts the two mainmasts were, with solid cages at the top of the shrouds, from where guns also stuck out, as indeed they did from every part, fore and aft. Whatever her present mission might be, she was plentifully equipped as far as firearms were concerned.

Along her exposed side could be counted eighteen large guns; three more lay flush with the maindeck; a double tier of twelves could be seen on the poop, facing the forecastle, to cover boarders; which, with the usual number on the stern, would make her a sixty-gun carrack, the description of vessel which explorers used for a long sea voyage in those days.

"Will she do, William?"

There were only three figures on the quay end, watching the approach of the ship.

An old gentleman, with thin, fragile figure, dressed plainly in black velvet, with rapier at his belt to denote his quality; a weak-looking, elderly gentleman he appeared to be, who trembled as he leaned heavily upon his ebony staff, with scanty white hair and beard, and watery, bleared eyes, which originally had been dark-brown.

His companions were a lady, who appeared to be as old as himself, and a man of about thirty-nine years of age, florid-faced and inclined to stoutness.

The lady was costumed plainly, and also in sable hue, and she too leaned heavily upon a staff of ebony. On her head she wore a black hood, which nearly concealed her face, allowing only the straight, thin nose and sharp chin to show, with the piercing dark eyes, which glowed in the shadow, and a single patch of white hair to show out amongst the black cloth—a sallow and withered-looking face, albeit showing very few wrinkles upon it.

The younger man at first sight looked commonplace and plebeian, and he carried no sword at his thigh; his dress also was perfectly plain and saffron-tinted, an overlapping linen collar and cuffs being the only relief to an otherwise monotony of uninteresting colours.

He wore his brown hair long and his beard short cut and pointed. Not a bad-looking face, but ordinary as far as features were concerned, with the exception of the large and bright blue eyes, which darted vivaciously from side to side, taking in every detail within range, and never for an instant keeping still.

It was to him that the old gentleman addressed his inquiry:—

"Will she do, William, lad?"

"As far as looks be; she is as gaily bedizened as a young bride; and so that she is sound within I can see no reason why you should not trust your fortunes with her."

"Good, William, good; she is sound, I warrant, for her age, which is under twenty."

"A good, seasonable age for a woman, Sir John, and not too old for a ship, either, so that neither have had rough usage in their youth. My friend, Sir Walter, took her from the Dons, didn't he?"

"Not Sir Walter, but the Admiral Drake."

"Ha! methinks I see an old friend on board," cried the younger man, shading his eyes with his hand. "As I live, my old shipmate Humphrey Bolin!"

"Ay, he is my master for the voyage," answered the old man; "specially recommended as a good seaman and an honest man, who has been well tried both at home and abroad."

"I have heard something of his trials at home," muttered William, with a laugh and a bright sparkle in his rolling eye. "Good old Humphrey, he hath a shrew for a better half."

"Ahoy there, ashore! lend a hand and catch a rope."

"Ay, ay, master," replied William, leaping forward and dexterously catching the line which the boatswain had flung towards him, drawing it hand over hand until he had the hawser well in, which he twisted round the post.

Next moment the anchors were dropped with a rattle of chains, and the carrack was butting and rubbing softly against the planks of the pier, while the master had left the wheel, and, followed by a couple of sailors and a boy of about fifteen, leaped ashore from the maindeck, which was almost level with the quay.

"Sir John Fenton?" inquired the master, touching his hat to the old gentleman.

"That is my name; and yours is Humphrey Bolin, I believe?"

"Yes, sir; old Humphrey I am now; and there stands young Humphrey, whom I took the liberty to bring with me as cabin-boy."

"And the dog Martin, Humphrey, where is he?" broke in the voice of the saffron-garbed stranger—a rich, clear voice, which made the master wheel round abruptly and examine him closely.

"The dog Martin is dead; yet I have a true son of his onboard. But who are you that asks the question?"

"Hast thou forgotten me, Humphrey?"

"Say that again, if you please."

Humphrey Bolin shut his eyes.

"Hast thou forgotten me, Humphrey Bolin?"

"That is the voice of jesting Will Shakespeare, my old shipmate on the *Revenge*. And now I see thy eyes, they flash the same merry light, although thou hast grown out of all recognition. Art thou the same lad?"

"No, Humphrey; but for all that my name is Will Shakespeare. When we chased the Spaniards from the Channel, methinks I was a different man."

"Ay, I heard that thou hadst turned mummer, and drank thy sack with lords. But, zounds! thou didst look better on Queen Bess's beer, bad as it was."

"Yes, Humphrey, lad, I was young then, without a feather-weight of care; and thou, also, hadst not married."

"Tush! let the past be, Will," growled out Humphrey gruffly, with a changed face.

"Is that thy son, master?" inquired the old lady, fixing her bright eyes on the boy.

"Ay, madam; my only child."

"So. He is a pretty boy, and will see some strange sights before he comes home again, if he goes with us."

"Ay, madam, his mind is set on going. Besides, I have no one to leave him with, so that it is as well that he should accompany me."

"Better, Master Humphrey Bolin, for I shall take charge of him, and make a man of him. Come, young Humphrey, give me thy arm and show me through the ship."

II

NECROMANCY

Sir John Fenton dabbled in the dark arts, and was known throughout the country-side as the Wizard of Witestaple. He was not a very formidable magician in himself—or rather would not have been, if it had not been for his familiar, the Witch of Canterbury, for so this dark-eyed and withered-looking companion who had watched the ship coming in was generally known.

It was not a very hard matter to win the reputation of a witch or a wizard in the days of Queen Bess or her Solomon successor, James,—a much safer time during the former reign than in the present for the possessor of the evil gift, as the kingly witch-hunter had a keen nose and an uncommon zeal in the game of fighting the devil and all his ministers.

During the reign of Queen Elizabeth Sir John Fenton had turned his attention to the study of astrology and necromancy. He had been a pupil of the famous Dr. Dee, and was fairly respected in the court of the virgin queen in consequence of his supposed gifts.

But with the crowning of King James men of his leanings considered it to be the best part of valour to put some distance between themselves and the capital, so he had prudently retired to a little estate which he possessed on the Kentish coast, and where he could continue his studies in secret, giving shelter to such-like professors of the forbidden science as came in his direction, with a smack always at anchor close by, in order to carry him out of danger, if the need for flying happened.

Penelope Ancrum had, some months before this, sought and found shelter in his mansion; she had fled from Canterbury, after making that place too hot to hold her, and in her Sir John had found a veritable treasure. All that Dr. Dee's young man had been able to accomplish this mysterious old woman had surpassed; where Sir John had been long fumbling in the dark and meeting only failures and rebuffs, Mistress Penelope cleared up with remarkable promptitude and success. Under her hands Sir John was able to call up whatever demon he particularly fancied, and see sights which had before been only vague surmises.

As Dr. Dee, in spite of his faith and enthusiasm, had never been able to arrive at any satisfactory results until he joined partnership with that gifted adventurer Edward Kelly, so Sir John had entered into familiar intercourse with many before the coming of Penelope, suffering grievous disappointments; for the spirits were most erratic in their coming and going, generally maliciously leaving him in the lurch when most wanted.

Now, however, the old gentleman stood upon a firm basis, and there were no more uncertainties or sportive tricks on the part of the Imps of Darkness. Penelope had them all under her complete control.

No magic mirrors were needed, as in the case of Dr. Dee and Edward Kelly, but a certain formula was required, as no crowned head likes to be approached *sans cérémonie*, and the devils who came to the call of Penelope were all princes of greater or lesser magnitude, from his Royal Highness Lucifer to the meanest of his imps; but as the times went Penelope did her feats with fewer preparations than most of her sisters in witchcraft used.

Before the coming of the Witch of Canterbury Sir John had been regarded by the neighbours as a harmless lunatic, and his magic dabbling as a foolish waste of time. But now that opinion altered; he was now allowed to have at last broken through the magic circle, and to have signed his name in the devil's private ledger. With the aid of his familiar, he could at length perform feats at which the strongest man trembled.

But never without the presence and aid of Penelope; indeed, he was never to be seen now absent from her when they walked abroad. The fishermen said that their spirits melted when she fixed her burning eyes upon them, so that they had to drop their lids; and that when they lifted them again, even in the broad daylight, they had seen her change herself, sometimes into a cat or a dog, or someother strange and uncouth beast.

She had fled for her life from Canterbury after a few weeks' stay there, but where she had come from before no one knew. She was white-haired and old-looking, with the exception of her eyes and teeth, which were singularly bright and well preserved; but few people could have told exactly what she was like after the first steady look into her dark and glowing eyes.

"She is not the devil," remarked Sir John to his friend Shakespeare, after he had been introduced to this domestic treasure; "for I have seen the Prince of Darkness in her company. And she is human, like the rest of us, for she is vulnerable to physical pain; but in all else she is a marvel. She has also the great secret of renewing her life and youth, and will take me where I can find the ingredients for the elixir."

"Has she tried it on herself?" inquired Shakespeare a little incredulously.

"Yes; thirteen times have I become a young girl since my first youth," answered Penelope, who had glided in upon them as they sat over their sack in the sitting-room of Sir John's mansion.

It was Shakespeare's first visit to his former friend since they had parted in London two years previously, and they were waiting upon the coming of Humphrey Bolin, who had been hard at work all day seeking recruits for the voyage; if he was successful, two more days would see them all afloat.

"How many years ago is it since your first youth, Mistress Ancrum?" inquired the illustrious guest, fixing his deep blue eyes upon the dark eyes of the witch.

"Eleven hundred and thirteen years, Master William Shakespeare. I was born in the year 370, just after the Emperor Theodosius drove the Picts and Scots from London."

Penelope spoke gravely, never moving her steady eyes from the twinkling orbs of her questioner. As she looked the humorous expression changed, while his glance became a fixed stare. Then, as his eyelids fell before her regard, a subtle smile of triumph curled up her thin lips and displayed her small white teeth.

"Yes, Master Shakespeare, I can show you afterwards, if you wish to see, some of the kings who have lived and passed away during my long life; they may help you in your future dramas."

Shakespeare gave a start, and passed his hand over his broad high brow, as one does who has been beset with a vagueness.

"Wilt thou try my skill?"

"Yes, Mistress Penelope; yet I seem already to have witnessed that battle of Valentia."

"It happened two years before I was born. Sir John, what do you see now?"

"My master, Humphrey Bolin, with his recruits and sailors."

"Where are they?"

"Entering the park gate."

"Now, Master Shakespeare, you will be able to prove Sir John; they should be here within five more minutes if he has foretold truly. How many of them are coming?"

"Humphrey Bolin and his son lead the way, followed by seven new men and five of the old crew."

Sir John spoke monotonously, with his head on his chest and his eyes half closed, while Penelope stood in the centre of the lamplit room, stooping over her crutch, which she held with both hands. She was for a woman very tall and thin.

"Good Sir John, are they willing to come here?"

"No, they come most unwillingly."

"But they are forced to come for all that. Listen, William Shakespeare; you will hear them knock in another moment."

As she finished speaking a loud knocking was heard at the hall door.

"Come, gentlemen, we will let them in, and see it they enter in the order which Sir John has described."

III

The Men Enlist for Long Service

The moon was shining brightly over the shingley walk and between the thinly-clad branches of the old oak trees in the park beyond, falling in chequered patches of pale green upon the tender young grass—such a landscape as only fair Kent could furnish in the beginning of the seventeenth century.

An old-fashioned, gabled, and mullioned-windowed mansion, surrounded by extensive grounds, with well-cared-for park of centuries growth, the grass soft and thick as the plot in front of Canterbury Cathedral, such a pile as is not easily disturbed or broken up; reaches of oak avenues, where the deer disported, and lovers had walked over under the summer suns and the autumn moons, losing themselves in that misty past, as they were lost now from mortal ken.

"Pity Sir John Fenton was a bachelor, and the last of his race, with so fair a heritage, unless his dream of renewed youth comes to pass," thought William Shakespeare, as he leaned against the doorway of the hall, and looked over this moonlit panorama of knarled oaks and bosky dells, with the silver mists creeping along from the distant sea, and mingling with the under-growth.

The seamen and recruits stood in the path, with the moonlight showing them up, and Humphrey Bolin and his son in advance, occupying the steps near to the open door.

Yes, they were standing as they had come, in the order that Sir John had mentioned, a most unwilling crowd, upon this enchanted ground; for the Witestaple recruits had communicated to the sailors the darkly mysterious character of their employers and the reputation of the house to which they had been invited; hence, although curiosity, with the mention of the high pay, had drawn them along, their superstitious fears were now tugging them backwards, so that they resembled very unhappy schoolboys just after the holidays.

"Welcome, my brave fellows; come into the light and be sworn to our service before supper," cried Sir John Fenton, as he showed himself bare-headed at the doorway, with his familiar, Penelope, at his side.

"So please you, Sir John," replied Humphrey, rather reluctantly, "my men have deputed me to ask a few questions before they decide to take service with your honour."

"By all means, Humphrey; that is only to be expected. But come inside and ask them."

"So please your honour, they would rather have the matter settled outside."

"Ha! let me manage these foolish fellows, Sir John," here cried Penelope, pushing past her master and taking her stand on the steps, where she could face the discontented group, the moon striking full upon her white tresses and pallid cheeks.

"You know me, men of Witestaple?"

"Ay, ay, the witch, the Witch of Canterbury, lads; let us get home while we can," shouted one of the recruits as they all shrank back.

"Stay where you are, fellows!"

Penelope, as she uttered the words, threw out her thin white hand towards them—a shapely and youthful looking hand it was which now pointed each one out in turn.

"Why, what ails the men? Are they afraid to go to sea?"

"No."

"Then come within without further parley, or I'll make tom-cats of you and send you all home mewing."

The threat was a singular one and seemingly took effect, for with a groan they moved towards her.

"Come inside, my brave fellows, and we will take your oaths and fix your time of servitude."

Truly Penelope, in spite of her great age and ancient appearance, had a majestic and taking manner with her which few could long resist. As William Shakespeare watched her now, stretched up to her full height, with her dark eyes blazing and her lips curling scornfully from her white even teeth, he likened her more to a high priestess of some pagan deity than to one of the poor witches which were so often seen at Smithfield. She had power, and knew how to exercise it.

When they were all within the study, which had been lighted up for this event, Sir John took his judicial chair, and placing himself within it, with Penelope on his right hand and his friend Shakespeare on his left, while the sailors and recruits stood before him, Humphrey Bolin and his son a little apart, then he addressed them in tones cheerful, if a little tremulous with old age.

"Men, we are going on a long sea-voyage, which may fill out one year and perhaps two; but I am willing to pay you from tonight at double the ordinary wages for three years, whether we return sooner or not. Is that fair?"

"Quite fair, your honour; only we would like to know where we are bound for, what we have to do, and who are to be with us on the voyage, before we join."

"Where we are going to is a secret for the present; we shall take South America on our way. Your duty will be to sail the ship and protect passengers; and as for them, why, they will consist of myself and my friend here."

"The witch?"

"Yes. You need have no fear of either of us, for we shall not meddle with you in your duties. The master, Humphrey Bolin there, will be your commander; and as for oaths, you will bind yourselves to his service. Now are you satisfied with my terms?"

"I should say they were satisfied with your terms, Sir John. Why, as the times go, you are treating them in a princely fashion—I would say kingly, only that the example set by his most gracious majesty the witch-hunter does not lead towards extravagance. Say at once, sirrahs, that you are delighted to sail in the good ship *Vigo*, and have done with it."

"We are delighted to sail in the good ship *Vigo*," answered the seamen and recruits with one accord as they fixed their eyes on those of Penelope, who had taken them so vigorously in hand, and with such complete success.

"That is as it should be with brave Englishmen who fear nothing, not even the devil and his devices. I promise you all merry times on board, lively adventures by sea and land, and well-plenished purses on your return. Master Humphrey, bustle with your muster-book. Master Shakespeare will help you at the writing of the names. And after the men make their marks give them a month's pay in advance, and then to supper."

This from Sir John Fenton, as he held out a well-filled purse to the master, Humphrey Bolin, who took it and laid it on the table.

Although there did not appear to be very much enthusiasm on the part of the men, yet none of them showed any longer reluctance to take service under Sir John. Shakespeare, always ready to oblige, and in no way dignified or raised by his already widespread fame, sat down at the table willingly, and dipping the pen into the inkpot, wrote out the names of each recruit as they came forward to give it, make their X, and receive from Humphrey a month's wages in advance. Not much alacrity, the temporary scribe thought, while he watched each face as it came forward and retired again apathetically. But there were no more murmurs or objections; they took their money passively, made their marks doggedly, and went back to their places with downcast eyes.

"Not the most enthusiastic crew in the world, Sir John, to go to sea with," remarked the poet, as he wrote down finally the name of the boy Humphrey.

"They will do their work well and faithfully, I warrant, for all that," replied the witch Penelope. "I have them all well under control. Would you like to have a specimen of my power over these uncouth rustics?"

"Not tonight, Penelope," answered Sir John from his chair, as he made a movement to rise. "We must not frighten our crew at the outset with your extraordinary gifts and controls; besides, I can smell supper in the distance. Give me your arm, good Master Bolin; while I shall be obliged if you will assist Mistress Ancrum, friend Will."

As Sir John spoke the bell of the tower was clanged for supper, and taking the lead, followed by the others, he marched solemnly into the dining-hall.

IV

An Old English Supper

Sir John Fenton was a dignified old gentleman, despite his dark pastimes and general tokens of bodily decay; he also held rigid principles regarding the duties of hospitality.

He was preparing to embark upon a long and uncertain voyage in search of the two great aims of philosophers in those days,—treasure and the elixir of life,—both of which had been promised to him by his assistant, Penelope.

Wealth he did not require so much as the gift of renewed youth, for as the times went he was considered fairly wealthy, and as he had long lived a retired life, without many expenses, much of his yearly income had remained untouched. But a man is never so wealthy or so old that the treasure-bait will not tempt.

He had another reason for wishing to quit England for a time: his daily and nightly studies had been noted by the new king, as well as his growing fortune, and his friends at court well knew that any hour might see him a prisoner and his estates confiscated. King James was on the watch, and only waiting until he had settled other matters of greater import before he pounced down upon this titled and wealthy victim.

Sir John had been all his life a patron of poetry and literature, and had done much to earn the gratitude of the great dramatist; so it was for the purpose of warning him of his danger that William Shakespeare had ridden down to Kent during one of his short holidays. It delighted him to know that the aged knight was taking time by the forelock; so, having leisure, he determined to wait now and see the venture safely away.

He was also greatly interested in the strange woman who had flung in her lot with the old knight, and somewhat awed with her weird influence over everyone, himself amongst the number. She moved him wonderfully when she looked at him,—an extraordinary female, who might have been anything excepting a common personage, for in all that she did or said there was a decided individuality that stamped her quite apart from other women, old or young.

For one thing, it was impossible to guess her age. She had the skin and hair of a very old woman, and when in repose she looked ancient enough, but when excited she seemed to fling from her the fetters of age, speaking and moving as actively as any young woman; her voice was singularly full and piercing, yet monotonous in its subdued tones; her eyes were clear and flashing, and the outlines of her face in no way worn or haggard; a firm round chin, with oval cheeks, sharply defined nose, and well-curved if thin lips; the teeth also were like the teeth of a girl, white and small, but sharp-pointed. If Penelope Ancrum had only been able to laugh, which she was not, she would have looked charming and almost beautiful, even with her parchment-like complexion.

The lacking charm was softness. There was no trace of womanly tenderness about that correctly shaped countenance, or in those brilliant dark eyes; they seemed able to pierce the watcher through and through when they turned upon him, and produce that peculiar fascination which possesses the imaginative when looking from a great height into a dangerous depth—a drawing-down feeling that was not to be resisted.

It was a relentless and scornful visage, expressing in every line and curl of the small mouth innate powers and self-control. During the supper she behaved as any other well-bred lady might have done, speaking little herself and listening with quiet attention. For the hour she had laid aside her spells; and as the supper was lavish, the men seemed to have forgotten their fears, and enjoyed themselves in a boisterous fashion at their end of the table. A good supper, with beer at discretion and a month's pay in advance in their pockets, gave quite a different aspect to the engagement to which they had pledged themselves.

It was a fine old English dining-hall, well lighted up with candles, the sides and roof wainscotted and panelled with polished oak, blackened by time, and hung with trophies of the chase, hunting implements, and armour of different periods; for the Fentons were an old race in the land.

There were two huge fireplaces, both plenished up with spitting and blazing logs, for the wind being easterly the night was chilly; and the centre of the floor was filled up with the long table, covered with good things of a substantial order—smoking rounds of corned beef, roasted sirloins, and pigs' heads, venison pasties, and sweets; and, as was the prevailing fashion, they were all spread upon the tablecloth at once, and served out according to taste. Great flagons of strong home-brewed ale stood at intervals between the sailors and servitors, while above the salt-cellar were the more choice brands of foreign wines for the quality.

Sir John, like the patriarchal country gentleman that he was, permitted no magic or mystery to interfere with the important duty of feasting. He did not eat or drink much himself, by reason of his tender teeth and troubled digestion, but he encouraged his guests in every possible way to do their utmost with the viands.

He occupied the head of the table, with Penelope on his right side and Shakespeare on his left; next to Shakespeare sat Humphrey Bolin, while Penelope had secured the boy Humphrey at her side. From the first she had made a special favourite of the lad, and helped him lavishly with the tit-bits.

"You'll spoil my son, ma'am, I fear," said Humphrey the elder, as he looked over to Penelope and the boy. "He ought to be with the men if he wants to become a good sailor."

"He'll be a good sailor, never fear, Master Bolin, all the better for learning how to behave like a gentleman at table," answered Penelope. "I mean to take him under my special charge, and teach him better things than the hauling of a tarry rope."

Humphrey looked a little troubled at this reply, but said no more, applying himself instead with more vigour to his platter.

They were all good trenchermen, with the exception of their host. Penelope proved by her performances that age had not spoilt her enjoyment of the good things of life; while the boy laid in with the gusto of healthy youth; Shakespeare and Humphrey behaving as strong men usually do about the age of forty: eating steadily and drinking deeply, while talking to each other and studying the traces which time had wrought upon each since the days when they had fought together.

"Ah, that was a great time for England, Will, and little did either of us think what we would have grown to in the few years that have passed,—you the player to his Majesty, and myself promoted to such a fine ship."

"What have you been doing all these years, old friend?" asked the bard.

"Married and become widower, for one thing," replied Humphrey gloomily.

"Ay, I heard something of thy fortunes in Hymen's market. Is the boy your only one?"

"The only one left, Will. I shall tell you anon all about it, but not to spoil a good supper like this. I have been a widower for four years now, and since then have been to foreign parts mostly—a wild life, Will, while you have been roystering at the court."

"Not all feasting and roystering there, Humphrey lad, but as hard steering through the envious tongues as you may have had amongst the shoals abroad. I carry the traces of many a stiff battle since we joyously chased the Spaniards, as you do, lad. We both show that we have lived, I think,—both somewhat scanty of hair at our temples and with some crows' feet round our eyes."

"But you have won fame, Will?"

"Ay, of a kind, as you won your old love."

"Tush! man; never speak of it now. How can you breathe the two together.

"Both are females, Humphrey, and uncertain."

"But you have your plays to comfort you, Will."

"As you have your son, lad; and a pretty youth he is—finer looking than you were, Humphrey, I fancy, at his age."

"Yes, he is a good boy, and has the makings of a man in him, if he is not spoilt before he gets his wisdom-teeth," answered Humphrey, looking fondly over to his blue-eyed, golden-haired son.

"He has his father's luck with the women," whispered Shakespeare; "see how he has won favour with our witch."

"Worse luck for him, I'm thinking," replied Humphrey, with a gloomy scowl.

Supper was at length over, and pipes with tobacco brought on, when, after a puff or two, Sir John rose from the table.

"Master Bolin and lads, the night is young, so I pray you all enjoy yourselves for an hour or so. There are some packages to take with you to the ship tonight. Do not forget this duty, or to return early in the morning for the rest of the baggage. Tomorrow night you may enjoy, in the town, saying goodbye to your friends; but remember that we sail first tide on Saturday."

"Ay, ay, your honour; we will not neglect our duty."

"Right. Now a full bumper to the success of our venture, and then I will bid you goodnight."

The bumpers were filled up and tossed over cheerfully. The men had forgotten that their owner was a minion of the devil, and their hearts were light with his generous fare.

"Come, Penelope, to our work."

V

Humphrey Bolin Tells His Story

The table was cleared, and the men were enjoying themselves in pot-house fashion along with the servitors, who were now released from duty, drinking, smoking, and spinning yarns as they crowded round the bottom of the table, where the lower fire was, leaving the upper end to Humphrey and his friend, while young Humphrey had laid himself down beside the hounds in front of the top fireplace and fallen asleep.

"When a man ships for a voyage like this, Will Shakespeare," observed Humphrey solemnly, when they had filled up their glasses and lighted their pipes, "there is no knowing what the future may bring forth; and it's the same with marriage. But there, you are a married man yourself, and of longer standing than I have been, and you must know more about it than I do."

"Not so much, Humphrey, if you have lived with your wife. You see, my Annie is at Stratford, and so I only see her occasionally."

"Ah, that makes a difference, mayhap. You saw my Dolly once, the prettiest and sweetest wench round Plymouth."

"She was all that, Humphrey, and should have made you happy."

"And so she did for the first eight years; no man could have been more so, which made the last four years all the harder to bear, for it was so unaccountable to a plain man of ordinary comprehension like myself.

"Our good old Queen—bless her memory for the greatest woman of any age—did not treat her defenders in the most generous fashion, but her captains made up for her nearness; and so, after my marriage with Dolly Shuttleworth, the old Admiral Drake found me out, and gave me a nice snug berth in the harbour, with a smack of my own to look after the waters, not much to do, and never a night hardly from home, with my wages regularly paid at the end of every month."

"You ought to have grown fat under those circumstances, Humphrey," remarked Shakespeare, with a smile.

"I did, Will, fat and contented, with never a wish or a care in life. Dolly was all that a man could desire—sweet-tempered and obedient, wishing for nothing more than the company of her husband, and thinking every hour during the day how best she could spoil him with comfort and love when he came home.

"Young Humphrey there arrived first, about a year after we were married; and then, following hard upon his heels, burst out a merry troop of boys and girls until we had six—six in eight years—three girls and two boys, besides our eldest, young Humphrey there.

"Dolly's hands, you may be sure, were full enough now of work, and the cottage was not such a one as an orderly bachelor might have fixed upon for repose; yet to me, coming from my short outings with the smack, there seemed to be nothing amiss that I could not find my sea-boots of a morning, or when I found them, after a hard search, that they should be filled up chock-a-block with cockle-shells and other treasures of childhood, placed there for safety. Ah, Will, lad, I have gone many a day, as the pilgrims did to their saint's shrine, with pebbles in my boots, and lain down many a night beside Dolly on sharp edges of mussels, without noting it as anything out of the ordinary. Lord! Lord! how those sharp corners haunt me, now that the little hands are gone which laid them so carefully between the sheets!"

Humphrey Bolin drew his horny hand sharply across his eyes, and tilted up his glass with a gulp, refilling it again from the flagon of sack before he continued.

"Did I grumble at the time? Of course I did; and swore lustily also, as is the manner of men when they are put out by trifles; but now, could I only bring back the sharpest shell, with the little hands that laid them, how blest a man I'd be tonight!

"Ay, Will Shakespeare, I have lain for four years in many a bed since, some of them rough, some of them well spread, but never a shell to remind me of all I have lost.

"When our sixth was born, Dolly had a hard time of it, and lay long afterwards weakly and without much interest in the doings of her household; but at last she mended, and then the change began which turned my heaven into hell.

"I married my wife for love, you know, Will Shakespeare, and I loved her straight through to the end; further than that, for I wouldn't even at this space put the finest lady in the land in Dolly's shoes, unstable as she has made me. You see, it is just this: eight years of heaven is enough for any man's life, good or bad, that's how I think now; and no other woman could ever reach up to her,—at least, I could not take the interest in any other woman to make it worth my while to count her like Dolly; and, after Dolly, give me war and adventure, with the thought of those eight years of bliss divine to make me fall asleep o' nights.

"I wasn't quite idle during these eight years—sometimes we weary even of happiness. I studied sea-craft during that time, and qualified myself as a master. I didn't know that there were anymore voyages afore me, but I made myself equal to them if they had to be done. I learnt the tides and the stars, and how to work the astrolabe, so that even Drake owned I was fit to take command of a ship and sail to foreign parts. Ah! how do we know what forces us to get ready against the future!

"The last baby which Dolly had troubled her sorely. That was the beginning of my unrest. She was long in mending, as I have told you, and took all sorts of curious fancies into her head, until I verily began to think that she had been bewitched by some malignant demon."

"Possibly the midwife bewitched her. They are mostly evil enough for any devilishness to vex and punish husbands," remarked Shakespeare gravely.

"It might have been," replied Humphrey. "They were all harridans that officiated at such times with us, and made rare havoc with our comfort while they reigned supreme. Most women, as a rule, are given more or less to jealousy, but I must say that Dolly had none of it until the birth of our sixth. It was after that time when she began to watch my actions at home and abroad, giving me no rest or peace, but filled with the most outrageous suspicions about people whom no one but a fool would have looked at with such a wife as she herself was.

"At the first I tried to reason with her on the foolishness of her ideas, but it was useless. She said that my explanations were lies, and all my endearments hypocritical. I had been free in my behaviour always with both women and men, as a man will be who loves confidently and knows that he is trusted and loved in return; now, for the sake of peace, I gave up my corner at the hostel and all my former friends, so that I might convince her that her company was enough for me.

"But naught could satisfy or please her now; her temper broke, and she reviled me because I stuck at home, for doing a wrong to my inclination.

"I never was a patient man, as you know, Will, and after a time, seeing that she grew worse everyday, either flouting me for my falseness or sulking for days at a time, I spoke rough when badgered beyond my strength; and so together we made such scenes as were bad for the children to listen to and see. It was a worrying war every week long, with perhaps only half a day of patched truce between."

"Did she drink?" inquired Shakespeare at this point.

"No more than a woman might with all safety, and that only honest ale, which can harm no one. She was bewitched, I tell you, and possessed of a devil that tortured us all to the verge of madness.

"Then the great calamity fell upon us in the midst of our unhappiness which parted us forever, although at the moment I thought it might have drawn us once more together. The spotted visitation came to the town and swept off the whole of our other children at one fell sweep, leaving us empty and desolate, with only Humphrey there to hold on by."

Again Humphrey Bolin paused chokingly, while his friend laid his hand tenderly upon his arm.

"After this her madness took a wilder turn: she accused me of cruelty to the children that were gone, and taunted me constantly with the cuffings that I had given them when they had misbehaved, as if every cuff was not already seared in my heart. It was harder to bear than jealousy now, for she spoke about them all day and all night too, often, as if she only had loved or been loved by them, charging me with hating them and wishing them dead. She loathed my presence, she said, and showed it by every action, lamenting constantly her ruined life, and wondering why she had taken me, instead of her cousin from London.

"I might have been more patient with her under her heavy grief, but wasn't it mine as well as her's? And no man can bear with patience the hatred of his wife, or to hear the name of an old rival constantly on her lips. I cursed roundly at times, and flung out of the house to seek comfort with my old bottle friends. But they also failed me, for I seemed to be a stranger now, and could take no pleasure in their jests, but sat with moody brow amongst them, spoiling all their merriment and drinking deeply without finding a whit of comfort in it.

"Her image followed me everywhere; not as she had been in the sweet past, but as she was in the present: sullen, revengeful, and unforgiving, flouting me with her family, whom she had taken to magnify, while she disparaged mine, until one would have thought that she had been a princess who had degraded herself by taking a clown to husband.

"It grew worse everyday and harder to bear, for I loved her more savagely than ever, and I could see that her madness and misery were sapping her life away, while it was out of my power to help her. During the last two years, so miserable was I when the drink was out of me that it is a wonder I did not finish it all up, and I think only for young Humphrey I would have done it.

"At last the end came, and the devil went out of her only with her life. She died cursing me and calling me her murderer and the murderer of her children, died with black hatred glaring out of her eyes and wild words of loathing on her lips, leaving me nothing to remember her by excepting horror at her unhappiness and injustice, for I was a true and loving, if a careless and rough husband, in the days of my contentment."

"My muse has not treated me so badly," murmured Shakespeare.

"I buried her and put my son to school, and then flung up my berth ashore and took to sea, with a horror for all womankind which has never left me, or ever will while I live, roughing it in all quarters of the globe, sometimes with Sir Walter Raleigh before he was imprisoned. We had some bracing work on the Spanish coasts, but mostly for the new East India Company, through the China Seas.

"The last voyage I made was with Captain Martin Pringe to America, under whose command I proved my seamanship so well that he recommended me as his best man to my present master, Sir John Fenton."

"And what about the old dog Martin?"

He died about a fortnight after the children. He was old and frail by that time, and moped about as if he wondered where they had gone, and so one morning we found him lying in the churchyard on their grave stiff and cold. Poor Martin! he was a gallant old growler to the end, but, like myself, took little pleasure in his life at the last. I have a son of his from a Cubian bloodhound mother, who takes to the sea just like his father. After all, Will, there is no life like the sea for adventure and the bracing up of a man. Come, old friend, one more glass, and then I must get my lads aboard.

VI

A May Dream

Folks rose early in those olden times, particularly in the country; and nowhere outside his own Stratford-on-Avon could a fairer prospect have greeted the waking eyes of the poet Shakespeare than this ancient park of Salterton.

The sky, luminous with the light of the yet unrisen sun, hung like a great pearl over the trees, clad in their mystery of young leafage and gnarled branches, the grass glimmering with the May dew and looking in the distance like early frost; while over it all lay a purity and hush which was irresistible to this lover of Nature so long confined to the haunts of men.

William Shakespeare, whose features and form time has hallowed so much that we dare scarcely desecrate their memory by describing; at whose shrine we are apt to bend down with covered eyes, and think of only as some vague and spiritual impersonation of dignity and grandeur, whom all men should at once recognise as their king.

Not the Shakespeare of Humphrey Bolin's recollection, who made sport for the forecastle of the *Revenge* when they were not fighting, and who fought as the rest of England's sons fought for their liberty, without a thought of anything beyond duty; who was there, as the rest were, because no young man held back,—Will Shakespeare the youthful, unknown jester of twenty-two, graceful of build, and slender, with nothing remarkable about him excepting a frank, open countenance and a well-formed forehead; who took life laughingly, and who made the most that he could from the pleasure of living.

Not the Shakespeare who was the light galleon to Ben Jonson's heavy galleon, using that ponderous scholar much in the same fashion that Drake used the Dons, who could not be frowned down to sober argument, but won the day through pure audacity and light repartee, who wrote about himself,—

> *"'Tis true, I have gone here and there,*
> *And made myself a motley to the view,*
> *Gored mine own thoughts, sold cheap what is most dear,*
> *Made old offences of affections new."*

This morning he was alone, and the poet, drinking in with chaste delight the deliciousness of Nature, saddened a little with the pity of friendship as he thought upon the end of that love match, but yet uplifted from the woes of humanity by the magic spell of the young day.

Shakespeare, at thirty-nine, getting stout in girth, medium-sized, with the face a trifle too florid for the modern ideal of a poet; but the eyes are unclouded and luminous as they look over the trees to that immensity of opalescent space,—quick eyes, which observe and retain impressions, with a brow above them massive and receptive.

He leaves his bedroom and unbars the front door, for he is the first up today. Sir John's canary had been strong the night before, and the fumes are still in his brains; therefore he walks forth with his hat in his hand, allowing the cool air to play upon his uncovered head.

Down amidst the dew-drenched grass, and between the vistas of opening glades, the park is well stocked with deer, who have grown bold with a long immunity from danger; or perhaps they recognise the poet who comes amongst them, for they graze quietly, and only look sideways at him as he passes.

He is once more with Nature, that has no intrigues, and away from the cabals of London life. There is no call for smartness here: he need not exercise his wits to appear clever. There is no envious Ben Jonson to brow-beat him, or try to make him appear small with the redundancy of his college acquirements and superior education. He has no need to think about style here; therefore his muse floats free and unconscious in her own completeness.

What joy it was to this lover of woods and meads to wander at will beneath those venerable oaks and gaze up through the twistings of the branches to the cross-patches of pulsing light. Last night he lay down a care-worn man, tired out with his efforts to please a frivolous public who could not understand him, who came only to be amused; disgusted with the vile crowd which he was forced to herd with, smarting with the clumsy buffets which his university rivals gave him at every turn, and over which he was forced to smile and jest like the motley fool they made him appear, writhing under his own defects as they were shown to him, diffident of his own powers and wondrous gifts before those merciless critics, yet ever compelled to wear the mask, and turn the sharp edges of malice and envy from him by a merry self-depreciating jest or quirk.

But with this blessed dawn enveloping his senses like cooling glory all these bitternesses of everyday life were quenched, and he was himself, the gifted son of God. He looked about him on the surrounding rugged trunks and mossy roots, then into the upper space, along which the thousand arrows and shafts of light were rushing, and spreading out his arms drank in all the sweetness of that soul-satisfying earth, thanking the Maker of all this excellence for His mighty gifts.

The birds were waking up and filling the glades with their voices of rejoicing; Nature sang, as the soul of Shakespeare sang, a universal harmony of pleasure. Through the trunk-spaces the golden rays travelled one by one, bringing out radiant lights and glimmerings of colour, and intensifying the same with the shadows which the opposing trees cast and trailed along the grass. In the light the dew-drops sparkled and flashed like minute diamond specks, in the shadows they still clung gauzy and grey.

"You are out betimes, bard Shakespeare," uttered a clear, sharp voice at his back, and he started and turned, half ashamed of his abandonment, to see the black-robed Penelope watching him with a sardonic curl of her thin lips. "Composing a new 'Midsummer Night's Dream' with the woodland elves around you?"

"No, Mistress Penelope; I was trying to grasp the visible."

"Are the fairies no longer visible to you, Master Shakespeare?"

"When I shut my eyes, they still come, sometimes," replied Shakespeare, smiling.

"Prithee, wherefore shut your eyes? Rather pray that I may open them for you. They are round you now, the pretty innocents, if you could but see them."

"That would be a gift, indeed!"

"Tush! That is a trifle. Come, give me your hand, and look at me steadily for a moment, and I will show you what is now invisible to you, dreamer that you are."

With an incredulous smile at the matter-of-fact manner of Penelope's announcement, Shakespeare permitted the old woman to take his hands in hers, and fixed his gaze upon the intense fire of her eyes. A minute or two passed, and then, with his lids closing, he slid to her feet, and lay there motionless.

"Go into fairyland, and see the merry court of Oberon, Titania, Puck, Peas-blossom and the rest. Nay, get them all while you are about it— nymphs, gnomes, salamanders and undines. You are with them now. Be

HUME NISBET

happy while you may. It is not often I deal with such harmless spirits, but you deserve it for some hours of pleasure which I have had in the past from these delicate creatures of your brain.

> *"Over hill, over dale,*
> *Through bush, through briar,*
> *Over park, over pale,*
> *Through flood, through fire,*
> *With Puck and his happy band*
> *Wander everywhere."*

As Penelope uttered the words she laid her hands upon the uncovered head of that prostrate figure; then, woman-like, spreading her handkerchief over his face to shade it from the rising sun, she left him on the ground, and going over to an upstarting root, sat down to rest herself and think.

"Big brains and empty heads, they all alike succumb to my witchcraft; and yet I know not what it is, or where it comes from, and I alone am shut out from the visions. Happy poet! He sees now in reality all that he before conjured up to charm outsiders; but I must plod on, grappling with my slavery and in dread of my life, flying from land to land at *his* loathed command, and as one accursed."

Very gloomy and brooding became the look which she fixed upon the grass at her feet, with occasional furtive glances to right and left, as if on the look-out for pursuers.

"Would that tomorrow were come, and a fair wind blowing us from these evil shores. Will I escape this time, or be caught and carried back to the torture and the fire? Oh, the horror of it! the horror of it!"

She put up her hands and covered her face, while she rocked herself to and fro and sobbed wildly with the intensity of that nightmare, the witch's doom.

VII

"Come Back, Bard Shakespeare"

C ome back, Bard Shakespeare." Penelope spoke in a clear, authoritative voice, as she stooped once more over the sleeper and touched him with her outspread hands; then she took up her ebony stick and stood back, leaning upon it and waiting.

With a heavy sigh Shakespeare opened his eyes and looked up for a moment, dazed, with the remains of a happy dream still lingering round his smiling lips.

"Ah! they have gone?"

"Yes, master poet; the little folks stayed an hour beyond their usual time to greet their best friend, but they dared not stay longer."

"Then it is real, and I did not dream it, after all?"

"Why should you think so, oh, you of little faith? Can a man write out a living thought which has not lived? Is the soul dead when the man dies? Get up, Shakespeare, and let me give you a glimpse into the past as I have seen it. Then you will know that whatever a man conceives is as real as what we women bring forth; ay, more real, for we give you shadows which pass away, while you give realities, which endure forever."

Shakespeare rose from the ground and looked at the woman with grave, questioning, and dilated eyes, which looked darker in their blue-greyness than was their usual appearance. He felt dazed and stupid still, as if he had been rudely awakened from a heavy sleep; but his senses were returning quickly to him.

"Yes, I saw them, or seemed to see them, all around me; just a little more tangible and real than I have seen them before, but the same creatures which I have called up by the aid of fancy. Not so glamorous, perhaps, or filmy, and more like to ourselves—earthy. And yet I wish I had not looked upon them as they are."

"Why, friend poet?"

"Because I can no longer see them with the finer vision of my soul. They have left that region of silver fancy forever, where they floated so airily, and trampled down the tissues with gross, mundane feet. No matter; I have beheld them with my grosser senses, and they are. Now, Mistress Penelope, let me also look upon the past that you have lived in."

"Come then, we will walk a little further, to where we can view the sea, for there I feel safer, on the bare cliffs, than here amongst the leaves, where prying eyes may be watching us. Give me your arm."

Together they walked along silently, with the morning sun laving them over and the birds twittering on every side. Through the woods they passed, until they came to the little turnstile which took them down to the cliffs, from where they could view the smooth ocean spread under them, with the sand and gravel glistening at their feet, against which the soft tide lapped gently.

Behind them the upper turrets of the old stone mansion could be seen above the trees of the park, with the smoke from the kitchen chimneys curling upwards and melting into the opalesque sky. The domestics were busy preparing the substantial breakfast of the times, when ale and baked or roasted meats took the place of the rashers of bacon and tea or coffee which serves to break our fast now. People drank fairly deep at nights, and started with fresh appetites for the same fare early, and there were not many dyspeptic subjects during the reigns of Elizabeth and James.

On the one side from where they now paused the clay cliffs broke up the coast-line with their rugged outlines, brown at their feet and blending off to hazy purple in the distance, low-lying cliffs which possessed petrifying qualities, and, as they became dislodged by the storms which at times beat against them, revealed many prehistoric and Roman remains, which indeed had been one of the first inducements for the old knight to bury himself in the quiet, old-fashioned hamlet.

On the other side lay the harbour, with the Isle of Sheppey in the distance, the waters dotted with the sails of dredgers, boats like a shoal of small fish hovering about some large sea denizen, the carrack *Vigo*, as she lay at anchor, while the men were hard at work loading her as fast as they could, and which work they had been at since daybreak under the direction of Humphrey Bolin.

"Dost think we shall be able to put to sea tonight, friend Shakespeare?" asked Penelope, as she shaded her eyes and looked anxiously towards the harbour.

"There is nothing to prevent you, if the wind holds as it is now doing," answered her companion.

"Pray Heaven it may!" she replied, with a deep sigh. "Every moment that crawls along seems an age until we get out of this fool-scholar's power, this Scottish deformity which the English have for a king."

"But you can read the future for others, Dame Penelope; do you not know what is to happen to yourself?"

"No; I can read that the ship *Vigo* will sail in safety away, also that Sir John Fenton will escape from England, but my familiars will tell me naught about my own fate."

"That is unfortunate; and yet you should have hopes, for you must have escaped many dangers in the past."

"That is it. I know how to continue life, if no untoward accident chances to hinder me from reaching the lands where the ingredients lie; but there are star chambers ashore and storms at sea which might cut short the long line of life. And as for the past, yes, it had its dangers also, but these, being gone, look trifles compared with the uncertain dread of the present."

She shivered violently as she plunged her ebony stick amongst a mass of hawthorns which overhung the park railings beside them, while her dark fierce eyes wandered restlessly over the wild flowers and gorse bushes to the breathing ocean beyond, showing a smooth but haggard face of mortal terror to the gaze of the wondering poet.

"Yet you must have looked upon Death in all his shapes during these centuries?"

"Yes; but always with his back turned to me. I have never met him face to face, as he seems to stand now. I was a young girl when Maximus was put to death for his treason. Then it was the fashion for the maidens to attend the temple of Diana on the hill of Lud. I took service under the protection of this goddess in my teens, and remained a vestal until the Saxons came to rule over us, for my father was a Roman, who was slain at Aquileia, and my mother a noble Briton, who followed the faith of her husband. London then was beautiful with its great walls, theatres, palaces, and temples, although in the country they still worshipped round the oak and mistletoe, and the new creed of Christianity was creeping in and making converts."

"Have you ever been a wife, Penelope?"

"No; I am still a votary of Diana. When I was first young and might have yielded to love, religion bound my spirit and chilled my heart; when I renewed my youth, experience kept me the icicle that religion had made me. No, I never loved a man or cared for the laughter of children; for nearly thirteen centuries I have lived alone and friendless, looking on the ravages of Death, and fearing him for myself only."

"What an awful doom. Why, the most ingenious torture which the

Star Chamber can invent could not equal the prolonged intensity of this punishment."

"Perhaps not. Yet Fate permitted me to live without inflicting *bodily* pain. That is what I dread now."

"I do not think that you need be under any apprehension for the next few days, because our king for the present is occupied in two more engrossing diversions even than witch-finding: to wit, the chase, along with a religious controversy. So that until he wearies the professors with his arguments and runs his hounds lame he is not likely to think about the Wizard of Witestaple with his companion the Witch of Canterbury. When he does call you to mind, I trust that you will be out of English waters, and myself once more safely back to the boards."

"Who knows what may next enter the head of this learned fool? Let us trust that we may not."

"Do you still put your trust in Diana?"

"No; I place the little trust I have in destiny."

"Tell me, how did you discover the secret of renewing life?"

"It was the high priest of Apollo, in the temple which stood where now stands Westminster Abbey, who gave me my first draught. We had both been driven out of London, and were hiding for our lives. For after the Romans left us the Christians became a power, and destroyed all the pagans who would not be baptized. This high priest was a native of Egypt, who had seen many lands and lived many lives, and with his own he renewed my youth; while, after a time, we made our escape from England, and worked together in the East, studying many magical arts while there. He taught me where to gather the herbs and how to mix them."

"Is he still alive?"

"No; he was killed at Alexandria by the falling of a loose stone from a wall as we were passing through a narrow street on our way to take ship for Constantinople. We were in slavery at the time, for we had been captured by Algerian pirates, and bought by a Greek sorcerer, who had recognised our gifts by his own incantations, and who wanted our assistance. This was during the reign of Edwy, when England was under the power of St. Dunstan, the Abbot of Glastonbury."

"Were you in England during the time of Merlin?"

"I was an assistant of his for sometime, while he lived as Merlin, and in many other characters, for he was my master, the Priest of Apollo."

"Then he was not enchanted by the 'Lady of the Lake'?"

"No. I was the only lady intimate enough with him and his secrets. We had made England a little too hot to hold us any longer, and so hit upon this device to leave it once more for the East, without suspicion, for we were both requiring a fresh draught of the elixir. I can call up my master as Merlin for you at anytime. Would you like to see him now?"

Penelope Ancrum had seemingly once more forgotten her terror of consequences in the recital of her wonderful past and her desire to impress her companion with her skill, for she looked at him eagerly, with her usual sardonic curl of the lip, as she waited for his reply.

"No. I do not think that I'd care about seeing Merlin, now that I know what he was. You have the gift of a critic to an uncommon degree, Mistress Ancrum, for you can shatter the most sacred illusions with fine words and tear a dream into tatters with a backward glance. I am of opinion now that there can be no myths or poetry left in a life of thirteen centuries."

"Nor before it either, when one has lived the contemporary of Hercules and Jason; who has seen Helen as she returned with her husband after the fall of Troy; who has laughed in his face at the heroic imaginings of the blind beggar, who sang about it; who watched Marc Antony playing the fool for a thick-lipped, middle-aged wanton; read the fortunes of Dido; helped Sappho in her love-spells; watched Egypt fall under Greece, Greece fall under Rome, Rome yield to the Goths. No; as love left me during the first fifty years of my existence, so sentiment and imagination died under the experience of my own life and the recollections of my master. But tell me what you would like me to show you the most at this moment, and I will call it up to you in its stern reality."

"Nothing of the past," replied the poor dramatist, with a slight shiver, as he turned his face towards the Hall. "You have entirely quenched any curiosity that may have been lurking in my mind by your recital; indeed, I have only one desire now left to gratify, and that is for—breakfast."

VIII

THE POWERS OF DARKNESS AND THE POWERS THAT BE

It is within two minutes of the witching hour of mid-night, and on board the ship *Vigo* Humphrey Bolin and his merry men wait, all prepared to put to sea.

The hatches are battened down, and the sails made easy for shaking out; the wind blows fairly from the nor'-east, the right direction to waft them into the Channel, a holding breeze which is just heavy enough to fill out the sails and send them along easy. Overhead the stars, with the moon, are well covered with cloud; yet the night is luminous and grey, with a fine light mist blurring distant objects, which might well make the heart of a smuggler or a runaway beat lightly within his ribs. It was just the kind of night which Captain Bolin would have fixed upon, had he been given the choosing of it, to leave the coast of old England.

Two hours more and the tide would be full in, and at the turn when they could lift up their anchors and start. He has an hour and a half yet before his company may be expected, so, like a sensible skipper of the old school, he is spending it in the best possible way he can hit upon for keeping himself, his officers and his crew in good temper, and from missing their friends ashore—by serving round the pannikins and getting them on the yarn. It will be time enough when they have got a mile or two of salt water between them and the shore to consult dignity and read out rules and regulations. English sailors are never spoilt by their captain being free and easy with them before duty begins; such a man can be as stern as he pleases afterwards. They honour him the more for it, for they abhor laxity at sea; but they always bear in mind, even as they take his cuffs, what a good fellow the old man is when off duty.

This is the sort of man that the sailors delight to honour and obey: who can rule them rigidly at sea and drink with them freely ashore.

At the Hall they were spending the hour of waiting on the tide in a different but equally characteristic fashion. Sir John Fenton, Shakespeare, Penelope and the boy Humphrey were congregated within the wizard's den—his study, laboratory, or whatever it might be termed.

A large apartment, which had originally been used as a loft or attic, and which extended over the upper bedrooms, with sloping raftered sides, for only the tiles were above them, and to get to it they were forced to use a stair-ladder.

It was a sombre-looking apartment, painted over with lamp-black, and with mystical signs picked out in white and red on every rafter, each division being dedicated to its own particular demon, who was supposed to be pleased with this attention and drawn from his shady sphere by this administration to his diabolic vanity.

The floor also was sable-hued, instead of being car-petted, while in the centre a broad white ring was drawn, within which the mystics were arranged. Other furniture saving that white ring there was none. Demons are not supposed to require seats; they stand when they attend a *séance*; come unwillingly, do not behave pleasantly while present, and clear out as quickly as possible. They object on principle to that white ring, which prevents them from becoming *en rapport* with their mortal friends; and certainly it isn't nice to be asked to assist at an entertainment and yet to be held at arm's length from the hosts. Devils have their pride, as well as mortals; and they are to be excused for being proud, seeing that they nearly all belong to old and patrician families.

Sir John had on his wizard's gown and cap, and held in his hand his wand of office. Penelope also was arrayed in witchlike costume: a silver band round her white locks, which fell loosely over her back; a Greek-like garb of dark blue, with silver designs over it, and clasped with a zone of silver, also curiously wrought with cabalistic signs, round her waist; and with bare feet, which shone singularly white and shapely under her gown,—at least, the bard Shakespeare thought so, as his eyes wandered down to them; and he ought to have been an authority on small and pretty feet, if any mortal ever was.

Shakespeare and the boy Humphrey, being novices, were attired in their usual garb, with high boots and travelling dresses, because after the meeting the one had to ride off to London and the other to wait upon his father.

Two fires were lighted inside the third of the charmed rings, for Sir John had now drawn two fresh ones, with about six inches between each. These were charcoal fires, and burned redly inside small braziers, and while the knight held in his hand a small box filled with powder, the others were unemployed.

"Twelve o'clock, Penelope," remarked the old knight, as they heard the hall clock toll out the hour sonorously. "Are you ready?"

"Yes," replied the witch, as she touched Shakespeare and the boy each lightly with her fingers upon their foreheads; then took her place beside the knight. "Now put in the powder."

As Sir John dropped a few pinches of the powder from his box into each of the fires dense clouds of smoke rolled up, while blue forks of flames darted out of the braziers, and a distant roll of thunder was heard.

"Who do you wish to watch over us tonight, Sir John?" inquired Penelope gravely.

"Your master—our master, Penelope. Call on Amenemapet," answered the knightly wizard, with a blanched face, while Shakespeare and the boy remained passive inside the ring.

"Amenemapet, my beloved master, come forth," called Penelope, stretching her hands out towards the misty space.

Nearer thunder.

"Amenemapet, come forth."

A close clap, with one blaze of wild fire.

"Come, Amenemapet."

In another instant outside the outer circle stood a tall form, lighted up by the blue flames, a figure draped in Eastern robes, with a clearly defined face.

"You know him again, Sir John?" whispered Penelope, breathing upon the back part of the knight's head.

"Oh yes,—our guide, philosopher, and friend," murmured the knight, in reply.

"And you, Shakespeare? What you see is Merlin, Nero, and a dozen historical personages rolled into one."

"Yes, I see," replied Shakespeare, in a sleepy tone.

"And you, my pretty Humphrey?"

"Yes, I know him also," replied the boy calmly.

"And you are not afraid of him?"

"Oh no; you tell me not to be afraid, and therefore I am not."

"That is right. Now manage the rest of the business for yourselves," muttered Penelope, squatting down in the centre of the circle.

She began to sing, as if to herself, a weird, wild, but monotonous air, which, however, the others did not appear to hear. It was like two lines of a song repeated over and over again without variety; while she waved her head slowly over her knees, as if to the refrain,—

> *"And Jack lies 'mongst the seaweeds in the deep and silent sea,*
> *And I am waiting on the shore, and nothing left for me."*

Two lines sung over and over again, from a low murmur to the full pitch of the woman's voice—a clear voice, but without melody or soul. It rang out to the night, while the old knight fed the braziers constantly with the powders, and Shakespeare, with the boy, looked out upon that shadowy form half wreathed in smoke.

The butler woke up in his bed and heard that mad voice pouring out the monotonous refrain, and, being a timid man, he covered his head with the blankets, and tried in this way to muffle his ears, for he had often heard it before during the past three or four months; the housekeeper heard it from her chamber, and having a turn for religion, said her prayers twice over; a housemaid heard it as she was leaning from her bedroom window whispering to her sweetheart, the gamekeeper, and she instantly cried,—

"Time you was moving, Jim, for the witch is at it again."

None of the other inmates heard that melancholy refrain, because they were all too tired, or too tipsy, to waken; except, perhaps, the deer grazing in the park. But if they did, they only raised their antlered heads for a moment to listen, and then went on calmly again; for it is wonderful how much deer can stand in the shape of monotony.

Meantime the incantations went on very satisfactorily to all parties concerned. Amenemapet, the Egyptian, did not appear to concern himself a whit more than did the herds outside about that song; possibly he had lived down all sensation for melody in his long earthly pilgrimage. The demons also came to command obediently with different varieties of thunder and lightning, and listened calmly to it, even while answering the questions obediently which the aged knight put to them. In their own domains possibly there were worse sounds, and where gnashings of teeth were more necessary.

Shakespeare had never seen or imagined so many devils before as he saw crowding into that chamber during the half-hour that the incantation lasted. Blue devils, scarlet devils, devils of all shapes and shades, they lurched forward to the outer circle and vomited flames in the faces of the audience; while the spirit Amenemapet held them all well in hand, and sent them to the right-about when they had prognosticated all they could. They came with a clap and vanished amongst the smoke: snakes of every dimension, dragons, apes, monsters with deformed faces, and flapping ears, and bat-like wings. Altogether it was the liveliest entertainment that the gifted player had ever assisted in, with the most dramatic and weird-like effects.

And the answers also coincided satisfactorily. They were to escape safely from their enemies and have a lucky voyage. The most appalling phantom was forced to answer in this way before he disappeared, clawing the perfume-charged air with his talons.

Hark! Other sounds break out clearly above the sing-song of Penelope and the anathemas of the conjured devils: the sounds of loud hammering at the hall front door, and a loud, authoritative voice along with the smashing.

"Open in the name of the king, Sir John Fenton; open in the name of the Star Chamber."

As the words travelled up to that enchanter's attic the guardian spirit Amenemapet, with his subservient legion of demons, vanished, while Penelope closed her song abruptly, starting up in the most frantic terror and passing her hands rapidly over the faces of her three companions, who instantly awoke.

"What is it Penelope?" demanded Sir John, as he looked at her glaring eyes.

"The officers of the King, Sir John, the messengers from the Star Chamber; we are discovered! we are lost!"

"Not yet," muttered the knight to himself; "they shall not catch me like a fox in a hole, if I can help it. But perhaps you may be mistaken?"

"No! no! listen again. We are lost!"

"Open in the name of his Majesty the King, Sir John Fenton; open, I say, to the messengers of the Star Chamber."

"The door is a stout one, and will not give way easily, and none of my servants will be in a hurry to open, unless I give them leave. Come, friends, follow me, and I will show you a way out of this."

As he spoke the aged knight threw off his wizard's gown and skull-cap, replacing it with his ordinary hat. Then it was found that he was equipped for his journey. Penelope also had under her robe her ordinary dress, and in a few moments had gathered up her tresses and donned her stockings and boots.

She did not display over much delicacy in tiring herself, and the poet, as he glanced in her direction, could not help noting that for an aged dame she exhibited a remarkably youthful looking and clean made limb.

"That comes of the extreme antiquity of the article, I expect," he murmured; "ordinary limbs would be shrivelled at her apparent age. I wish I had seen this witchly specimen before I thought out 'Macbeth'; however, it may come in for someother incident of the kind."

They were now ready and eager to follow Sir John, for to one and all there was extreme danger in any further delay, with that disturbance at the front door and the sounds within of the servants waking up; so without any further remark they scrambled down the ladder behind the knight, and ran after him into his bedroom.

IX

THE ESCAPE

I t did not astonish any of the followers of Sir John Fenton to be taken into his bedroom in search of a mode of escape. Every old mansion of the period had its secret chambers and underground passages; the only wonder was that the soldiers, who must have known of this as well as the inmates did, should be standing sounding the alarm outside the main door, instead of stealing quietly in, or surrounding the park; that is, if they did not wish to aid in the escape, which perhaps in reality was the purpose of making all this outcry and causing the servants to get up and stand shivering in their night-clothes in their different chambers.

The old knight, when they had entered the bedroom and double-locked the door behind them, did exactly what they expected he would do under the circumstances, and with the customary amount of caution and mystery.

He fumbled about the frame of a life-sized portrait in one of the panels of the wainscot, and pressing upon one of the ornaments, made the picture slide out of its frame, revealing behind it a secret doorway leading into a dark and cobwebby passage that had not been used for many years.

Into this dark passage they all passed one by one, the leader, shutting the picture panel behind him carefully; and then, bidding them tread softly, he once more pushed on in front.

There was no fear of them going astray in this passage, for they could feel both sides of it as they pressed along. Their footsteps also were deadened in the thick matting of dust which lay on the floor, while across their faces flapped many a soft, filmy, dust-laden spider-web. If betrayed at all, it could only be by the sneezes which this cheap snuff produced.

The passage was narrow, dark, and evil-odoured, twisting about the house in all sorts of eccentric curves; so they traversed the maze of chambers along the top storey, then, descending a narrow staircase, came to the second flat, and again round that to the servants' rooms, from where they could hear their muffled cries of terror, with the smashing in of the front door, for the soldiers had grown impatient, and had found a beam of some sort lying about, which they were using as a battering-ram.

The shaking of the old boards which this beam caused was not the least unpleasant item of that secret journey, for it sent down whole avalanches of accumulated dust upon them, and nearly choked them before they were able to dive to the lower level of the cellar. This, with the colonies of over-confident mice, rats, and other small game, added to their discomforts; and the terrors of Penelope, who, although a witch and of rare antiquity, had not yet learnt to subdue her feminine terror for these underground pirates and housebreakers; so that more than once Shakespeare, who was nearest her, was forced to put his hand over her mouth and stifle the shriek that broke from her as she felt them dashing against her ankles in their frantic efforts to get out of her way. However, there was little fear of her voice reaching the ears of the besiegers, with the din they were themselves making and the loud squeakings of the disturbed vermin.

As they proceeded further underground the air became more noisome, and the sides of the passage damper and nastier to the touch. They had now left the mansion, with its oak wainscotting, and were treading their way along a rough, stone-built tunnel, the walls of which were wet and slimy to the touch, and the uneven floor covered some inches in slush and mud, while chill, earth-bred gases wafted over them, and turned them sick and faint.

"Where does this passage lead to, Sir John?" asked Shakespeare, surprised at the hollowness of his own voice.

"To the stables at the far end of the park, and where I always keep some extra horses. We are not far from them now; and once there, I hope we may steal out without being perceived."

After what seemed to be hours, although it was only minutes, of groping along blindly in the dark, they began to ascend some stone steps, and then once more got to boarded-in sides, and away from the chilly damps into the close and steamy atmosphere of stables. They were nearly at the end of their underground journey, for they could hear the hoofs of the horses trampling against their stalls, disturbed doubtless by the vicinity of breathing and unseen humanity.

For a moment they stood still and listened for other sounds, but only the champing and kicking of the horses met their ears; then, with another touch at some secret knob, the doorway slid aside, and revealed to them a roomy stable, lighted only by a single candle-lantern which hung up against the wall, and with none of the grooms in sight.

"At last," remarked Shakespeare, in a relieved tone, as he stretched himself and drew in a long breath, looking round on his dust and mire-stained companions.

"I think we are almost disguised enough to pass in safety through the midst of our enemies."

"Not so loud, friend Will," said the old knight nervously. "Let us reconnoitre before we venture to speak or leave this shelter."

Bidding them stand well in the shade, Sir John crept up a ladder to the hay loft, and cautiously opening the window, looked out on the silent park, now dimly lighted up by the cloud-covered moon.

All seemed quiet and deserted in its envelopment of mist, while from the Hall the battering had ceased: the soldiers had either broken in the door, or else had it opened to them from within, and were probably at that moment ransacking the rooms. So, satisfied, he once more shut the window and descended to his companions.

"Now let us make haste and saddle four of the horses. You can ride, I suppose, boy, the short distance from here to the ship?"

"Yes, sir," replied Humphrey the younger; so, without further parley, each of the three set to work saddling the horses, who, recognising their master, submitted patiently, Penelope crouching meanwhile in silent terror under the shadow of the lantern.

"Now let us go."

Softly they led the horses out of the stable and between the trees, until they came to the side gate which led to the roadway on the land end of the estate. They were now close to the square-built church of "All Saints," which loomed up darkly on the top of the hill.

"We must take a circuit through the fields, so as to avoid the highway and the town. Wilt ride farther with us, Shakespeare, or hie thee back to London? for that is your straight road."

"I will see you safely away before I set my face towards London," replied Shakespeare, as he helped Penelope to mount, and then got into his own saddle.

"Thanks, friend," returned the old wizard, as he lifted himself stiffly on to his horse and touched it gently with his heel.

Over the fields they cantered like shadows, with the mist blurring objects around them, in the direction of Heron Hill, and then down towards the cliffs. Here they would have to pass close to the Hall once more, but trusted to chance that if met by any of their pursuers they would be mistaken for strangers.

"Pray Heaven that they know nothing about the ship," fervently muttered Sir John, as he cast his eyes in the direction of his property.

"I think not," replied Shakespeare, "or I should have received some hint of it."

Silently they rode along after this, until they came to the part where Penelope and the poet had stood that morning. They could see the Hall now through the trees. It was brilliantly lighted up, with dark shadows coming and going in front of the windows, as the soldiers searched about for the birds that had flown, in the same methodical fashion which is still pursued by our civic guardians when they are after an escaped criminal; while outside could be heard the murmurings of the disturbed villagers, who were assembled in force to witness the capture of their lord the wizard and his accomplice.

The knight looked sadly upon the house which he was leaving forever, and where he might have spent the remainder of his days in comfort and honour but for his infatuation for the forbidden arts, and unconsciously owned to himself that up to now the demons had not done much for him. He was going out upon the waters and leaving all that was dear to him behind.

"Farewell!" murmured the exile, in a melancholy voice, as he halted his steed and half turned in his saddle towards the mansion.

"Let us hasten, for God's sake!" whispered the votary of Diana, husky with acute terror. "See, they have set the house on fire, and will be coming out presently."

It was as she said: from the upper windows the flames were beginning to curl out, while the mob below roared out their hoarse approval.

With a heavy groan the knight gave his horse the reins, and together they trotted down to the beach and past the deserted cottages, until they came to the harbour.

The tide by this time was nearly at its full, so that as they rode up they could see how the carrack floated, and that the men were only waiting on them. Hurriedly they flung themselves from their saddles,— all except Shakespeare,—and then turned to say goodbye.

"Up anchors, captain, without the loss of a moment. We are pursued."

"I heard the din at the Hall, Sir John, and we have only the last anchor to get aboard," replied Humphrey, as he turned to his men and gave his orders.

"Farewell, friend Shakespeare. If I live, you will see me again; and if I can, I will write to you from some port," said the knight, reaching up his hand to his friend and giving him a firm clasp.

"Farewell, Sir John, and a safe voyage to you; the same to you, Mistress Ancrum, and to you, old friend Humphrey; and as for you, young Humphrey, do not forget all I have told you about improving your mind: take notes of your foreign travelling and keep a book."

"I'll remember it, Master Shakespeare," shouted the boy from the deck, where they were now standing looking at the solitary rider who held the reins of the three left horses, while the seamen pushed the ship from her moorings and shook out the sails.

But the old knight kept his eyes fixed upon the part where his house stood, now lighted up with a fierce glow of fire, while the trees stood out blackly against the glare, every instant increasing in intensity and brightness.

The sails had caught the wind, and the *Vigo* began to move from the shore,—slowly at first and then more quickly, the fire-glare lighting up her topsails, while those below were still in shadow.

Now she seems like a golden swan gliding into the silvery haze, her bulwarks and rigging glittering in that ruddy glare. The rider still sits in his saddle watching her as she sails majestically away from the shore with her living freight; then, hearing a loud shouting from the cliffs, he turns in that direction, letting go his hold of the bridles of all but his own horse, which, when the beasts find that they are free, they move away towards their stables, shying aside from the glare and quickening their pace until they break into a wild gallop across the fields.

The soldiers have been questioning the fishermen, and have just learnt about the ship, and now they are gathered on the cliffs watching her disappear with their prey on board.

Shakespeare glances quickly towards them and the blazing mansion behind the trees, then, with another look at the golden ship, now a dim and misty spectre, he turns his horse's head in the direction of London and rides off, pursued by the shadows of the trees and the crimson reflections of the nearly demolished house of his old friend.

BOOK SECOND

Journal of Humphrey Bolin the younger, written at the request of and addressed to one Master William Shakespeare, actor, of the City of London, and found at sea in the year 1612.

I

The Island

I never thought it was such a hard matter to begin to put upon paper what one has gone through during several years of wandering in savage parts. Master Shakespeare told me to take notes as I went along, and so I tried to do day after day for the first week or two; then work came in to interfere, or I felt too tired to hold the pen, or else the ship rocked too much, so that I would miss a day, and then, when I sought to trace back to it, I found that I had nothing to say. Thus I left off that task, and could not take to it again.

Now I must try to remember all that happened since that night we left Witestaple Harbour, until now, when I sit amongst savages, with plenty to eat and drink, it is true, and paper enough saved from the ship to make a goodly book, if I am only clever enough to fill it up.

I suppose that I ought to begin with the day of the month and the year; but, faith, I have forgotten both months and years in this land of perpetual summer. My friends here reckon by moons; but I have seen so many grow and wane since I left my native land that I cannot count from them.

I feel that I am a man, from having a man's beard on my chin, and which has never been clipped since it began to grow; whereas I was only a stripling of sixteen when we first sailed away upon our many and dark adventures; also that I have gone through and can remember enough to fill all the sheets which poor Sir John left behind him. But the difficulty is to know how I am to begin.

If I had only someone who could understand me, handy to tell it to, it would come out all easy enough; or if only someone less great than Shakespeare had asked me to do it, then I might have used the first words that came to me. But it is like writing an exercise for my old schoolmaster, when one has to hunt out and cudgel his brains for the most intricate words, in order to make it look erudite and flowery; drag in all the gods and goddesses of the heathen mythology, with a host of other figures of speech, so as to make my descriptions pleasant, all of which require books of reference.

And yet here I sit beneath the leaves of a native hut, with only some black-letter books on magic to turn to, which I do not understand, with a radiant landscape about me, and lots of naked gods and goddesses at hand, without a scrap of memory left in me of any of the heathen names, whereby I might make my description plain to English readers.

The cocoa-nut trees are drooping above in the fierce midday glaring eye of—of—— There, I stick at the name of the god who ought to stand for the sun, and there is no use asking my poor friends the natives about it, for they would only give it a name that no one could understand, or be able to write down.

It is beautiful though, for all that, Master Shakespeare, if I could only describe it properly, or you were here to see it with your poetic and far-reaching eyes. There is a ravine close at hand, with flower-clustered cliffs, over which a silvery waterfall dashes cool, and clear, and shady, even in the hottest day, with a deep pool of the freshest, where one may plunge into and banish fatigue.

There are gardens and groves, where the most rare and delicious fruit hang for the gathering, with never a winter to strip the leaves.

On the sea-shore are rare grottoes, where the light filters in green and soft upon rosy seaweed and wondrous shells. And out in the bay rots the old ship *Vigo*, weighted down with treasure enough to purchase a dukedom: chests and ingots of solid gold, jewels and ornaments of the most precious; every doubloon or glistening gem won at the price of a more precious life. She lies on the sands, everyday sinking deeper in her moorings; not so much with the weight of gold as with the blood and crime that is pressing upon her.

On the dark and starry nights when I look at her from the beach, I can see the blue flames licking round her broken masts from the gaping caverns of her treasure-crammed hold, and they take on the shapes of the murdered hundreds of victims, and hover round as if they were watching over their own lost property; until I have to cover my eyes with my hands and rush back to the living savages for comfort, to my island bride "Quassatta," who hides out the terrible vision with her beautiful arms.

We were mad, they tell me, when we came here floating on the *Vigo* to their hospitable shores,—mad with the fever which had killed the rest of my shipmates and left me sole master of all this useless wealth. Only Quassatta and my dog, young Martin, as I am young Humphrey— middle-aged Martin now and full-grown Humphrey. Dear old mastiff! He still shares my exile, and has learnt to favour Quassatta.

They tell me now, when I can understand their language, that the equinoctial gales drove the rudderless ship in through the narrow passage of this reef as if spirits had been guiding it, with the white god and goddess—they call us that—standing upright on the poop, singing wildly, with the dog crouching at our feet, and around us a cluster of dead and putrifying bodies, which they buried.

Was Penelope amongst that dead and buried? or shall she start up once more alive to draw me back to her with the chains she forged about me? Can this evil witch die and be buried? I for one ask this question of the winds that sing amongst the palm trees?

I was mad for many moons, they tell me, for so do they mark off time, and at last, when I woke up, I felt as if my youth had fallen from me, and that, with my beard grown, I had become another man, only for Quassatta, the dog Martin, and my blood-dyed recollections. But, thank God, I am not quite alone, for I have still my beautiful Quassatta to be my own forever; thank God for His infinite mercy that He spared us twain out of the rest.

Quassatta, who knows me at last, and who has learnt her husband's tongue, and can now tell her love as she looked it before, yet who never seems too sure of her prize, for she watches me constantly, and sighs with relief when she holds me once more in her arms. When sleep separates us, I think she wakes up each morning expecting to discover that I have floated to the stars; and this fear is both her torture and her delight.

But thus I am, Master Shakespeare, tackling the end before the beginning, as I knew that I should do in my ignorance of the proper way to start a story; so pray pardon my faults, and let me try to hearken back to the moment when I saw the last of you, and the burning mansion of Seasalter.

II

Shipmates

It was a sorry sight to our master, Sir John, to look upon his old mansion burning down as we sailed away from it. He made the best of his way up to the poop, and hung over the side and watched it long after the mist had swallowed up the flames, and had become tinted only with the glow; which, after a time, also died out, and left us only the grey night. Then he staggered below to his cabin, and we saw no more of him for three days.

Nor were any of the fresh hands much seen during those three first days; for we were all sea-sick and despairing of our lives as we rocked about the rough waters of the Channel and into the Bay of Biscay.

It was not very comfortable in any part of the ship during the first three days; and I had not much to do, for, although I was booked as cabin-boy, and, besides, was under the strict surveillance of my father, our two passengers, Sir John and Mistress Penelope, did not give me much trouble, keeping all the while strictly within their own berths, without calling for either bite or sup; while father was nearly constantly upon deck, looking out for danger and strange sails as long as the fog lasted and we were within English waters.

Every hour the wind blew harder as we got into the full sweep of the Bay, while the waves rose and broke over us with yeasty fury. But we had a pretty tight vessel under us, and a fast sailer also, in spite of her Spanish bulwarks; so that, seeing father so calmly confident, I soon got over my own fears, as well as my sickness, and went more amongst the seamen; for I knew them all, more or less, excepting the Witestaple recruits, having sailed from Plymouth with them on our way to the dry docks at Sheppey, where we had had her over-hauled and thoroughly refurnished.

We had a fairly complete complement of ordinary sea men and fighting men with us; many of them honest and well-known Plymouth comrades, and the rest made up from all sorts and nationalities, as we could get them—characters not so much thought about as working abilities or strength of muscles. So that I used to spend most of my spare time in the forecastle, getting acquainted with their names and trying to read their different nations from their faces.

We had four mates under father, the first, second, and fourth being fellow-townsmen and old friends of his. The third mate, having been specially recommended by Sir John, had been appointed to the post without any questions being asked about his qualifications or antecedents; yet that he was quite able to fill his post he proved to father and the rest of the men during the first hour of his watch.

He was a singular, and perhaps, in his own style, the handsomest man on board. Not too tall, but of an exceedingly shapely and well-knit frame, with fine features and a clear, musical voice. In age he might be about twenty-eight or thirty.

It was the utter absence of colour in him that first made me take notice of him, for his cheeks and lips were absolutely bloodless, like the countenance of a dead man; with snow-white, fine, straight hair, and eyes which gave out a reddish light, like those of a rabbit. Afterwards I knew that he was what they called an albino, and a Greek.

It gave me a great shock when I first looked into his face, and saw the long white tresses trailing over his shoulders, like the locks of a very old man; for I had never seen anything like him before. But by-and-by I got used to his appearance; and as he often talked to me with his clear, musical voice, and gave me many instructions in sea-craft, I grew to like him very greatly, although I never felt comfortable with his strange eyes. During the day, however, he used to wear coloured glasses, for he said that he could not bear the daylight; but at nights he took them off, and then he could see better than any of the rest of us.

Sir John Fenton greeted him kindly when he came aboard, and Mistress Penelope seemed to know him well, for she gave him her hand, and permitted him to lead her to her cabin, addressing him by his name, Alsander, which was the only name he had shipped under; when afterwards on the voyage she always talked with him in his own language, although he could speak English as well as any of us.

The other mates did not associate much with Alsander, for, being Englishmen, they resented, as Englishmen always do, the companionship of a foreigner. William Giles, the first mate, was a strongly made, full-bearded man of about forty, who had been shipmate before with father. Peter Claybroke, the second mate, was about twenty-five, fair and florid, who, beyond some coasting passages, had not sailed far out of England; whereas Jack Howard was a little over twenty, stalwart as a young giant, and as good-tempered as he was brave. He also had learnt most of his sailorship ashore, but, for all that, knew how to handle both a ship and a cutlass, and liked both exercises dearly. His duty consisted mainly in serving out the provisions as purser.

Besides these officers, there was another personage who was well known to us all from Plymouth, who had slipped his cable from a termagant wife, and come out with his old friend Humphrey Bolin on this strange venture—little Robbie Crooker, the surgeon-barber. He acted in the capacity of ship-barber and doctor to the expedition,—a very able man, although undersized and shrivelled up like a mummy, with a most atrocious squint, yet filled to the masthead with conceit. He was never tired of telling about his conquests over the female sex; and, indeed, to my own knowledge the lasses of Plymouth used to come much about his shop, which had been the cause of many a domestic storm. Therefore, those who knew him in the past were inclined to give him credit for some truth in his stories, even although appearances were so sadly against him. Yet he was a merry little fellow, and a good fiddler, which made many a weary hour to pass pleasantly.

In the forecastle I always felt at home, for there were so many of the faces that I had known all my life: Tom Blunt, who was the son of a coastguardsman, and Nick Shilling, and Rowland Pring, with half a dozen other bold boys, to whose adventures afloat I had listened each time they came ashore, and between the sweethearts of them all I had run scores of times with messages, and for doing which I had earned many a sixpence. They were all here serving loyally under father, and eager to make a good sailor out of me. So that, although it was a gloomy and evil-smelling hole to herd so many men in, I liked that dingy forecastle better than the gaily-painted cabin.

The Witestaple recruits were mostly quiet and honest fellows, with whom it was no trouble to get along; but there were others, who had been picked out of crimping houses, or had volunteered with the third mate, who never could be favourites with any man—vile, hang-dog wretches, who slouched about in their dirty rags, hating work, and muttering as they scowled at their officers, and who had to be kept down with a strict hand. But this father and his mates were thoroughly able to do.

Tom Blunt was our boatswain, and owned a right heavy and willing fist of his own, so that whenever he saw a sign of skulking or insubordination he promptly struck out, and felled the mutineer like an ox.

These black sheep the honest men kept at arm's-length, and made them mess together, dividing them as much as possible into different watches, and working them hard, so that they had not much leisure to hatch mischief. I knew them all by their ship-names, and used to watch them whenever I had the chance, wondering what kind of lives they must have led to cause such sin-stamps to be fixed into their features, for I could not think that human beings could be born so.

Yes, with a little difference in face and sizes they all bore a striking family resemblance to each other: heavy seams over the brow, and wrinkles round the shifty eyes; they all looked sideways, and hung their heads forward, with restless hands fumbling about their waist-belts, as if they had been in the constant habit of playing with knives; dark, sunburnt faces, some of them had, others puffed out and pasty-hued; some of them weakly-looking and undersized, who made up in cruel cunning what they lacked in strength.

There were two of these hang-dogs that used to impress me most disagreeably, and for the reason that they were forever trying to force their company upon me and cajole me with wheedling flattery.

One was a tall, lank man, with a skin yellow as brass, as if he suffered from jaundice, and yellow, lack-lustre eyes; while, whenever he opened his long lips to speak or laugh, he used to show great discoloured fangs. They called him Indian Jos, on account of his coarse, straight black hair, which looked like an American Indian's.

The other was short and boyish in his appearance, with a pink skin, like that of a freshly scraped young pig; thin-faced and sharp as a razor, and without a vestige of hair upon him anywhere: eyebrows, eyelashes, chin, and head were as bare as the body of a new-born child's; so that one could never have guessed at his age. He always spoke soft and husky, and walked about the deck with the lightness of a shadow. I hated Indian Jos, but always heard the husky whisper of Gabrial Peas with a shiver and a sudden faintness of the heart.

Our cook was a gigantic negro, who had come aboard with these two men. They had sailed together in other ships, and referred to the third mate for their characters, which he gave an excellent account of to father: they had served under him, and knew their duty thoroughly.

So they did as sailors; while Sambo, the cook, in spite of his exaggerated features and blood-shot, evil, small eyes, in the galley did all that could be desired of him. He moved about amongst the kettles and pots, a perfect mountain of ungainly black flesh, yet managed to turn out the most toothsome dishes for the cabin, and to keep the seamen in good humour by his punctuality and cleanly cooking.

Yet they were a fearsome looking triad, for all these good points; and although it was impossible to avoid speaking with them at times in that narrow space, I always felt easier when honest Tom Blunt joined us, and made my escape easy, without giving them the chance of offence.

III

THE EVIL EYE

On the eighth day after leaving England we got to the sunny weather and into shipshape sailing order.

We had been hailed once or twice during this time both by English and foreign vessels, and also chased, but this had only gone to prove to my father's entire satisfaction that our ship was the swiftest sailer, as we had run from them easily—that is, the large vessels; and as for the smaller fry, we had only to show them our teeth to get a wide berth.

Penelope and Sir John were now on deck everyday, enjoying the warm sun and the balmy winds, which wafted us on towards our destination—South America; for this was where Penelope had told her protector that the life-renewing herbs were to be found.

Mistress Penelope exercised a strange influence upon nearly every man on board, from my father and Sir John down to me, the youngest.

She was an old woman, although her voice sounded young, like Alsander's; but it was not so ringing or musical as the voice of the Greek mate, and I don't think that her voice had much effect upon us unless when she sang. Then it seemed to dance through our brains and bring out all our worst passions, as bad drink does sometimes. She only sang, however, when the moon was at the full, which had been the night after we left Witestaple. Then we all heard her in her cabin, and for a while lost our self-control, and might have murdered each other but for her timely appearance amongst us, with Alsander, which quelled the mad riot.

She had only to raise her hand and point at anyone to deprive him of all power, or look at him without raising her hand and he became as one dead before her.

It was the evil eye, we all knew, which had conquered us, and which we could not resist.

There were three men on board, however, over whom she had no influence, and this I heard from one of the three—to wit, Tom Blunt. Sambo, the negro cook, and Alsander were the others.

One morning one of the gaol-birds became mutinous to the first mate, and he was ordered up to be whipped. They had stripped and tied him up, and our purser, Jack Howard, stood with the rope-end in his hand ready to lay on cheerily, while we all stood round to see the punishment given, for the mutineer was one of the vilest and most contumacious dogs on board, and all the honest ones amongst us enjoyed the sight.

Just at that moment the old woman came up to the deck and looked over at us, pointing her hands with a sweep towards us.

For an instant I felt as if a hot wind had blown over me like a fevered breath and a gripping at my heart; and then the punishment went on, and I saw the wretch take his three-dozen with abject howls, while Jack laid on lustily.

Then another hot breath laved me for an instant and blurred objects in front; and then, as I looked again, I saw the criminal standing with his shirt in his hand scowling like a fiend at his whipper, who, to my astonishment, wasn't Jack Howard at all, but our burly boatswain, Tom Blunt; while Penelope stood beside the third mate looking with burning eyes at the laughing boatswain, as if in a fury of baffled passion; and the negro rolled his eyes about and bared his white teeth in an unmistakable grin. The rest of the men were looking dumbfoundered from Tom Blunt to Jack Howard.

"Well," observed the pallid-faced mate, "you have all seen this man punished, have you not, boys?"

"Ay, ay, sir!" answered the men, in a chorus.

"And you are satisfied, I hope."

"Ay, ay, sir! *Jack Howard* has laid it on proper."

"And you all saw this?" asked Penelope, harshly glancing round the faces. "You, Humphrey?"

"Yes, Mistress Ancrum; I saw Jack Howard laying it on."

"It's a cussed lie!" roared the whipped sailor. "It was the boatswain that marked me, not the mate; and I'll not forget it, either."

"Quite su' ob dat," chuckled the negro hoarsely, while he looked at Penelope out of his half-closed lids.

"What did you see, Sambo?" asked Penelope anxiously.

"Same as all de odders, missah, ob course; su' you no tink poor nigger like me make himself out liar. My ole mudder was witch too, and showed me dat trick often. Evil eye no good on dis child; he know all 'bout it."

Penelope Ancrum stole a lurid side glance towards the cook, and then retreated to her cabin without saying anymore, while the men went to their duties, and the punished man to his bunk, cursing savagely under his breath.

"Look here, Humphrey, my boy," said Tom Blunt, drawing me aside; "who was it you saw whip that mongrel?"

"Jack Howard, of course," I replied promptly.

"And what was I doing all the time?"

"Looking on, like the rest of us."

"Then you were all wrong, my boy," Tom replied sorrowfully; "and this ship is bewitched, from the shipper down, with the exception of the witch, that Greek piratical friend of hers, the cook, myself, and your dog Martin there. Say, did you hear anything?"

"Yes; I heard the man yelling out lustily from the first stroke Jack laid on."

"Witchcraft all through, and I wish I saw the end of this voyage. Now I'll tell you just what happened. You all fell asleep and tumbled about the deck at a word from that old bag—all excepting those I have mentioned; while I took the rope-end from Jack and laid on the bare back. And, as for him yelling, I might just as well have laid on to a bit of dead meat, for he never budged except at the last two strokes, when she had woke him and the rest of you up. That's how the villain knew who struck him, and that's how I know that you are all under the devil's spell, all saving myself and the witch's mates, barring the good hound there, who nearly choked himself trying to break from his moorings and get at her. Good dog," he continued, stooping down and patting young Martin. "You and I haven't yet got into the devil's clutches; but the rest have, and it strikes me that we are a doomed ship."

IV

SHARK FISHING

Young Martin had his prejudices, as all good dogs have, and showed them so strongly that I was forced to keep him constantly on the chain during the voyage.

Penelope Ancrum was one of his special hatreds. Whenever she appeared on deck he tugged wildly at his chain, showed all his teeth, and bayed with fury to get at her. The Greek also was an object of aversion with him, mixed with abject terror. Whenever he caught a glimpse at that fine and impassive, but death-like face, the poor beast shrank down with horror, as if he had seen a ghost, and with his tail hidden, howled wildly.

A strange figure and face that was as it paced the deck, with its snow-white hair, and red eyes, hidden by day behind those blue spectacles, or blazing out like rubies in the dark; an unearthly sign it must have seemed to the terrified dog. Without a smile for anyone and hardly ever a word, up and down he paced during his watch, like a resuscitated corpse, with the dead white lustre of a soulless body lying on him. I don't know how I ever got used to it, so that I could walk with him and listen to his even voice without shuddering and shrinking, as my dog always did.

Martin showed his dislike in different ways to the gigantic negro, Indian Jos, and Gabrial Peas; for he disliked those three gentlemen as heartily as I did; a snarl and baring of the teeth towards Sambo, a low growl, with lurid side look, at Jos, and a shrinking back from the light approach of Gabrial.

Toward Sir John Fenton and the friends he had grown used to in the old town, however, he was always amiable; and to the strangers passively indifferent, so long as they did not attempt any familiarities with him.

He was now full grown, of a handsome tan colour, with black joints, an equal mixture between the mastiff and the Cuban bloodhound—that is, his mother had been a pure bloodhound, and his father, dear old Martin, the hero of a hundred fights.

Like myself, he had never yet tried his mettle at anything greater than a street fight, but he had it in him, anyone could see, when the time came, so long as his enemy had nothing supernatural about him. We both drew the line at ghouls and demons.

We were now nearing the tropics, and the winds were failing us; now they came in little spurts, sending us lazily along for a spell and then leaving us in the lurch.

At last one morning we woke up with nothing to do except to roll about the blistering deck, while the *Vigo* rolled about on an ultramarine ocean of heaving oil under a bleached-out sky; we were fairly becalmed, and must just content ourselves as best we could.

We had out our paints and brushes, and oakum and pitch, which needed no fire to melt it, and then we set to work scraping the blisters off and revarnishing the masts and yards until they shone again. Inside the ship was thoroughly over-hauled—forecastle, cockpit, and main-hold—while still we lay under that burning sun and on that rotting waste of heaving blue, and never a breath of air coming to revive us day or night. The sails hung in heavy folds from the yards, but without a flap of motion. We walked about the decks at midday without a shadow, and that seems to be something important that a man has lost when he misses it for the first time.

We tried next to play some old Plymouth games on deck—bowls and such-like; but these went languidly in that breathless heat, where no one could move a pace without panting as if he had been doing hard work. Generally we settled down to cards and dice under the awnings, where the men gambled with peas with each other for their future wages. At these games the black sheep showed up the most adroitly. Indeed, before the wind came the honest portion of the crew had become debtors to these sharks for much more than they ever expected to earn during the voyage.

Sometimes one or two would take out a small boat and row away from the ship. I liked to go on these excursions and look back at our wooden home, as she lay upon that plain, with her reflection under her. When we got a little distance from her, she seemed like two ships joined together at the hull, one upright and one reversed, and floating on the blue sky; for where the ocean and space met there was always a thin gas which hid the line;—two ships floating with drooping sails, and two suns blazing out of the blue.

Mistress Penelope was always very gracious to me, and seemed never satisfied unless she had me near her side, finding a hundred duties for me to do, if I wanted to join the others. She liked the great heat, and used to lie on deck, very lightly clad, with half her body in the sun-glare, and only the upper portion under the shadow of the awning. As we got into the tropics, she discarded her black costume, and took to rich thin stuffs and gandy colours, spreading a tiger skin mat under her, and glittering with the tinsel and flimsy drapery which lay about her.

For hours she would lie spread out full length on her rugs and cushions, a fine woman as far as figure went, and, when one looked at the arms or feet only, surprisingly young and shapely.

She did not frighten me so much at this time with her evil powers, nor seek to hold me near her, as she had done at first, with a word or a look; indeed, I think that to me her eyes had grown softer, and had lost a great deal of their power, as I did not so often feel them burn, or that heat-wave pass over, which made me unable to think or move but as she desired. She would ask me gently to sit beside her, and hold my hand or stroke my hair as she looked tenderly at me; and as being an old woman who might have been my grandmother, and I a young boy, I took these passages of kindness without much uneasiness or thought.

"It is a glorious land that we sail towards, my pretty boy," she would sometimes say, as she lay at my side and looked into my face from her pillows; "covered with fruits and flowers, where the herbs grow which make men and women young again and lusty. In a week after we get there I shall be young enough and perhaps fair enough even to win your heart."

"Where is this land, Mistress Ancrum?"

"It is an island to the south of the equator, and not far from the Spanish main, where I am well known and *respected*. You will meet brave fellows there who are able to drink their wine from cups of gold, and who are heroes, every man of them, as you will become."

"It is on the same Spanish main where all the buccaneers sail for, is it not?"

"Yes, Humphrey lad; bold rovers who call no man master, saving the captain they fix upon themselves—friends of Drake and Hawkins, some of them."

"Then they must be old friends of father's?"

"Most likely. We will soon find out when we get there."

My father did not look pleased when I told him about these things, nor when he saw me sitting so much with the old witch; but he had other duties to look after, and could not very well refuse to let her do as she pleased, for, like the others, he always grew helpless when she looked at him, as also I did when she looked fixed and fierce; yet it was seldom she did so with me, but seemed to like better to let me see her skill shown upon someothers.

"Would you like to see your friends win that game of cards, Humphrey?" she asked one day, as she pointed to the card players on deck.

"Yes, vastly," I replied.

"Then watch, for now they will win."

She never moved while she spoke, but looked steadily at the group, until they seemed to fall asleep for a moment, and then wake up with the cards all placed so that the honest boys won easily. She made the sharks shuffle out the losing cards for themselves and give the lucky ones to the others, without being aware of their folly.

"Ha! ha! Humphrey. You see what a gift I have over men. I could make any of them jump overboard amongst the sharks, if I liked."

"Don't do that, Mistress Penelope; unless if you like to send Indian Jos."

"Ah! you don't like Indian Jos?"

"No."

"Yet he is a brave fellow; and if you had seen him fight you would say so. Come here, Jos."

Jos came up from the game which he had just lost.

"I want you to show this young gentleman how to catch a blue-nose."

"Right you are, ma'am," replied Jos, going coolly over to the side and casting off his shirt. "Be ready with the rope, Gab, to fling when I give the word. And now, youngster, come this way, and I'll show you how we fish in the tropics, and the sort of bait we use."

Penelope rose and went with me to the ship's side, while Jos began to climb up the shrouds, with only his breeches on, and his uncovered body gleaming like brass in the sunshine; the hairless Gabrial Peas in the meantime fastening a whale hook to the end of a coil of rope and chain, and waiting beside us, ready for the throw.

By this time the main body of the idle seamen got up from under the awnings, and, leaning against the bulwarks, watched that half-naked climber. My father had gone below, and was busy with his charts, over which he and Sir John were bending, otherwise I knew that he would have put a stop to this foolhardy feat—that is, if Penelope had not spellbound him. As for the fourth mate, Jack Howard, or Tom Blunt, who were both on duty at the time, interfering, no one thought about such a thing in the case of Indian Jos.

Slowly the ungainly looking object climbed the shrouds until he reached the lower yard, along which he crept until he was beyond the ship's side and directly over the still ocean. Then, taking out his stiff dagger-knife from his belt, he put it between his fang-like teeth, and rose to his feet to make the plunge.

Here then he was, with his jaundiced skin drawn over his bulging ribs, and his bones all shining out in hard knobs as he clasped his hands above his head, and stood for a moment balancing himself above that spar-end, while the space grew bleached around him, and below slumbered the intensely blue depths.

Then, slowly bending forward like a bow, he suddenly made the spring, dropping like a lump of lead through the light air and into that fathomless ocean, while a bright silver column went gyrating after his heels as he plunged down—down, as the disturbed waters fell out into rings, which grew bigger as they receded, wide circles, like lines of dark blue paint, drawn round a paler blue surface.

I could count a great many beats of my heart while he still remained below. As Penelope leaned against my shoulders, with her bright black eyes fixed upon that silver spiral cord, and her breath softly laving my neck; I could count her heart-throbs also through her thin drapery, as she pressed closely to me—steady, full throbs, that caused mine to beat faster, while minutes seemed to pass as she looked through my hair down to the sea, with her arm over mine.

At last he bounded half-way out of the waves, and shook the brine out of his eyes, while a little way from him appeared a black, three-cornered speck, towards which he swam vigorously, the knife still between his teeth.

"Yonder is the shark," murmured the old woman, while she pressed her dry, hot lips against my sweltering neck. "Now, pretty boy, you will see some sport."

As she spoke, both Jos and the fin disappeared simultaneously, and then for a little space there was silence and a strange disturbance of the waters, while Penelope's breath came faster, and I felt the flash of her burning eyes as her arm tightened round me, and my heart beat time with hers. All the while I was dripping with perspiration.

"Ha! ha! Do you see it, my pretty boy? Blood—blood mixing with the blue and changing it into purple."

I saw it with a shiver.

"Whose is it?—Jos's?"

"What matter, so long as it flows? Ah, it is the shark's."

It was Jos who once more appeared, with an awful laugh stretching his wide mouth and wrinkling his yellow jaws, as he waved the dripping knife over his head and shouted for Gabrial Peas to fling the hook and rope.

Then, catching it with his free hand, he once more dived with it out of sight, while we waited on what next was to come.

Again he appeared, the knife in his teeth, swimming with one hand, while he passed his hand along the rope, and so on, until he reached the side of the ship, up which he scrambled, and made towards his shirt, which he proceeded to throw over him quietly.

As he did so I saw the body of the monster float to the surface, belly upwards, and gleaming white where it was not gashed and torn, with the blood pouring from its wounds and dyeing the ocean for yards round, its horrible mouth half gaping and showing awful rows of glittering, zigzag teeth.

"That is the way to fish for sharks, youngster, only it takes a man to do it; don't it, ma'am?" said Indian Jos with a grin, as Penelope released me and once more laid herself down listlessly on her pillows and skins, without looking at him or thanking him.

"Would you like to try it, sonny?" he continued, turning to me. "There will be lots of his relations up presently to look after him, if you want a chance to distinguish yourself."

"No," I replied, with a shiver, as I once more looked at the evil thing which the men were slowly hauling near. As I watched it, suddenly I saw the ocean covered with fins, all crowding eagerly towards the quivering carcase. Who could have thought that this silent ocean held so many monsters, or that they could be so vicious? In a moment they darted close, and threw themselves on it, tugging and tearing it into pieces with their sharp teeth, while the sailors played with them, drawing it from them and they following it foot by foot until I could see their wide jaws and dull eyes right under me—a horrible sight of slaughter, which made me grow faint, and glad to sink once more down by the side of the witch.

"You are not used to blood yet, pretty boy," she murmured, patting me softly on the cheek, while she looked at me with half-closed eyes.

At this moment Alsander came out of his cabin, pale and cold, like a being which no tropic sun could warm.

She drew her hand from my cheek quickly, and looked at him uneasily as he approached, while I, now feeling better, was glad of the chance to leave her and go amongst the men.

So the days passed, while we rocked above that shark-crowded ocean, my dog lying panting, with lolling tongue, inside his barrel, and the smell of food hateful to us, the men whistling for the wind that never came, and the sun going down each night blood coloured, with strangely shaped vapours gathering round it, and the night, before the moon rose, filled with luminous sparkles that clung to our masts and yards like ghosts, while the waters seemed to crawl with loathsome yet shining monstrosities.

V

The Resurrection of Alsander

It was during Alsander's watch on deck that I always got my liberty from Penelope Ancrum; she always let me go from her the moment he appeared, and devoted herself mostly to him. What they talked about I never knew, for they always spoke to each other in that strange language; she sometimes eagerly, without, however, disturbing his calmness. But one thing I could see, and that was that he appeared to exercise as great a power over her as she had over the others.

One day when I was beside her, and he was below sleeping, I said to her, with the freedom of a petted boy,—

"Have you known Alsander long, Mistress Ancrum?"

"Yes, Humphrey, many years," she replied, with a slight shiver and a backward glance in the direction of the cabin.

"Where did you first meet him?"

"On one of the islands of Greece, eighteen years ago."

"How old is he?"

"No one knows, my pretty boy; he looked the same age as he does today when we first met."

"And did he always look as he does now?"

"Yes, Humphrey."

"Like a dead man?"

"Hush! Humphrey, or he may hear; and he would not like us speaking about him," she replied, lowering her voice and bending near to me.

"Oh, he will not hear; he must be asleep just now."

"He never sleeps, and he can only look like what he is," she whispered, her dark eyes looking into mine with a film of horror over them; but I was curious, and her indulgence had made me pert and bold, so I pushed on with my questions.

"What do you mean, Mistress Ancrum?"

"What I say: that he is a dead man—a man who has lost his soul."

"Oh!" I had read about vampires and ghouls, who were made up from dead bodies, and who sometimes were permitted to walk the earth, and I shuddered as I thought upon these weird stories.

"Do you mean that he is a vampire?"

"Listen, my boy, and I will tell you about Alsander as much as I know; and then never ask me again, for I am in his power, and can never be free from him, unless someone can free me by love. And even then it must be a heart never before possessed by woman—a young heart fresh and pure, like yours, Humphrey."

I looked at the old woman with a sudden fear. Was she mad? or could she expect any boy to fall in love with his grandmother? I began to regret my curiosity, and wish that Alsander would only appear and set me at liberty. Her next words showed that she had read my thoughts like a book, for she continued in a low voice, while she held me from going with a hand which, I must admit, was both small and pretty,—

"No, I could not expect such a sacrifice—at least, not yet, as I am; but wait until I get my youth back again, and my beauty, and then perhaps you may."

I sat silent, thinking that to me she could never appear other than what she was—a very old woman, only pretending to be young, as Alsander was pretending to be alive, if she was not telling me a lie.

"Eighteen years ago I landed upon the island of Milo, where I had gone to seek a sorcerer, who was reputed wonderful in his dark wisdom; but I was too late to see him alive, for the natives had killed him, and left him unburied in his cave. He had been over a month dead and lying in that cave, with all his potions and books about him, for none of them, although vindictive enough to kill him, dared to go near it afterwards.

"I had come a long way to see him, and therefore I determined not to be disappointed: I would go alone to his barbarous sepulchre and secure his books, since I could not learn from his own lips his fateful secrets. So one night after sundown I stole out of the village and sought the mountains.

"The moon was shining brightly—a full moon, which always affects me strangely, and from which I think I gather the power to work on men, although I am losing it with you, Humphrey, for I am growing to love you too well, and that always robs me of my spells."

Had she often loved, this strange old witch, to know the effect so well, I thought, as she went on with her story.

"The moon was streaming down over the plains and hills, strange, fibrous tissues of silver, that seemed to draw my heart out towards its white soul, and deprive me of my own volition and personality, as I rob others of theirs when I look at them. I stole along the plains and into the shadow-buried ravines until I came to the priest-cursed cavern where lay the body of Alsander.

"I saw him lying within as they had left him, with a streak of moonlight falling upon his naked, white body, and the stake which they had driven through his heart. I looked at him, and saw that he was as fresh as if newly slain, but no blood came from him as I drew the stake from his heart—that had all escaped long before.

"Then I cast a spell, and summoned my old master to my aid. With the dead body of Alsander beside me within the magic ring, I called up my familiars and my master, and asked them to revive the body, so that I might ask his secrets from him.

"They did so, and Alsander rose up from my side as you see him now, and walked out with me. They had given him life, but his spirit had been past recall, and none of the demons would enter into that church-banned tenement; so he came back to earth with only the sparkle of life which had never left him, but without a soul.

"I made a compact with him that night. No matter what; you could not understand what it was. But it bound me to him forever, unless a young life and a fresh soul can set me at liberty, and make me content with life and Alsander satisfied with death. Hush! pretty one; go away, for he is coming; but never speak about this secret."

I rose and ran from under that awning as if it had been a graveyard as I saw the white, handsome features of our third mate lift up from the companion stairs. I felt as I sought out honest Tom Blunt as if I never wanted to ask anymore questions while I lived.

That night the moon was at the full, and as we lay on deck, trying to find a cool plank, we were spellbound by the clear but monotonous voice of the witch singing down in her cabin the melancholy refrain of that air which incited us all to homicide:—

> *"And Jack lies 'mongst the seaweed in the deep and silent sea,*
> *And I am waiting on the shore, with nothing left for me."*

VI

Raising the Wind

We were prevented from using our knives on each other for the second time by our third mate, Alsander, for with the blood mounting into our brains we felt that we must let it out somehow—I as bad as the rest, young though I was; while Sambo and honest Tom Blunt were the only two who were not driven mad by that wailing refrain. We wanted to howl out our reasonless rage and fly at each other's throats, like rabid dogs.

As for Sambo, that heaving mountain of blackness, nothing either human or supernatural appeared to be able to astonish him or move him to emotion. He lived and slept either in the caboose or on the maindeck beside it, greeting all comers with the same distorted grin, or rather, folding back of his enormous lips, and the baring of his white teeth; while his little eyes went nearly out of sight behind the layers of fat which that grin sent upwards. He was the tallest and most obese figure that I ever beheld, as well as the most emotionless.

Tom Blunt was the hardest hitter, the hardest swearer, as well as the hardest-headed man on board, yet withal the most religious. He never missed his prayers, or the saying of a grace over meals; and for relaxation he occupied himself with two books only—the "Church Service" and the "Laws of Navigation." For he had learnt to read, and was vastly proud of this accomplishment. Perhaps he was a little over-fond of argument and liking to have the last word, but he was a man who never committed himself to a promise that he could not perform, and who was never afraid of holding to his own opinion. Short-built and broad-shouldered, with bushy black eyebrows hanging over keen blue eyes; a deeply bronzed face, surmounted by a perfect forest of crisp dark hair and beard; he always walked with his head well thrown back, and with a straight look in the face. As he said of himself, he trusted in the Lord, and despised the devil and all his works. To win the friendship and protection of Tom Blunt was something that anyone might feel proud about. The dog Martin and he were alike in many points: they never disguised either their likes or dislikes.

Tom drew me out of the snarling crowd in the forecastle while that dirge was going on, and into the moonlight, where he made me walk with him until it ceased and I had become cooled down.

"Say your prayers, Humphrey, when you feel like that, or you will be damned with the rest of them; and keep from that evil witch, if you are wise."

That I couldn't keep from her wasn't Tom's blame, nor did he blame me for it either. He knew by instinct what she was, and watched vigilantly over my welfare. Although he owned that he had little hopes of how the voyage would end, yet he went about his duty calmly, saying little about what he thought.

Our owner, Sir John, did not often appear on deck, and when he did I noticed a great change for the worse on him. He was ageing swiftly, and tottered feebly when he walked, with his head bending over his thin chest, and a dejected look in his dim eyes. I think that he had never recovered from the destruction of his mansion, and his exile from the land of his birth. Old men feel these trials worse than young folk.

It was at this time that the sailors began to speak aloud about the ship being haunted as well as bewitched. We had been over three weeks without budging a foot, and the water in the casks was rotten and almost undrinkable, even with all the pangs of thirst which we suffered. Sir John was generous with his wine and beer, I will allow, at this season; but it is water that men crave mostly for when they are becalmed at sea; and even that, vile as it was, had to be served out sparingly, for we were running short, and unless we got into the doldrums soon, would be left without any.

Strange noises were heard coming from the body of the ship, which affrighted the sailors: shrieks, and wailings, and the rattling of chains, which no one could account for excepting as supernatural.

The sailors told how they had been buffeted about by unseen hands when they were on their watch. We had sailed on a Friday, which was the most unlucky day that could have been taken; but for that we had no choice.

Pale ghost candles on our mast-heads and bowsprit were seen by all, but they were counted good as far as they went; and the strange lights which moved on the waters, Tom said that they were the spirits of all who had lived and died on board the *Vigo* looking after her, for spirits always haunted the ship which they had died in, and never left her as long as she could float. And none wondered at that, for a ship is like nothing else for getting round a human heart, and already I felt that

I loved every plank and spar of the old *Vigo*, and would willingly forego ease and comfort for the pleasure of going with her over the ocean.

"Yes, the ship was haunted; and by spirits good and evil. She had been a Spanish craft at the first, and, they said, knew the journey well that she was taking now; so that it was our Plymouth boys who suffered the most from the buffetings of ghostly hands, for none of the black sheep ever complained about being hurt by these unseen souls of pirates. Indian Jos used to laugh grimly, and say in his grating tones that we'd have no good luck until we hoisted the flag that the *Vigo* had grown used to—the "Jolly Roger."

"Ships are just like men, boys, after a free life: they don't take kindly to square sailing—at least, not while they are in their prime."

And it appeared like this with the *Vigo*, for she lay obstinately on that haunted ocean, as if she was waiting for us to re-christen her, and give her employment to her liking, before she would go on.

One night, as I was lying in the shadow of the water casks, while the little barber was trying his best to amuse them forward with his fiddle, I saw the cook, with Indian Jos and Gabrial Peas, come over from the crowd and squat down close at hand without noticing me.

"What's come over our queen lately, that she ain't raising a wind and getting us out of this?" growled Jos, as he sucked savagely at his pipe. "I'm getting about sick of it, and think she must be losing her power."

"No fear ob dat," replied Sambo, with a hoarse laugh. "That witch know what she's about, I 'spect, as well as anyone. She jist knows the right moment to set to work, you take my word for dat."

"She is soft on the boy, and is forgetting us, I fancy," remarked Gabrial, in his husky whisper.

"No blamed fear o' that!" cried Jos; "she dar'n't for her life look past the commodore."

"Ah! Captain Alsander ain't always to the fore. It's when he is off duty that she claws round the young one. You know, Jos, that she always had a liking for innocent boys when he wasn't there to look after her."

"Ah! that's just it. But, hush! mates; here comes the king."

I heard the steady footstep of our third mate as he strode along from the poop, and presently I saw his dead-white face and snowy hair gleaming in the moonlight as he paused beside them.

"Well, lads!" he said, in his rich, clear voice, "you are getting tired of waiting here, I expect."

"Yes, sir," replied Jos.

"Tired of doing nothing, tired of winning from the fools."

"There ain't no more to win, sir; every man Jack of them is owing us five years' service, and there's no fun playing for more."

"No; you have won enough for our purpose," he said, looking round and up at the distant lightning, which was darting about the other lights, and at the corpse candles, which were sitting on the yards and masts in clusters. "Penelope is getting ready to raise the wind, and we shall be moving before morning."

"Right you are, sir; that's what we want."

Alsander walked slowly from them, and as I still lay wondering what it all means I heard Tom Blunt's whistle calling the men together. Then, as the three rose and joined the others, I crept along in the shadows until I could also get amongst them without being observed where I came from.

The moon was getting into the third quarter, and beginning to grow thin at the edges, as we all clustered up to the maindeck, where Penelope, Sir John, my father, and the mates stood. At Sir John's request, the witch had at last consented to call up those spirits who haunted the ship, and ask them for a fair wind.

As we stood waiting, Penelope came down amongst us; her body covered with the same robe that she had worn on that night when she summoned the demons at Witestaple, and her white hair hanging loosely over her shoulders. Sir John also had on his wizard's robe and conical cap, and held his wand in his trembling hand.

The witch took each man by rotation and gazed at him fixedly as she held him by the hand. When she came to Sambo, she only glanced at him, and passed him over without touching him, at which he grinned.

When she came to Tom Blunt, she said, "That man must go below and be locked in, or else I cannot work."

Tom only looked at her with a scornful smile, and turning his back on the crowd, tramped away to his own bunk without a word.

"You will come with me, Humphrey," she said, taking my hand and leading me on to the poop, where the officers were standing.

When we reached the group, I saw Alsander turn his glowing red eyes on me, while he said to her,—

"Don't you think that the boy had better join the boatswain, madam? He is rather young to witness the sights we may have to look upon."

"Yes, Mistress Ancrum; let me go along with Tom Blunt," I replied, eager to get away from her and the vicinity of the vampire mate.

"No," said Penelope sullenly, without looking up; "I want to try him, Alsander, and he has courage enough."

"As you like," replied the mate, with a gentle shrug of his shoulders as he retreated to the side of Sir John.

The witch now clasped both my hands in hers, and turning me to where the moon fell upon my face, looked at me steadily with her burning glance. At first I experienced no sensation, but in a short time I felt my heart begin to quiver as if it was being drawn from its place out of my eyes. Then the warm wave passed over me, while things became blanked out, and after that a stillness and courage came into me that was from her.

"That will do, pretty one," she whispered softly in my ear. "Now you are no longer afraid."

"No," I answered confidently, as I took my place with the others and prepared to look on.

Sir John now began to read out of a book in a strange language, and make passes and signs in the air with his wand, while Penelope sat at his feet clasping her knees with her hands, and looking stedfastly towards the bows of the vessel.

"Heavens! what is that?" I heard my father cry, as he looked in the same direction, and at the cry every head was turned the same way.

"A 'Jack-Harry' lightship!" shouted the sailors from below. "Look! she is going to board us!"

There in the distance I saw a large vessel loom up, with all her sails set, and from every point blue lights hanging like stars or spangles of silver.

She was gliding on softly without ruffling the still waters, which were burning under her keel like fired brandy, with scaly shapes twisting about, as if a swarm of huge serpents were twisting round each other to get out of the way.

How light and thin seemed the body of this ship, as if it had been made from transparent paper, while the sails and shrouds looked like silver gossamer, through which one could see the stars, for the moon was at our stern—the flimsy shadow of a ship more than a reality.

Nearer it drew, and then I could make out its figure-head—a female saint, with her arms crossed over her breast—the same figure-head that our own carrack carried.

It was the double of the *Vigo* in every particular, only that, whereas our ship lay like a heavy log upon the waste, with lumpish sails dangling about the solid masts, this ghostly vessel moved lightly and easily along.

So she floated on until she drew to about ten yards from us, when, without a sound or the shifting of the yards, she turned about, presenting her stern to our bows, and lying, as we were, motionlessly on the sea.

Something made me change my gaze from the phantom to our own decks, and then I saw what they were waiting for.

From the closed hatches and open forecastle doors crowded out a procession of pallid, fleshless figures, all clad in shining dresses—seamen, richly dressed gentlemen and ladies, with the difference of their stations and sex shown in the cut of their clothes, but of the same luminous texture. I saw them passing us also from the cabin behind and floating away towards that spectreship, which they boarded.

The gentlemen and ladies went first, and after them followed the mariners, bearing with them silver ropes, which they had fastened to our bows and which they carried over to the stern in front of us.

Then the ghost-laden carrack began to move ahead and the shining strands began to grow taut, and after that draw us behind them.

Yes, we were moving on over that fiery sea with our strange pilot in front of us, slowly at first, while the surge began to furrow from us, and leave a moonlit track behind.

Then faster we sailed, with the waves curling up as we forced our way through them, after that craft, which cast no furrow.

While still watching this strange sight, a darkness fell behind me and blackened the deck, which had been silvered with the moonbeams.

I turned quickly about, and noticed that the moon was dimly battling with crape-like clouds, while heavier masses were welling up from the horizon, now copper-tinted, like the heated doors of a great furnace, and thickly charged with fierce lightning flashes.

"Reef sails!" shouted my father, starting into sudden animation at the sight of that sky behind. And at the command the sailors sped like monkeys up the shrouds and began to haul in all canvas with a will, never looking in front of them.

In the far distance sounded a long, melancholy wail, such as a dog might utter when he foretells a death. It smote upon my ears and filled my heart with nameless horror.

I looked ahead once more; but the phantom ship had vanished, with its ghostly crew and silver ropes, and only the glowing stars were visible, with that crape-like drapery of clouds, hustling over us and dropping in front, putting them out one by one.

We were still sailing on, but sluggishly, with the top-sails, not yet furled, bulging out, and with a light wind, which hadn't yet reached the decks.

Now it came eddying down and playing upon my fevered head, so fresh and gracious, after the long spell of heat.

"Get below, Sir John and Mistress Ancrum," shouted my father, as he sprang to the wheel and caught it in his strong hands, shoving the man who had held it out of his way.

"Take me below, Humphrey," said the witch, putting her hand upon my arm, and drawing me with her to the cabin doors, which were immediately closed behind Sir John and us, closed and barred from the outside by Alsander.

I led Penelope to one of the sofas, and was turning to go, when she pressed me down beside her, saying, "You must stay here, child, or you'll be washed overboard. They have asked me to raise the wind, and I have done it."

VII

Father Neptune Boards the *Vigo*

For a few moments there reigned deep silence in the stuffy cabin; then I heard that death-howl once more from behind, only nearer and louder than before, as if a pack of wolves were coming on at full speed.

Nearer and shriller the awful yell came; then, as it filled my ears, and almost deafened me, a sudden shock sent me full upon Penelope, who clasped me tightly in her arms, and drew me closely to her heart, kissing me savagely, and screaming out as she did so,—

"Nearer, my pretty one; closer. It is the tempest—the tornado—that is with us: to fill our blood with fire, to give us life and motion."

I could not break from that fierce embrace, and she was stifling me with her kisses, while the lightning flashes blazed every instant through the cabin, and the thunder claps rattled through the horrible shrieking of the wind; a wild confusion of tumbling articles around us, and outside the mighty thudding of those hellish waves.

I was blinded by the swift flashes of the lightning, and dazed with the turmoil of the tempest, as well as being nearly suffocated by the fury of her embrace, so that I could neither look about me nor pause to grasp the situation, for the ship rose and sank, and swayed from side to side as the waves fell about her, and thumped her about unceasingly, until my heart grew sick and faint, and I was fast losing my senses, when all at once I felt her clinging arms grow slack and leave me free. Then, after a breathless gasp or two, I managed to get hold of the legs of the fixed table, and raising myself up, looked round me as well as I could.

Sir John Fenton, still in his wizard's robe, was lying on the floor, clinging wildly to the curved foot of the sofa from which he had been cast—now almost perpendicular, as the ship made a sudden dive, like one hanging to the roof of a house; now with his head down, as the ship rebounded. There was no time given us to rest before the next change came.

In the centre of the cabin stood Alsander, with his legs wide apart, and steadying himself upright, as only a sailor or a fly could do under the circumstances; while at his feet, where he held her with a firm clutch on her shoulder, crouched Penelope, with a wild glare of abject and reasonless fear in her black eyes as she looked up at his luminous red ones.

His face was steady and coldly white, as usual, with the same still expression upon the features turned towards her; but the eyes were brighter, and more like two rubies with a light behind them. As I watched him I seemed to see two scarlet rays shoot from them and reflect themselves on the staring inky balls beneath, until they sparkled like drops of blood.

The lightning was flashing at longer intervals by this time, and the thunder-peals rumbling away into distant growls, while the vessel began to ride more steadily.

"The storm has passed, madam, and Sir John. Now you may get into your berths and go to sleep quietly."

Alsander uttered the words slowly and clearly, releasing his grasp at the witch's shoulder, upon which she crawled away on her hands and knees towards the door of her private cabin, like a whipped cur, with her head turned back at the mate, and her eyes still glaring on him as if they would leap from their sockets.

"Permit me," he said quietly, going after her and opening the door, within which she disappeared, while he closed it again after her.

"Are we dismantled?" gasped Sir John, getting up all trembling, and still holding on to the couch.

"Not at all. We were prepared for the first gust, and now we are driving along bravely, with a fair wind, in the right direction, and nothing damaged. Let me help you to your berth, Sir John."

While the old man took the arm of the mate, and tottered along with him to his side of the saloon, I made the most of my opportunity, and ran up the companion steps, and out to the poop, where my father still stood at the wheel, while the men tramped about the slopping decks in full activity, with the mates and boatswain shouting out their commands, plentifully garnished in the fashion that seamen expect.

The strength of the tornado had gone by, and we were now chasing its tail, which was rapidly leaving us behind. Away to the front rushed the lurid thunderclouds, belching out from their distended sides their artillery of fire and sound as they retreated; and behind us the waning moon was sailing through dark-blue rivers, which cut continents of snowy clouds, into soft, windy bags of fleece, that changed their outlines as they rolled and choked up the rivers, burying the wan moon behind them for a time, until she once more broke free, and found another passage all unimpeded.

The ocean was no longer sluggish, but foam-flecked and champing in its impatience, as it tossed against us, and drove us on.

The men were hauling down the topsails, which tore wildly as they filled and sought to escape from the control; but at last they were fastened to the yards, and then they bellied out steadily, and gave us the advantage over the waves.

It was a full and lasting breeze we were having, after all our waiting—a breeze which stirred up the blood and made us feel active, yet warm, as it blew over us, as new-drawn milk.

I did not linger on the wet poop, but sought the main-deck, where the men were working and singing their chants as they hauled at the ropes. I had no desire to meet Alsander on his return, for now I understood the meaning of Indian Jos's words, and felt afraid of his ruby eyes and rigid whiteness. So I took a hand at the ropes, and kept as well as I could within the shadow.

Before long we got the ship under full sail and all taut. Then the men who were off watch went back to their bunks, and I lay down beside my dog and went to sleep, while the ship flew merrily upon her course.

Next day we were into the doldrums, and made ourselves busy spreading our spare sails to catch the rain and fill our casks. It fell steadily and heavily for two days, while we stripped ourselves naked, and washed our bodies and our clothes in the warm downpour, feeling as if we were drinking in fresh life at every pore as we danced about and jested, playing pranks on each other, and preparing to welcome Father Neptune on board, for we had now crossed the line, and expected him and his court the first dry day.

Mistress Penelope and Sir John kept to their berths during this time, for which I was well pleased, for I was ashamed to look her in the face after what had passed in the cabin. Indeed, when I thought of it, I felt a loathing at both myself and her that I could not overcome.

Alsander I saw at times when he was on duty, but I gave him a wide berth, and he did not appear to notice me. I knew now that he held the witch in his power, and that, whether he had a soul or not in that cold, dead body, the power and will to do evil were alive enough in him, and that he had cause to hate me, if hatred is not, like virtue, a quality of the soul.

However, it was a merry day of pastime when old Neptune boarded us, with his wife and attendants, to claim his dues, and judge those who had crossed the line for the first time.

A fine old fellow King Neptune was, with his tow beard, and tin crown, and three-pronged sceptre in his hand,—very like what Tom Blunt's grandfather might have looked; his wife also, with her ragged ringlets, was not unlike Jack Howard in the face and voice.

They made two thrones for him and his wife on the poop, with a platform for his barber and doctor, which he had brought along with him. In front of him they had fixed a large sail half filled with sea-water, and beside the barber stood a bucket of shaving mixture and an enormous razor of hoop-iron; the doctor also had his pills and potions all ready at hand.

Sir John was tried in his absence, and let off with a substantial fine and half a dozen flagons of rum, for King Neptune and his court liked this drink best when above water.

Robbie Crooker, the little Plymouth surgeon-barber, was the first man called, and a wild chase they had after him before he was caught and led up by Sambo, who had been sworn in by Neptune to act as bathman. Mercy on us! What an awful monster that black man looked as he stood naked and waist high inside the sail, waiting on the victims being flung down to him!

Neptune first examined Robbie as to his qualities and profession, and then turned him over to the queen, who decided that, if the doctor thought him strong enough, he should be shaved and washed, an operation that the little man certainly required, for he had been a stranger to water since he left his shrew wife.

In vain Robbie howled for grace. The doctor decided that he required a strengthening pill, and manfully forced the largest and blackest-looking lump of medicine I ever saw down the poor man's throat; after which he was handed over to the barber.

It was a nasty shame, and no mistake, for while he was being lathered the barber plied him with questions, which, as the little man opened his mouth to answer, the brush was crammed where the pill had gone, so that he could only spit and splutter.

Then he was shaved with that formidable razor, and pitched without ceremony down to Sambo, who gave him such a bath that Robbie did not get quite the better of it for a week; and after this he was allowed to crawl away to his bunk like a half-drowned rat.

The other fresh hands followed, fighting vainly for their liberty as they were maul-hauled. And then my turn came. But, being young and beardless, they let me off the shave and pill, and only gave me a ducking. But that was quite enough to make me feel glad when it was over, and that one had only to pay tribute to Neptune once in a lifetime.

But, for all that, he was a right genial fellow for a sea-king, and stayed with us all day, enjoying himself, with his wife, free and easy amongst the men, sharing his rum all round, and bellowing out spirited ditties which we all knew, and could join in the choruses. But of course a sea-god is expected to be up to date in such matters.

Robbie Crooker brought out his fiddle, after he had got over his sulks, and, under the stimulation of a couple of glasses of stiff grog, almost forgot his troubles, and played while the others sang or danced.

We kept it up till long after dark, and then the merry god bade us farewell, and with his wife, himself, and his mermen all pretty much intoxicated, they disappeared over the ship's side.

VIII

The Home of King Death

That witch-raised wind carried us right on without accident or delay until we sighted the island which Penelope had fixed upon as our first destination.

It was a beautiful island, and well chosen by the people who lived upon it for their own purposes,—a tropical gem, resting within a tropical sea, and which I shall try to describe presently.

We knew that we were approaching some kind of land two or three days before, from the birds that we saw and the floating vegetation, with the seaweed, like rare, dyed grasses and ferns, which clung about our bows, as well as from the number of small vessels, caravels, pinnaces, and junks which ran out to meet us, and, after hailing and boarding us, shot off again to herald our approach.

At Penelope's request, another dark-blue flag with silver devices was kept floating at our masthead as we advanced; otherwise we might have been shot at, for even the lightest smack carried long-range guns. But this insignia they appeared to know, for after the first flotilla had boarded us and the captains had talked to Penelope and Alsander, whom they appeared to know well, as also they did the ship, they went off again cheerfully, after welcoming us heartily to their waters, and we were troubled with no further questions.

A queer insignia that was which floated at our masthead—a skeleton wrought in silver, holding in one hand a writhing snake, while with the other fleshless arm he embraced the waist of a woman; while around the two figures were the symbolic signs of the different stars. Not exactly the "Black Roger," Tom Blunt remarked, as he cast his eyes up to it, but as near to it as might be, for it looked black enough in the distance.

I was on deck when we were first hailed by the half-dozen of swift sailing vessels, and saw the captains and some of their crews as they were rowed aboard. A sprinkling of all nationalities, they were made up from black, yellow, and brown; for, although some of them may have been originally white, they were now reduced to the shade of tanned leather with their long basking in the hot suns.

They all bent their heads respectfully to Alsander, and stooped to kiss the hand which Penelope held out to them, speaking to them in the same language that they used themselves when together. Sambo and Jos they also greeted as old friends and boon companions, with a tight hand grip and hearty slap on the shoulders. And then looking round at my father and his other mates with curious smiles, they dropped over the side into their boats, and were rowed away to their own vessels, which at once shook out sails and went off like swallows on the wind—a villainous looking lot, with crews ugly enough to give an honest man the shakes.

Penelope had never spoken to me since that night of the storm, and when our eyes met she merely smiled faintly and turned away; but it was only as we drew near to the island that she came up on deck at all, and only then when Alsander was on duty and could be near her, a change that I was not at all sorry to see.

Slowly loomed up from the horizon that miracle of an island which I was to know more of in the future; first a blur of blue haze, which changed to gold and emerald as we advanced, then the barrier walls of surf-fringed reefs, with the lofty mountains, great forests, and high precipices of coloured rocks.

It took us sometime to get through these different circles of reefs in our way. And here I noticed that Indian Jos had the wheel, while Alsander acted as pilot.

Through one narrow gateway we would glide, with the white surf thundering on each side at a few yards space from the ship, then we would shift our yards and run along for a mile or so before we came to another passage, and back again to the third and fourth; after this it was all zigzag, steering along twisting rivers of blue, with the waves round us bright, green, and pink, while fish of every hue darted over the clear waters in countless shoals. I could have hung over the taffrail watching them for hours without wearying, there was such a bewildering variety.

It was afternoon before we reached clear, deep water, and then we had to sail along steep cliffs without seeing an opening anywhere—cliffs filled with small caves and covered with sea-birds, so that they looked white in some places, with the tops of dense forests above, but never a sign of humanity,

At last we came to a part where the cliff became a promontory with other wall-like cliffs behind; into this we passed, then round other points. I counted eight of these headlands as we passed round them, enclosed as we were amid precipices.

We were moving slowly, for the wind had failed us, but the tide was fairly strong and running inwards, so that it drew us on. There were two ways to the heart of this island, as I afterwards found; and, according to the tide, they could use either for coming in or going out.

All at once we burst into the harbour, and for a moment I blinked my eyes with wonderment at the rare sight before me: it was so like an enchanted scene and so little expected.

A vast lake, surrounded on three sides with precipices, and in the distance the most beautiful shore that I ever looked at or could dream about.

Golden sands near the water's edge, with a long sloping hill all terraced reaching behind and green with lush grasses, where it was not cultivated or built upon, here lay a town as large as Plymouth, with verandahed houses of wood and stone placed on the terraces, and reaching one above the other half-way up the hill,—gaily painted houses, all glowing in the subdued light, for the cliffs hid the setting sun, and already twilight was beginning to settle down upon it,—a warm, golden twilight, that was far from being darkness. Yet from many of the windows shone bright lamps. As for the gardens, they were everywhere, trees drooping under their load of fruit, flowers, the like of which I had never before seen for largeness and beauty of colouring.

The streets, terraces, sands, and harbour were dotted with figures of men, women, and children, all gaily costumed, while about us, as we rested, for the tide also left us here, lay carracks, galliases, and smaller vessels by the hundred.

While we waited, a dozen or so of rowing boats and canoes darted out to meet us, crowded with figures; at the same moment from each of the ships and many of the terraces and walls thundered out a salvo of cannon, belching out their smoke until the whole picture was buried for sometime in white fog. It was such a welcome as a king might get on his coming home.

I looked to where Penelope and Alsander were standing alongside of Sir John and the others. She had spread out both arms towards the shore, while her mouth was open in an ecstasy of joy; but Alsander stood quiet and emotionless, with his arms crossed over his breast and his snow-white hair falling down his dead-white cheeks, and only the glow of two red lamps in his awful and sightless-looking eyes. I shivered at the sight of that joyless face and the rigidity of that handsome figure.

Then the shoal of boats joined us as the smoke was clearing, and heaving their towlines up to us, they began to pull us in.

Slowly we glided past the galleys and small craft, each crew cheering us as we went along, to which only Penelope responded by waving her handkerchief, for the mate never budged.

Up to the harbour wharf, and there we were moored, while a score of men dressed like noblemen leapt aboard and surrounded Alsander.

"Welcome, King Death, to home. So you have brought back the old ship."

"Yes, friends; I said that I would bring her back," replied Alsander quietly, as he prepared to step ashore.

IX

A Merry Night

That night my father and Tom Blunt stayed aboard, while the rest of us went into the town to see the sights and, as is common with sailors, spend some money.

The men who had won from our Plymouth and Witestaple boys the whole of their ready cash, as well as their wages in advance, came out free enough on this night with their offer of loans. All they asked in return was that each man should give his written bond for the money lost and borrowed. These papers the landlord of the first inn we dropped into witnessed, along with a few customers who were present; and then we were right good friends, and equal in the way of pocket-money. I borrowed five pieces of eight straight away, giving my written bond to Indian Jos for the pieces right willingly, and feeling like a man, ready for any game which the others proposed.

And we had our games that night in this gay and festive city, where never a clergyman could be found to correct, where wine flowed like water, and men and women roystered about without regard to decency, losing and winning gold pieces as if they had been farthings, singing, blaspheming, and fighting, as the inclination seized them, all through the lamp-lit hours, until the sun rose over the hills and gilded the tops of the fruit trees.

Penelope and Sir John went with Alsander, or rather, King Death, to his palace, where he entertained them right royally, along with the captains of the different vessels now lying in the harbour. We joined some of the crews, and, under the able leadership of Indian Jos, were shown all the sights, introduced to his old friends, male and female, and made welcome to the rights of the colony.

Of course we were mighty curious to learn all about our old mate, Alsander, and Indian Jos wasn't at all backward in telling us.

The *Vigo* had been captured by him from the Spaniards, and fitted up for the buccaneer service, for he did not require to tell us that we were now amongst the pirates, and that Alsander was the recognised chief.

The *Vigo* was his favourite ship; and when she had been captured again by the English, he swore a mighty oath that he would have her again, even although he had to take her from London docks. And so, with a few of his most trusted followers and Penelope, he had left the island on his perilous mission.

It was under his directions that Penelope induced Sir John to purchase the *Vigo*, by means of my father and some Plymouth merchants, from the Government of cash-loving King James. A high price it had cost the old knight to secure the prize, but after that the game was easy. Sir John realized all the money that he could, and shipped it on board at Witestaple; so that his entire fortune now lay in the holds, an easily acquired treasure for this pirate king.

He informed us that Penelope was the wife of Alsander, and had sailed with him always for years, taking her place beside him in the hour of battle, and doing her part as well as the best, and a great deal better than many a man. Indian Jos, and those others who knew her, respected her mightily, and called her King Death's tiger, for they said that she adored the smell of blood and battle.

I was not so easy in my mind when I heard this and thought upon that night in the cabin. Had Alsander seen her arms about me when he entered? and was he of a jealous disposition? It all depended upon what he had seen, and how he had taken it, the kind of life I had to expect amongst the pirates. However, these were questions which the future must decide, so that I shoved reflection from me, and determined to enjoy myself while I could.

There were no lack of means or boisterous company to help to make one forget trouble of any kind, particularly a boy fresh from school, to whose eyes each object was a novelty and a wonderment.

The flaring of the torches and bonfires in the streets, round which crowds of revellers sat on empty puncheons, or lay on gandy mats, which the landlords had spread out for their accommodation, and near them great barrels of wine and spirits, from which their own servants drew the liquor as it was wanted, into rare flagons of chased metal and costly ware, while the glasses from which they drank were of the richest, and most quaint or delicate.

They were mostly faces upon which cruelty, lust, and debauchery could be read plainly enough, while many wore the deeply stamped mementoes of hard fighting—an ear missing or a cheek slashed, or someother token of old wounds. They had devilish eyes, the whole of them, whether blue, black, or nondescript in hue; and as they had been recruited from all nations on the face of the earth, there was no such thing as a sameness of face, feature, colour, or intonation.

Their dresses, also, were extravagant as to colour and texture, and of great variety, although as a rule they mostly took after the Spanish planters—that is, light loose trowsers and gaudy silk sashes, with embroidered shirts open at the neck, and loose, gold-trimmed velvet jackets. Their head-dresses varied, according to the taste of the wearer, but turbans of the richest and lightest texture were mostly the vogue.

The women who kept company in their midnight revels were, without exception, young, and nearly all good-looking, although all, more or less, bore visible traces of the life they led—bold, shameless hussies, who drank glass for glass with the rovers, and swore as coarsely. Jos, our guide, told us there were no ugly women permitted to land on the island, and that those who could not please the eyes of the men were made to walk the plank, and keep those men, who would not join with the pirates, company at the bottom of the sea. Therefore it no longer surprised me to see so many pretty children swarming about.

Both women and men were armed, as one might say, to the teeth, and fairly bristled with daggers and pistols, while cutlasses and sabres lay on the ground or over the barrels, ready to be used at a moment's notice; and as in the course of an hour's walk we witnessed half a dozen savage duels and one general scrimmage, it seemed that these were not useless ornaments.

It was all a dazzle and bewilderment from the moment we set foot ashore until daylight came to change the garish splendours into chaster beauty: men drinking, singing, swearing, dancing, or lying about indolently smoking cigars, while they listened to the whispering of girls, or to the music of guitars or flutes, which many of them played; women who had been originally forced into captivity and now were used to it, with women who had come with the pirates, or found them out from vicious choice—the northerns with their melting blue eyes, the southerns, brown-eyed and flashing, like tropical flowers, with forms lithesome as panthers, and skins soft as velvet, glittering like serpents with costly jewels on their bare arms and necks, and plumaged out with all the stolen treasures of the east and west—a veritable paradise of ravishing and soul-destroying sirens.

No wonder that the most honest amongst our lads succumbed under the charms of these wicked daughters of the devil, after passing months at sea with only the sight of an aged witch; and small blame to them that before the night was half over they had to borrow once more from the men they had despised on board. The spells of Penelope were nothing compared to the witcheries of these silvery-voiced, sleepy-eyed, dazzling demons who swarmed about us, picking out their victims with the same ease that a girl might lift up a tame tom-cat. Jos laughed like an ogre when he saw us so quickly mated, but shelled out the expenses without a murmur, so that even Jack Howard began to blame himself for being so prejudiced against the yellow man.

I laughed to see Sambo waited upon by three of the youngest and prettiest. They were all white-skinned, and bloomed up against that enormous mass of ebony like lilies sewed on black velvet. Robbie Crooker also had been daring in his choice, and was half carried along by a robust Spanish beauty adorned in crimson satin. They are fond of music, these Spanish women, and the scraping of his catgut had fired her inflammable heart. There is no accounting for female tastes, and experience goes for nothing with some men.

To me it was only a merry jest, and no more, for the kisses of Penelope were too fresh in my mind to care for anymore; so that, although I had to be in the fashion and take a girl, yet I'd rather have been left alone; and to keep the others back, I chose the ugliest I could find—a coal-black young negress, who amused me with her pleasant grins, and who took my plain hint that it was to be arm's length between us if we were to be good friends, while, as neither of us could speak a word in common, the conversation was none of the briskest.

Most of the drinking was done in the open street; while inside, where the lamps shone brightly, we got rid of our money in throwing the dice, and other games of chance. Then, as daylight was beginning to break, we staggered back to the ship, to get an hour or two of much-needed sleep before we began to explore the other parts of the town.

When I woke, the sun was shining brightly over the harbour, and as I sat up, blinking at the light, and wondering at the strange spinning round of objects, I saw some of our boys sitting in front of me, holding their aching heads with their hands, and looking particularly solemn, while they listened to the grating voice of Indian Jos, who was explaining something as important as it was evidently unpleasant.

"There's no gammon about it, lads, as you will find out for yourselves, and I only speak now as your friend. It is the law of the island, to which we are all bound, from the king downwards, that if a man is in debt and unable to pay up, he belongs to his creditor, and must be sold into slavery. Now I don't suppose you are going to deny that you are all deeply in debt?"

"No," replied Jack Howard dolefully. "We can't, and that's the plain truth."

"It would be useless for you to try, mates, even if you wanted, with those papers ag'in ye. Now the question is, have ye money enough amongst ye to square up?"

"Devil a piece!" returned the boys in a dismal chorus.

"I knew this, lads; and so I thought the kindest act I could do for you was to go up and see our king, and lay the matter to him before the town came to hear of it, for then your chances would be gone: you'd have to be put up to auction and sold to the planters, for that's our fixed law in such cases as yours."

"And what did he say about it?" asked Jack Howard, without looking up.

"Well, boys, our king is a stern man where duty is concerned, but he is the kindest and indulgenest man when off duty. After considering it over, he told me to keep it dark till you had decided, for it's all free-will with us, and we want no unwilling recruits; so he up like a father and made us a downright generous offer."

"Yes; what is it?" again asked Jack.

"It is this. He says that he is willing to pay me and my mates the money you are due to us, if we will say nothing about it, so be as you are all willing to volunteer heartily in his service, and take the oath of fidelity. Then you shall be at once put on the ordinary wages, which is a fair division of the prizes, and according to results; so that, if we are lucky, you may wipe off the score with one voyage, and be then at full liberty to do as you like. Otherwise he has no option: you must go off to the plantations for six years."

Our follies had found us out with quick despatch, As we heard the ultimatum, and knew that we were trapped, there wasn't one who did not feel sober enough.

As for me, I owed Jos ten pieces of eight, and I knew full well that neither my father nor Tom Blunt had a farthing of their own with them, for they were both prudent men, and had put their money out to interest before leaving home. Besides, I was too heartily ashamed of my conduct, and too frightened of my father's and honest Tom Blunt's anger, to dare face them with my confession; and, moreover, I had not the smallest doubt but that they were also trapped, according to someother law of the land, and would be quite unable to assist me.

As for Sir John Fenton, our owner, he was already in his dotage, and completely under the spells of Penelope; while, after what I had heard about her from Jos, the less I looked at that lady the better for my chance of life, far less liberty.

The others were in the same strait; so, after a solemn look in each other's eyes, we decided unanimously, and Jack spoke out for the rest.

"We don't want to be slaves, that's flat; so, as there is nothing else to be done, we agree to take the oath willingly, and become pirates. Is that so, lads?"

"Yes," the rest of us made reply mournfully.

"That's right, boys, and just what we expected from plucky fellows as you are. Now let us go and have a drink at my expense to steady our nerves, and then we will march up to the castle and see the king."

X

The Palace of the King

We were not a very cheerful party as we left the ship and went for that nerve-sustainer, nor after it either, for that matter. I was also filled with foreboding when we left the deck without seeing either my father or Tom Blunt. Where could they be? was filling my mind as we marched through the streets where we had passed such a jovial night, and thought how different the rich hangings and tapestries which were screening the verandahs looked in the sunshine from what they had appeared in the glare of the fires and torches.

We passed plenty of jovial revellers still at the casks with their lovely companions, while cherub-like children rolled about half-naked amongst the warm dust. But they no longer struck us as being the same; all the fascination was gone for me, now that I was a bondman and going to enlist as a pirate. Things look different in daylight from what they do at night, particularly after a spree which has still to be paid for.

The pirate city of Laverna had been founded and named by Alsander after the Greek goddess of thieves, and built without much regard to arrangement of order; so that from the main street, which spread along the shore, to reach the heights where the stronghold and mansion of the king had been placed required a considerable number of windings along lanes and past gardens, with much climbing of steps cut out of the rock.

After we had left the shore street, we did not come to many more shops, for these garden-surrounded houses belonged to those members of the community who had been saving with their prize-money and had settled down to take life easy with their wives and children and beautify their estates.

We passed and were greeted by many of these retired buccaneers from their open verandahs, where they lay within swinging hammocks with black and white slaves waiting upon them, like Turks in their harems; for they had adopted the luxurious lives of the Orientals, and did not stint themselves in the matter of wives. Their gardens and houses were in beautiful condition, for the overseers used the whip lavishly about the shoulders of the half-naked slaves, who mostly, as Jos informed us, had gambled away their freedom, and were now paying the penalty of over-indulgence in stripes and hard work. A wretched and hopeless fate, we saw for ourselves, these slaves led; so that what remaining scruples we might have had vanished from our hearts long before we were half-way up the hill. To be pirates might be risky, but to become slaves was to abandon all hope.

Up we climbed between gardens filled with fruit trees, palms and bananas meeting overhead, and making cool shadows, orange and lemon trees, speckled with their golden balls, peaches, apricots, quinces, figs, clustering vines and passion fruit overhanging the porches and verandahs. All well watered from fountains and cascades which trickled down from the hill streams. It was a place where every want of man was fulfilled by lavish Nature; while inland, as Jos informed us, they had their plantations and cattle farms, where the slaves were worked and tortured to death, for merciless masters these retired pirates were, as might be expected.

We came to one or two strongly fortified esplanades on our way up, where the harbour could be overlooked and unwelcome visitors destroyed, and had to own, as we looked down on the town and shipping, to those walling-in cliffs, that it would not be an easy task to storm this citadel. We could also see on the distant heights look-out towers erected, where the ocean outside could be watched. To reach these posts they used rope ladders, which they hung over the precipices, while the trees on the ocean side screened their watches from the observation of vessels sailing along. I thought, as I looked over all these advantages, was Nature the friend of free-booters, that she fashioned such a complete stronghold? It seemed like as if she was the most indulgent of patrons, with all these evidences of security and comfort around me.

As we advanced up the hill we could see the great gardens of Laverna government house. What spacious grounds they were, and how deliciously laid out! High walls surrounded them, over which masses of jasmine, honeysuckle, and other spreading flowers hung and concealed the bare stone-work; while above them towered lofty palms, nutmeg trees, and pendulous canes, making an almost impenetrable thicket.

The gate-posts were of a barbarous character, with solid and massive gates of filigreed bronze. Jos told us that they had been brought from a king's palace, as indeed most of the ornaments of the house had originally belonged to. Alsander did things on a large scale when he was at it, and had sacked the city and put the inhabitants to the sword for the sake of the palace, which he brought away piecemeal to this island. Only the builders and masons were spared from that ancient city, or secured from other parts, and made slaves of afterwards, which accounted for the rich and strange heathenish designs of many of the houses and walls we had passed, so that although beautiful to the eyes, each stone had been cemented with blood and tears.

The outer gates were open today, and many captains and sailors lounged about the grounds or lay under the shadow of the trees with their giddy light-o'-loves, while tables were set in all directions with awnings of flowered silk over them to keep the sun-glare from the meat and drinking vessels, which were spread out so that anyone might eat or drink when and what they listed. Chairs and hammocks also were standing or swinging under shadow of the covered boughs, some occupied, some ready for whoever chose to take them.

Fountains plashed into marble and brazen basins in various parts of the grounds, with strange monsters vomiting out the silvery floods. Repulsive and obscene figures some of them were when one got up close to them, but making a rich effect amongst the foliage, fruit, and flowers.

It was designed artfully, this garden, with many winding labyrinths and hidden paths leading off to arbours and grottoes, half buried in vegetation, or to small lakes, where floated lilies and where swans with other birds swam.

Down these avenues and vine-covered paths we could see fluttering dresses of females and gaily clad men, for they were all in their best on this day. We strode on our way in single file, with Jos at our head, explaining the sights as we went along; now coming upon green lawns and raised banks, now upon images of strange-looking gods, or crossing the bridge of a running stream. Every turn we took we found some fresh variety.

At last we came to the inner park, and saw the massive house with its carved balconies, cupolas, and domes, its painted pillars, and fretted windows, with the silken blinds and fringed shades, and the steps leading up to it inlaid with rare stones.

And all this grandeur belonged to our third mate, Alsander! As we looked about us, with eyes aching from the very splendours and delights of this earthly paradise, we grew humbled and abashed that we should ever have been so familiar with such a magnificent prince of robbers, and so blind as to take him for only the third mate of an honest trading carrack.

We saw him—the centre of an admiring and obsequious crowd, amongst which were Penelope and Sir John Fenton—on the outer balcony as we advanced. He was the plainest dressed man amongst them; but how majestic and uncommon he looked as he stood there, so silent and cold! I have often thought since that kings ought to be uncommon in their appearance, so that all their subjects might know them at a glance, like Alsander was—the pink-eyed king, or the cat-faced king, or the leper king, for even an uncommon disease would be better than nothing about them to distinguish them from ordinary men. But in what was our poor Scottish gift of a King Jamie different from the humblest serf of a poltroon, who shuddered at a naked sword or howled piteously for a stroke of the belt? King Death, with his white lamb's-wool hair and ruby eyes, was a signpost of royalty wherever he went, let alone his bloodless cheeks and lips. No man could go about and boast how like the prince he was, with Alsander. And since I had witnessed his exhaustless wealth I no longer felt inclined to judge him harshly for adding the fortune of Sir John to his store, or question how he had gathered it all. It was there, and that was enough to make him worthy of respect; while as for his strange appearance, that appeared now to adorn him with greater attractions. So that I wondered in my abasement how the witch had ever dared to turn her eyes from him even for a moment to such a clod as me, as I also marvelled how he ever could rest contented with her, for Jos had told us that he was the only man in the island who did not have half a dozen wives, at least.

You will perceive from these reflections what a glamour the sight of so much wealth and power had thrown over me all of a moment, and how ready I was to excuse murder and rapine when I saw that the reward was a throne, instead of the gallows'-tree, which makes all the difference between a hero and a murderer; how also that, although a freak of Nature may be viewed with distaste in an ordinary sailor, that it must be an additional charm to be admired when it distinguishes a monarch. For it is bred in us to lick the hand of greatness and riches, no matter how free-born we may be. So that there is no use trying to hunt for excuses for my newly fledged humility and veneration.

Alsander, when he saw us, left his crowd of courtiers and came down the stairs toward where we stood with quiet, slow grace and majesty—at least, I expect that is how kings ought to show off their majesty before subjects—and flinging himself easily into a hammock, gently waved his white hand as a signal for us to come nearer.

"Well, lads, have you come to offer your services to us freely and willingly, to swear fealty to our rule, and to fight loyally in our battles?"

"Yes, your majesty, they are all willing and eager," replied Jos humbly.

"'Tis well. Now kneel and take the oath which Jos will read over to you. After which he will conduct you to our steward, who will pay over to each man a hundred pieces of eight, with which to settle any trifling debts which you may have incurred in ignorance of our laws."

He spoke carelessly about the money, as if it had been a matter of no consequence; and after the horrible oath had been taken by each man, he said,—

"Enough. Now go inside, all except the boy Humphrey. Let him wait upon us for the present."

A horrible fear crept into my heart at these words. Was he now going to take me to task for that never-to-be-forgotten night? With a face almost as blanched as his own, I stood in front of him, watching my friends file away, leaving me to my fate.

XI

The Keeper of His Jealousy

Alsander leaned back in his hammock and looked at me in silence for a few minutes, during which I vainly strove to still my beating heart, or at least keep him from seeing the horror that was shaking my limbs.

"Art afraid of us, Humphrey?" he inquired, in an icy tone, through which I traced a ring of contempt.

At the words all my ebbing courage rushed back with a flash, and my legs became firm once more, while I threw up my head and looked him full in the eyes, feeling as if I had received a slap on the cheek, which no true Plymouth boy could stand, from king or clown.

Afraid? I had left home to die, if need be, for my profession; and why not now, as well as at some other time? He was no longer the lordly master whose very imperfections seemed to be attractive, no longer even the vampire mate who had scared me on board the ship; but a soulless pirate apeing at tinsel royalty.

"No, Master Alsander; I am not afraid of you or of any other man."

"King Death, my boy, and thy master now," he corrected gently.

"Yes; that I own frankly, king. I have forfeited all right to hold up my head until I have worked off my obligations."

"Nay, my brave boy, say not that; surely we have been friends enough in the past for you to take a paltry hundred or so pieces from our coffers as a memento of kindness."

"Not from King Death."

"Then take it, Humphrey, from the mate Alsander, and go free. Choose thy own course, if our life does not suit thee."

"I have sworn, king, and a boy has as much right to keep his oath as a man."

"Of thy own free will, surely?"

"Yes, free and hearty; to act up to my oath or else to die."

"To Alsander?" queried the king softly.

"No; I have sworn to King. Death," I replied, as bravely as I could, for his questions were worrying me sorely.

"And what wilt thou give to Alsander, Humphrey?"

How rich and musical his voice sounded now, as he raised himself up from his hammock and took my hand. It was too much for my strained nerves—the thought of torture, and now this sudden and unexpected kindness; so that I broke down and blubbered like a baby, and burst out,—

"My life, an thou wilt, Alsander."

"Now, child, I claim thee as the subject of King Death, and as the son of Alsander. Deal with me as thou wouldst with a father,—fair and honest,—and I promise thee a fate that thou little dreamst of for delight; for I can judge boys' hearts as I do men's, and I can lay the blame on the right shoulders, and excuse the guiltless as I can punish the guilty. Wilt thou be my friend, Humphrey, and deal with me fair and open?"

"Yes, Alsander; fair and open—fair and honest always so that you do not awe me over much with your majesty."

"You are my adopted son from this hour, Humphrey. Be true to me, and I will reward you; betray me, and as there lives the devil, my master, I will plunge you into a living hell."

I knew all that he meant by these words, for I had seen men before who were thralled by a single passion, young as I was, and who were blind enough to fancy that their jackdaw was a turtle-dove; and their cabbage a rare rose, which all creation must envy them for and covet also to possess. And I could afford now to humour him in his delusions, and pledge my heart to what he asked. I was no longer afraid of King Death, for he had placed his heart under my eyes.

So it chanced that this strange, cold-blooded man, with the dull jealousy gnawing at his sluggish vitals, and I went in together to his palace as father and son, as master and slave, only that now he had become my servant, so long as I could be true to myself and to the oath which I had sworn.

Penelope saw the change in me, and shrunk with a sullen despair into herself. She could conquer me by her eye only at his bidding; and I think he was sure of me from that hour, and therefore had leisure to meditate upon my punishment.

What a strange thing is mad passion, and how near akin to savage hatred. I was easy and cool because I was heart-whole, and could watch all the movements of this engrossing game.

That day I was taken and dressed like a prince, with a retinue of slaves to wait upon my slightest wants, and heralded to the community as the king's adopted son and heir, with the treasury placed at my disposal. It is curious, when the worst of men take a notion, how doting they become, and that was so with Alsander as far as I was concerned. I lodged at the palace, and had every indulgence and liberty to do as I liked, while Penelope looked at me with lurid eyes, for he had made me the guardian of his jealousy, and built up a wall which she could not get over.

But what of my father and Tom Blunt? They were not in the town, and no one would tell me about them or their fate.

XII

How the Pirates Lived at Laverna

Thus I, in my simple innocence and boyish importance, went on my guileless way, feeling assured that I had sounded the depths of the heart of this most devilish Greek vampire, as he had been able to look through me, now that I was treated as his son and loaded with kindness. A boy's fidelity is not more difficult to win than is a hound's love; and if he is played upon both on his heart-strings and the blow-pipe of his easily sounded conceit, the older man must be vile and mean beyond compare, who cannot become a hero to such a follower.

I took him on trust at sight then, and it was long before I could realize the coldness and satanic cruelty of his monstrous nature, or the wonderful quality he had of never forgetting the most casual offence, or how completely he could concentrate his mind on paltry devilishnesses, even while planning out great deeds. He was a born leader of men— cool, calculating, remorseless, and daring, with a keen eye upon every item, able to pick out the most minute slip in his network of plans, and who never forgave or forgot.

And this Penelope knew full well. He was now punishing her for that fatal partiality which she had shown to me; and he had my punishment also carefully planned out, for he loved to amuse himself with his victims when he was in no need to hurry them out of his way.

Now that I felt safe in my mind as to the past, between my master and myself, it became to me an easy matter to guard myself in the presence of the witch; for whether she had lost her power over me, or did not dare to use it, I know not, but I could speak to her and gaze at her now without the slightest fear.

One thing I did miss, besides my father and Tom Blunt, and that was my dog Martin. He was near me, only I was forced to have him constantly on the chain in a distant part of the grounds, for he still kept up his animosities towards my new friends and companions; so that, for the sake of peace, it was only when I went to feed him that I could enjoy his company.

Of course, in such an extensive and public palace, we were never free from company day or night. I knew that they were getting ready for another filibustering expedition, for they had their spies all over the ocean, and could tell when the Spanish treasure-ships were to sail from the mainland; so that there was always a large crowd of captains and recruits coming or going, or lounging about enjoying themselves, as there had been on the day of my admission.

One of these captains attached himself particularly to me, and whom I could rarely shake off. His real name was Pierre Denis, a half Frenchman, who was sometimes called "The Scribbler," because he kept what Master Shakespeare advised me to keep,—a note-book,—and was always to be seen jotting down something or other when in the company of others. He was a prime favourite of Alsander, but not much liked by the pirates, who always spoke of him, when out of hearing, as "Judas Denis." Why, I was to find out for myself.

He was a large-made man and somewhat bulky and soft-looking, with goggling grey eyes, which protruded from their sockets, and looked watery and ready to shed tears. Indeed, he was the easiest man to break down and melt into the weeps that ever I met.

He was not very socially inclined as far as drinking was concerned, but took his bouts in solitary fashion and at unexpected intervals. Then he would drink himself into a hoggish state of dirt and delirium that was disgusting to see; while at other times he would grow morose and argumentative, as selfish and solitary drunkards always do.

He was very mighty in his behaviour though, whether drunk or sober, and spoke so morally and uprightly, as well as so ponderously, on all subjects relating to learning that I very naturally considered him at the first to be a very honest and outspoken man, for a pirate, and gave him the friendship which he appeared to desire so ardently from me. Although I did not find him a very agreeable companion, either in his maudlin or his aggressive moods.

He also considered himself a genius, who was lost in his present occupation through lack of opportunity; and used to speak contemptuously about the works of Shakespeare and Ben Jonson, as very commonplace fellows indeed compared to him. He told me in confidence that he was writing a play about the Spanish main, which would eclipse their work for grandeur, diction, and style.

I didn't know much about diction or style, but it chanced when I saw him writing so much that I also took the idle fit on me; and having a turn for rhyme, I knocked off a song or two, which made me rather popular with the other captains, who set them to music, and sang them over the town. When Pierre Denis heard about this foolishness, he grew strangely quiet and disagreeable towards me, yet forced his company upon me more than ever, and watched all my actions like a cat. It took me a long time to know for certain that "The Scribbler" was jealous of me and hated me like poison for my paltry gifts, and only waited for the chance to do me an ill turn.

For a full week we lived thus in luxurious ease and festivity, Alsander and Penelope acting the hosts right royally, with every want we could express gratified, and the sun shining all day long, without a cloud to mar its glory, and the stars burning at nights like white lamps over the gardens.

All within the palace was rich and extravagant beyond compare: gold, silver, and copper carvings, vases, idols, and other ornaments met us at every turn; spacious chambers, with almost priceless hangings, tapestries, and carpets placed about them lavishly, the softest and costliest of couches, with ivory and ebony supports, and the lightest spun silk for coverlets; paintings and sculpture, for which churches had been ransacked and razed, and the priests and holy sisters butchered indiscriminately as the price of their attainment. We went to bed hazy with precious vintages, and opened our eyes in the morning to be greeted only by objects of beauty and immortal art.

Then the slaves came in and bathed us with perfumed waters, and, to make our limbs flexible, kneaded our flesh about, oiling and dressing our hair and decking us up like Roman patricians, while we lay, or sat, or stood passive under their trembling hands.

We had nothing to think about, saving how best to pass the hours, and cultivate appetites to be appeased, either in the eating, the drinking, or the other pleasing of the carnal senses.

Outside we could overlook the city and the waters of the harbour from the balcony, for we sat high on the hill, or drink in the balmy breezes which wafted over us; for such was the life of a favoured pirate when taking his ease in the city of Laverna.

XIII

The Inland Ride

One afternoon, while we were all taking life as easy as possible upon different hammocks, Alsander announced that on the morrow he was willing to go with Sir John Fenton and the witch Penelope in search of the life-renewing plants. In two days more the new moon would be in the proper quarter for the ingredients to be gathered, mixed, brewed, and swallowed.

I have not said much about the poor old knight, for the simple reason that he had made himself of such small account since leaving his native land that no one appeared to notice him. It is our own estimation of ourselves, to a great extent, that the public is apt to take of our merits. Sir John Fenton was a modest and retiring gentleman, in spite of his magical leanings, who was always ready to take a back seat, with a "Thank you" for the favour bestowed; and now he had come to the wrong community for anyone else to shove him farther forward than he desired to go himself, each pirate being over eager for a front seat himself to be able to recognise modesty in any other way than to take advantage of it.

Now, although he had come expressly to this island to secure these herbs, and was visibly failing everyday, he was much too courtly to urge the matter upon his hosts, but contented himself during the days we were idling with roaming about the palace and examining the stolen works of art through his magnifying glasses. Sometimes I was his companion, along with that jealous "dramatist" Pierre Denis, who never left me long alone. Then Sir John would deliver to us a homily upon the artists or sculptors who were there represented, with a learned criticism of their qualities and the leading passages of their lives which he appeared to have at heart, and which interested me greatly.

Pierre, as usual, would either contradict the knight flatly as to his assertions and canons of art, or else make trumpet of his hands and blow into it "toot, toot, toot," to signify to me that the speaker was a wind-bag and a liar. But as these were his usual methods of conducting an argument, I did not mind much, and the old gentleman would only pause and regard him with gentle surprise for a moment, and then continue his remarks as if he had not been interrupted. Oh, a rare old nobleman this venerable knight was, if foolish in somethings, who never lost his temper with this envious, vulgar, and ignorant boor, no matter how gross he became in his offensive behaviour!

What an envious and puffed-up toad this man was, to be sure, in his blatant conceit! For he was not satisfied with wishing people to think that he excelled the most noted men of letters, but he was also forever saying, with a snifter of contempt,—

"That a painting or statue worth setting up in a house! Why, if I had only brushes and paints, or proper carving tools here, I'd very quickly fill the palace with a hundred better works of art; only that I haven't got the right materials nor the time to devote to such silly rubbish."

"Then you have never been able to capture a painter or sculptor yet, Pierre?" I would ask innocently.

"Yes, I've caught heaps of them," retorted Pierre, savagely; "but I always made a rule to send them and their tools overboard the first thing."

"It's a pity, though, that you did not save the paints and chisels, even if principle compelled you to drown the artists, isn't it, Pierre?" I would reply mildly, as I turned to listen again to the interesting remarks of Sir John.

On the morrow, after the king had announced his decision, we all got up early and prepared for the journey inland. It was a small party, composed of Alsander, Penelope, Sir John, and myself, for I had expressed a desire to go with them to see the country, and Alsander gave his consent without demur. He also took with him Pierre Denis, Indian Jos, and the bulky Sambo, besides half a dozen body servants to carry provisions.

So all, saving the slaves, being mounted on good steeds, with our provisions on the pack-horses behind, "which the slaves led, we started up the hill while the stars were still in the sky. Alsander and Indian Jos went before, with Penelope and Sir John in the centre, and Denis and myself behind. Sambo brought up the rear, straddling over the back of a sturdy mule, with his huge feet nearly touching the ground, the horses of the island being too small and delicate to carry such a ponderous weight.

We rode past a high-walled and massive stronghold on the peak of the hill. This was designed as a final retreat in case of a surprise, and considered impregnable to cannon shots. As we came up to it the sentinels challenged us, and permitted us to go on after getting the password.

Then our course lay downwards for a time on a winding bridle path cut from the rock's face; for it was precipitous in the extreme—a path which only very sure-footed horses and mules could take, and in many places walled in or tunneled, and lighted up with lanterns for our accommodation. These passages were also well guarded and covered by guns, so that only friends could traverse them in safety. I could see at a glance that there would be little chance for an enemy to take this side by surprise, for at the open portions the cliffs rose straight above us, and sheer down farther than I could calculate in the darkness. A low wall had been built on these exposed places, to prevent travellers from rolling over, but not high enough to stop us from seeing what lay beyond.

At last we reached the plain, while the sky began to lighten in front of us, for our course lay easterly. A pleasant ride that was, past fields of maize, tobacco, sago, cotton, sugar, and other tropical produce, with the workers being driven to their work from their huts—silent processions of hopeless men and females, who had been too old or not well favoured enough to win their exemption.

Then the light darted upon us, sudden and glorious—a yellow glow behind the distant mountains, with rosy shafts shooting up and blotting out the stars, while the crops lay white with the night-mists, like hoar-frost. Next the sun itself, like a cauldron of quicksilver, glowing down upon us and drinking up the dews with a visible suction, as the thin vapours floated off the fields and melted in steam-wreaths.

I could see these poor slaves beginning their day of ceaseless labour after their short rest, with the cruel drivers lashing the sleep from their heavy eyes: sullen-looking men and women, with scarce a rag upon their lean bodies, bending down with their hoes and other implements; while they gazed in our direction with side-long glances of hatred out of their blood-shot, hollow eyes. But never a sound except the cracking of the whips or the call of a bird as it flew over our heads.

For hours we rode along through those fertile fields, or through the fording places of wide rivers and shallow streams, for the land was well watered, halting occasionally to drink, then pushing on again, until we reached the edge of the forest, which, being marshy, was devoted mostly to sugar, sago, and rice-growing.

Here the mosquitoes rose about us by myriads, stinging us viciously and forcing us to gallop on as fast as we could to escape their hungry importunity. But even here, as we rushed past, we could see crowds of poor wretches toiling away knee-deep in malarious mire, with their naked bodies covered with the venomous insects—poor broken wretches, with their ribs bulging out like gaunt skeletons, the females without a trace hardly of their sex left, saving the pendulous empty breasts and hairless faces.

Then we got into the dense forests and to higher ground, where we called a halt for breakfast, which our servants took from the pack-horses, and spread out for us, along with soft mats for us to rest upon.

After regaling ourselves with meat, wine, fruit and other delicacies, those who indulged in the weed lit their cigars, and once more mounted, puffing out as they rode along. Alsander still led us; and as he did not converse with his companion, the rest of us followed his example and said little.

A great forest that was, with mighty trees and closely laced tendrils, which completely shut out the sun as we got into it, leaving only a grim and dark twilight. Sometimes we heard a heavy crashing of the underwood, and knew from that we were disturbing the sleep of some wild beast; or what we took to be a massive vegetable tendon would detach itself from the branch and glide out of sight with an angry hiss and rustle. Otherwise it was a silent and dreary region, like an enchanted wood, where life had been crowded to excess and then arrested into an everlasting sleep.

We halted once more for refreshments in this forest, and then pushed through it again, until by the time it grew thin enough to see patches of sky we found that the day was drawing to a close, and the earth was growing cool and grey.

Another hour and we had come to open ground, with a dark range of mountains before us, all rugged in outline and broken into defiles and rocky gorges, while the stars were once more coming out upon a sky deeply grim and dusky.

In front of us we could see a low, flat, wooden cabin, with lights burning from the windows and a camp fire in front blazing merrily. It stood close to the entrance of a great dark valley, with rocks rising steeply behind it.

"There is our shelter for tonight, gentlemen," said Alsander, as he put spurs to his jaded steed and dashed off briskly in front of us.

When we got up to the fire, we found our leader standing at his horse's head speaking to a hideous-looking negress of great dimensions, and who uttered a howl of delight as she clapped eyes upon Sambo, who grinned broadly while he submitted to her extravagant embraces.

"My Sambo come home to his ole woman!"

"Yes, Dinah; an' he hopes you hab a dam good supper for him and his friends."

"Yes, Sambo; de best in de land. Dere am roast pig and fowls, yams and boiled maize—ebberything dat a long-lost husband could expect to find at home from his lubbing and lonely wife."

XIV

Through the Valley of Serpents

After supper, which, with the additional luxuries that we had brought with us, was really all that Dinah had said,—a meal worthy of famished travellers and long-lost husbands,—we lay down in the common apartment, upon the mats which our slaves spread for us, and went off to sleep in company.

I was tired out with my long ride, therefore it was late before I woke up and the sun already high up in the heavens, while I found the hut empty, and all the mats removed excepting the one I had slept upon.

Rising and going outside, I discovered Sambo sitting beside the fire leisurely gorging himself, while his grateful spouse served him with tit-bits, using her own ebony fingers to lift them from the platter to his wide mouth.

He paused to bolt down his last mouthful as he saw me, and then informed me that Alsander had allowed me to sleep on, and left him to follow after with me when I woke.

The rest had gone about three hours in advance, but he knew the place where they were to camp; while, as Penelope had to gather herbs by the way, there was no hurry: we would easily come upon them before night.

I was perfectly satisfied with this explanation, and thought it very considerate on the part of my adopted father to let me have a proper rest; so, telling Sambo that I'd be with him shortly, I made my way through some trees to where I saw the gleam of water.

Here I discovered a nice deep pool of the river; and, throwing off my clothes, plunged in and had a most refreshing bath. After which I got to the shore, and sat down for a moment in the sun to dry myself before dressing.

As I sat here looking on the river which flowed slowly past the banks, I noticed all at once a couple of tree-trunks rise to the surface and begin floating at a pretty rapid speed towards me; and what struck me as most peculiar, they were breasting against the stream.

I watched them until they were almost close to the bank, and then, all at once, the key to this curious puzzle came to me with a flash, and caused me to leap up in double quick time, make a grab at my clothes, and go off at my hardest speed towards the hut; and not a second too soon, for as I rose to my feet the long, open jaws of two enormous alligators were lifted up to the bank with a horridly expectant grin, while their scale-covered bodies prepared to follow.

I was always rather shy and modest, but there was no time for modesty now, so I raced off with the monsters after me, and appeared before Dinah and her lord in much the same guise as Joseph must have shown off to the servants in the palace of Potiphar, when he ran away from that gentleman's wife.

However, Dinah did not cover her face with her hands or scream, as many ladies might have done. She had looked beyond me, and seeing the causes of my alarm, promptly caught up two blazing fire-brands, dashed past me, and stuck them into the open jaws of the advancing enemy.

With a snap the beasts closed their teeth on the warm gifts; then, looking at her stolidly for an instant with their small eyes, winked rapidly to her, as if in appreciation of her kindness, and opening their jaws, dropped the charred embers as a dog might do a hot morsel, and turning slowly from her, they both made off to the river again as fast as their short legs could carry them. Meanwhile, I had pulled on my shirt and was busy hauling on my breeches.

"Dat serve de foolish brutes better than nice white boy for breakfast," remarked Dinah, coming over to me and giving me a hand to brace up.

After cooling down and enjoying a substantial meal, Sambo and I, mounting our respective steeds, set out upon our journey.

We rode slowly into the rocky defile, picking our way amongst the fallen rocks, and once more leaving daylight as the precipices above closed in and overhung us. A dreary ride that was, up the sterile glen, like entering into a doomed place.

"Dis am de Snake Valley," Sambo explained; "you see 'em presently— all sizes. But they mighty shy if you let 'em alone."

Truly I saw them before long, and shivered in horror at the gruesome sight, so that I could hardly keep my place in the saddle,—great, loathsome reptiles, hanging limply from holes and crevices, or trailing their slimy bodies over the stones on every side; bloated serpents, some of them forty feet in length, who lay torpid in our path, from recent gorges, so that we had to step over them; others rearing themselves at us as we advanced, with red, open jaws, and waving, forked tongues, while the gloomy space re-echoed with their angry hisses.

I felt sick and faint as I looked at them, and clung to the pommel to keep from falling amongst them; while Sambo rode calmly by my side, flicking at the nearest of them with his heavy whip, as if they had been thistles, and laughing hoarsely as they fell from it with broken backs and wriggled viciously on the ground.

"Are they poisonous?" I gasped in my horror.

"Some of dem am, very; de little ones am de worst," replied Sambo coolly. "See dat fellow running away—he copper-head. One bite from him enough to settle you."

At last we got out of this devil's den, and on to the ridge of the hill, along which we rode, with a deep and desolate valley below us, where no other vegetation grew excepting one great tree, which spread its roots in all directions.

"Dat place called Hell Valley," observed Sambo. "Worse den snakes, dat tree am. No one get out of him clutches, once he catch 'em alone: he suck 'em blood dry in no time. See all de bones down dere scattered about?"

"Yes."

"Dey am all dat is left ob runaway slaves. Ha! ha! Think 'emselves safe down dere; so dey am," and he chuckled hoarsely to himself as we rode on.

After we had traced the ridge of this deadly valley, we descended by another but more open glen, in the heart of which roared and foamed a noisy torrent, which, after the silence and gruesome sights, cheered me vastly, for it seemed to babble of life and activity.

"We must take rest here and eat something," said Sambo, rolling from his mule and tying it up to a small tree, while he took from his wallet some cold meat, and bread of Dinah's baking, and began to divide it leisurely; while I dismounted, and following his example with my horse, sat down beside him to take my share.

Sambo had no great taste for delicacies or wine, but he had not forgotten to bring a flask of rum with him, so that we made a substantial lunch, washing it down with the strong liquid; after which I felt my cheeks getting back their natural colour, and, while we rested, began to ask my companion if he knew what had become of my father and Tom Blunt.

"Oh, dey am all safe and well cared for, you bet," he replied, rolling his little eyes about.

"But where are they, Sambo?"

"Well, you see, our king wanted two very honest men whom he

could depend upon to go as ambassadors for him to some place, and so he fixed on de captain and de bossun as the two honestest men he knew."

"And so they are, Sambo."

"Yes. He knows men as well as boys, does our king. He very great man. So he tells 'em what he wants 'em to do, and they does it willingly."

"Then they have left the island?"

"Oh, yes, they have both left the *town*; of dat I am quite sure."

"And they may be back soon?"

"Oh, yes, they may; it all depends, of course, on their secret mission and how they get on how soon they am back."

"That's why the king wouldn't tell me, I suppose, it being a secret mission," I replied, feeling easy at last about their fate.

"Yas, dat so; and dat am why you must never speak 'bout it, or tell anyone what Sambo let out. You understand?"

"Yes, Sambo; I'll hold my tongue until they come back."

"Dat de very best thing you can do, my boy. And now I must have five minutes' sleep; so hold it fast now."

Sambo laid himself down and shut his eyes, while I looked round me and listened to the merry singing of that mountain torrent, while the afternoon clouds sailed overhead, and gradually grew mellow and golden, as the horse and the mule nibbled the grass round their tethers contentedly.

He slept longer than five minutes; indeed, he must have lain with shut eyes for hours, for, as evening drew on, I was just about to wake him, when I heard the sound of a horse's hoofs against the rocks below us, and he suddenly sat up and rubbed his eyes; while the next moment the rider came upon us, who I saw was Penelope, and alone.

"We are waiting for you, Humphrey; and I feared that you had lost your way, so I came back to seek for you."

She had reached us and dismounted, and was now standing beside me, holding my hand, while she gazed into my eyes with the old, fierce tenderness that had frightened me so much.

I shrank back from her and looked towards Sambo; but he was once more lying back with his eyes closed.

"I was sent for you, pretty boy. *He* sent me, so don't be afraid. But I wanted to see you all alone first, before my reincarnation."

I drew my hand from hers and pointed to where the negro lay.

"Don't mind Sambo; he is ray friend, and yours also, if you like; for he hates my master and yours, as do many more of the pirates, who only wait for a chance to come over to my side. Say, Humphrey, will you not save me from a great misery?"

"Yes, if I can, without being false to him, for I have sworn to be his true friend."

"But he hates you, my boy, and will never forget or forgive. Can you not like me enough to take me with you, away from here, if I make you rich and set you free? Can you not care for me well enough as I am to make some sacrifice for me?"

"What do you want?"

I asked this coldly and with a boy's brutality, for I abhorred both her and her tenderness at that moment, and determined to be true to my friend Alsander.

She looked at me long, and with a changing expression, during which the softness melted out of her gaze and became an icy ferocity.

"Nothing—at least, nothing that you can give me, I see now. I must look elsewhere for what I want; and yet,—yes, you can give me something."

"What is it?"

"A last kiss. Will you?" There was sudden tearful tenderness in her accents.

"No," I replied stoutly and harshly, for I was getting afraid of myself.

"Then I will not ask even for that. Come, look at me, boy."

It was the old, imperious command that I could not resist, with the hard, hot flash of her black eyes, which forced me to look up and feel myself slipping away into a giddy dream.

Then I woke up with the same old feeling of stillness and obedience to her wishes. She was still gripping my hand, but she now pointed to the tree where I had tethered my horse.

"What is that beside your horse, Humphrey?"

"A tree, of course. No; it is one of the great serpents which we left in the valley!"

I shuddered violently, and hid my eyes with my hand, while she laughed shrilly, touching me lightly on the forehead.

"That is all right. There, you foolish boy, I have banished the serpent. Now you can get up and loosen your horse with perfect safety. Come, Sambo; we must get back to Alsander."

I looked again towards my horse; he was still nibbling calmly beside the tree, while the great snake that I had seen had vanished. With trembling hands I unloosed the reins and sprang upon my horse's back; then turned with him to follow Penelope and Sambo, who were already mounted and waiting for me.

XV

Quassatta is Born

Penelope rode first down the glen, and at a silent signal from her I took my place behind her, while Sambo brought up the rear.

She rode swiftly, and I followed, with the same old exhilaration at my heart, and the same lightness and recklessness of spirits which I had felt before, after she had put me under her spell. I could see and mark each object which we passed—at least, so it appeared to me; only, somehow, things were different. The trees, rocks, clouds, outlines of landscape grew more fantastic or grotesque as they danced before me. I saw strange and living shapes of monsters in the twilight, clouds behind me like the spectres of a nightmare; and yet I was not afraid of them—rather the reverse, as if I gloated upon the fact that I could behold these visitors from the unseen world. The rocks and boulders changed under my eyes into strange forms, which grinned, or sneered, or scowled upon me as I flew past.

The spreading branches of the trees grew into imploring or menacing arms, with outstretched fingers; while their leaves became floating tresses, and the trunks into heaving breasts of women, with the heads bending forward or thrown back.

The wind wailed up the glen in warning gusts, which seemed to sob, "Go back! go back! go back!"

The stream rushed and roared at my feet. "Return, boy; return! be free, boy; be free! Return, and be free!"

The twelve hoofs of horses and mules clattered out of time to a singular refrain, which was unvaried in its constant recurrence:—

"Take her offer! take her offer! Go back, Humphrey; go back! Take her with you; take her with you! Escape! escape! escape!"

But my heart beat lightly through it all—with that grey-haired woman in front of me, and the lithe figure swaying gracefully over her saddle, and the friendly negro behind; and I never thought about asking her to halt, while the voices of wind, stream, and hoofs fell upon a callous ear, and the outspread arms of the branches provoked me only to contemptuous laughter.

She was leading me on, on, to the man to whom I had pledged my word, and who had bound me past the power of mortal or spectre to liberate me. Only he could accomplish this, as he was now drawing me to him, for I felt that she was but an instrument in his potent hands, as we all were, against whom it was useless for us to struggle; against whom I had no desire to fight, only the passionate wish to serve.

Penelope never turned her head as she rode on, but kept her face, as mine was, fixed in the direction where I knew he stood waiting for us, with that lumpy shadow, Sambo, swinging along behind.

Down through the valley, with the daylight swiftly going from us, into the blackness of a narrow chasm, where I could see nothing; over a bare mountain peak, with the clustering planets and stars above our heads, and under our feet the low-lying, new moon—a silver sickle, thin as a curl of new wire.

Down the crumbling sides of that volcanic basin, with the cinders and pumice-stone crunching under our feet; while away in the bottom we could see, through the cracks, the lurid glowing of the internal fires.

"Halt!"

It was the cold, clear, musical voice of Alsander; and as our horses drew up, and our eyes got accustomed to the semi-darkness, we could make out the figures of our friends and slaves. We were standing upon a flat plateau overlooking the core of the crater, with the lurid cracks about twenty feet below us, and vapoury wreathes of smoke stealing up, and making that thin crescent moon, now overhead, to waver like a reflection upon trembling waves.

When we had dismounted, the slaves came forward and took our horses and the mule from our hands, and disappeared with them up the sides of the basin. Alsander waited until the shower of loose earth and cinders had stopped, which proved that the servants were out of hearing, then he spoke:—

"We are ready now to begin. Light the fire, Sambo; you will find it there prepared for you. While you, Sir John and Penelope, prepare yourselves."

I waited anxiously, and feeling a little giddy with the sulphurous fumes which were rising from the bottom of the crater, so that I was fain to sit down on the ground, while Sambo knelt by the firewood mound and began to strike his flint and steel.

At last, after a few sparks had been sent out, the powder caught fire and flared up suddenly; then the leaves caught fire and communicated the blaze to the saunder-wood branches, and so on to the dry logs that had been put under and round the small brazen cauldron, which, already half filled with some kind of liquid, soon was boiling, and sending up a cloud of violet-coloured steam.

I could now see my companions as they sat around me, all excepting Sir John and Penelope, who stood together at the cauldron, throwing in sprigs of different herbs, with their backs to us; both almost of a height, and slender, although Penelope looked the taller, by reason of the old knight's stooping shoulders; and both dressed in their fantastic robes.

Round me the fires flashed on the eagerly watching faces of Indian Jos, Pierre Denis, and Sambo, while Alsander sat by himself beside a little mound which was covered by a dark shawl, which I supposed to be more materials wanted for the incantation.

My head, as I have said, was giddy with the almost over-powering fumes that were steaming slowly up and surrounding us—strange vapours which the blazing logs lit up with all sorts of rainbow colours, that to my mind took upon themselves weird and demoniacal forms, which, however, did not appall me, for I had been expecting to see a few evil spirits come to this incantation.

"It is ready, Sir John. Quick! help me off with the cauldron."

As Penelope said this I saw her and the knight take each a side of the pot and swing it from the embers, while Sambo stepped forward, and with two or three vigorous kicks sent the fire scattering over the plateau into the crater, so that we were plunged into darkness. At the same moment a dismal rumbling was heard under my feet, while the ground shook violently, and a fiercer gust of sulphur blew into my face, and sent me headlong to the earth.

"Quick! quick!" I heard the voice of Penelope, as I lay half choked and dazed. "Quick! or we shall be too late and doomed!"

A wild shriek burst on my ears, followed by a heavy groan, then an interval of deadly silence, only broken by hurried breathing and moving of feet. I could not, even if I dared, look up, for my brain seemed to be whirling round with the potent fumes I was swallowing at every gasp.

"Up! up! Humphrey, and run for your life; the crater is beginning to fire!" I heard the voice of Indian Jos, as he caught me by the arm and raised me to my feet, as a fresh and louder rumbling was heard, followed by a violent heaving of the earth, and a spurt of yellow flame from the crater.

Then fear gave me strength, and clutching at the arm of Jos I rushed up the side of the basin along with him; while in front I could see the indistinct figures of our five companions struggling up wildly, and behind us the hot glare of the rising fire, pulsating, but every instant waxing brighter.

We at length reached the outer edge, where we found the slaves standing, holding our frightened horses, who were kicking and plunging madly.

"Are we all here?" asked Alsander coldly, as he seized his horse's bridle and looked behind him at what we had left.

"Yes, King Death," replied Indian Jos.

I also looked behind me for a moment into the crater, which was growling ominously, while the flames spouted out and leaped high above our late resting-place from every crack; while others were breaking out and widening with fearful rapidity, as with the flames waves of red-hot lava were beginning to pour out and eddy upwards like a stormy ocean.

The plateau, our last resting-place—I saw it for a moment before it crumbled down like a lump of melting lead—brilliantly illuminated, and upon its surface the naked figure of an old man, with his long, white tresses dabbled in blood; then mound and figure dissolved like a snow-flake into the glowing and seething sea.

"Sir John Fenton! We have left Sir John Fenton behind us, and he is swallowed up!" I shrieked, as I pointed down to that awful quicksilver.

"You are mistaken, Humphrey, for I am here," replied a voice at my side like, and yet unlike, that of Sir John's.

I looked round amazed, to see looking upon me with a smile a young man with clean face and jet-black, short, crimpy hair, dressed as I had last seen Sir John before he put on his wizard's robe.

"And Penelope?"

"This was Penelope five minutes ago," answered Alsander, pointing to a figure close at hand; "but now that she has been born again we must re-christen her, so let us call her Quassatta."

Heavens! could that radiant vision of fresh young loveliness be the Witch of Canterbury? I had a lightning, but vivid glimpse of a halo of golden hair, surrounding the perfect face of a girl of about fifteen, with starry-like, dark eyes fixed wonderingly upon mine, when I again heard the clear voice of Alsander:—

"To horse! to horse! for we are in danger here. Help Quassatta to her saddle, Humphrey, and guide her down; but"(this in a low whisper to me only) "remember that you are the keeper of my jealousy. Come, Sir John Fenton, to horse and away!"

XVI

The Escape From the Volcano

There was not much chance for deliberation now, with the volcano boiling up towards us, and which at any moment might belch out an explosive blast of fire and fury and overwhelm us where we paused; so with a bound I sprang to the side of the lovely girl, heedlessly letting go my own bridle in my amazement. In an instant I was horseless, for the beast took advantage of his release to bound away into the darkness.

"Never mind," shouted Alsander. "Take up Quassatta behind you, Humphrey, and ride that way; but don't pause for a moment."

Next instant I was astride the horse Penelope had used, with that light, slim young figure at my back clinging to my waist as we galloped headlong down the mountain side.

As we turned into the cleft gorge of the next mountain ridge, I heard a loud burst, like the explosion of a gun-powder factory, while the earth vibrated violently under our horses' feet, and the boulders began to dislodge themselves from their long undisturbed resting-places on the sides of that narrow but lofty gorge, and crash down with thunderous sounds in front of us, while the light was so vivid that we could see each other and those avalanches as distinctly as if it had been broad daylight—or, rather, the intense glare of a crimson sunset, which made objects appear the more terrible and distorted.

The volcano, after those few growls, had burst forth in the full splendour and anger of its eruption, and was shooting up a great column of fire, mixed with stones, cinders, and lava, two or three hundred feet into the air; also rising up and cresting this fire-pillar curled a dense cloud of ruddy-tinted smoke, which spread out as it rose like a great awning; while down the sides of the black cone there began to pour a series of streams and waterfalls of quicksilver-like liquid; inexpressibly beautiful in their dazzling brightness against the jet-black mountain, appallingly deadly in the torrent-like speed with which they were racing towards us.

My horror-stricken companion had hidden her face against my thinly covered back, so that I felt the thrilling warmth from her fresh young breath; while her slender arms clutched me with nervous closeness and tenacity. That glorious wealth of golden hair caught my backward glance as it floated behind, all ruddy with the fire glare. Only a second's backward glance at the lurid spectacle and those floating ripples of red gold, and then we had entered the blackness of that chasm and were riding blindly on at full speed.

Our slaves—ah! they had been left behind us, and we never saw or heard of them more: the volcano had given to them their freedom.

On through the dark, with the rocks crashing down on every side of us, some perilously close, although we were too excited to take heed of this; up the sides of that valley adown which the torrent roared and foamed, the sky above us all dusky with the distant glare, and smoke-covered. While the fine ash-dust fell upon us and covered us thickly, so that we could hardly breathe from that close, dense atmosphere, but choked as we were forced to swallow it in.

Along that ridge we rode, below which I knew lay the Valley of Hell, the glare and the cloud still enveloping us like a river fog, only so arid that our throats felt cracking and our nostrils clogged up.

Through that fearful serpents' pass we rushed one behind the other, and reckless of what we quashed under our hoofs. We all rode down these horrors furiously; even Sambo's mule, in its panic, kept pace with us, in spite of its unequal load.

At last we drew reins at the hut by the river, where Dinah lived, and where she was now slumbering heavily, not expecting us that night; so that there was no fire or light to welcome our return.

Dinah was a sound sleeper, and only woke up when Sambo had burst open the door and roughly dragged her from her virtuous couch. Then, in the most scanty of night-robes, she realized the position, and bustled about to supply us with what we all required—water to slake our burning throats. This want satisfied, we flung ourselves down without ceremony and went off to sleep without uttering a word.

XVII

A Dangerous Dream

The next morning, when we were all refreshed with a goodnight's sleep, a good bath, which the males took together, looking out sharply for crocodiles, who are shy about attacking a company, and as good a breakfast as we could get from Dinah, I had leisure, before resuming our journey, to examine more closely the renewed Sir John Fenton and Penelope.

I reckoned, when I came to think about it calmly, that the swift glimpse which I thought I had of a human form lying on that volcano's ledge had been all a trick of my excited imagination; possibly a run of molten lava along the cracks, taking the outlines of a white human figure, with the glitter of a scarlet spurt of flame on the extremity, caused the fancy to start that it was blood soaking through long, thin hair. Yes, that must have been the cause of the ugly impression. So, with an easy effort, I pushed this matter from my mind.

Now that I saw the revigorated knight in the full daylight, I could trace the resemblance to his former self quite distinctly. 'Twas as if a son of his, if he had one, might have appeared before my wondering eyes. Tall and exceedingly handsome and graceful both in face and figure, with features regular and complexion fresh-coloured; coal-black, piercing eyes and short-cut, wavy, dark-brown hair. He had excessively bright red, finely curved but rather sarcastically shaped, thin lips, with a perfect set of snowy small teeth behind them; a rather long but oval face, with pointed chin, with hands white, and, like the feet, excessively small and well-shaped.

I don't know exactly what age he might have felt himself to be now that he had re-entered life. Perhaps twenty, or under; perhaps thirty, or a little over. But as the face was perfectly devoid of hair, excepting a very slight dark down on the upper lip, it was impossible for me to guess even remotely. He wore, as was his usual habit, a black velvet suit, without ornament, stuffed at the hips and chest, as was the fashion amongst court gentlemen since the crowning of King James, which made him appear full-like at these parts, with a feminine slenderness of waist. What I took particular notice of, however, about him, and remarked as a change for the better,—he was bolder in his demeanour and more assertive than he had been in his former old age, answered questions shortly and sharply, and snubbed Pierre Denis curtly whenever that gentleman attempted to air his opinions. And, what was more wonderful still, Denis took his rebuke meekly, a quality I had not observed before in this literary buccaneer, unless to Penelope and Alsander, to both of whom he had always truckled obsequiously.

Sir John, however, spoke as gently as usual to me, although he did not appear to care for my company so much as formerly, being mostly taken up with the king, his friend. I could see, before I had been half an hour in his presence, that with youth he had become fiery and impetuous in his motions, and was eager to throw in his lot with Alsander and take share in some fighting. And for this I liked and respected him all the more, for I felt that sorcery no longer had a charm to him; it was the young and gentlemanly desire for action which possessed him now.

As for the new Penelope, or, as I should call her, Quassatta, how can I describe that pink of perfection! that matchless piece of loveliness! who was given so trustingly into my charge, to guard safely and amuse, by the man who had been the husband of her former life.

As to years, she looked about my own age, or perhaps a few months younger. Of course I knew that she had seen centuries of changes; but this did not trouble me now, as it had done with the old and vanished Penelope.

She was tall for her years, with a straight and growing figure, supple as a willow wand, and light in her step as a fawn of the forest. It must have taken centuries of progression to produce that perfect shape: those exquisite small hands, with their tapering fingers, those arched and slender little feet which danced so lightly over the ground.

Her face was oval, yet full as a young maid's should be; with dimpled chin, short upper lip and full under lip, ever ready to laugh and show the dazzling rows of pearls within; her nose was straight, and joining her small broad forehead with just the faintest depression between the eyes, as we see in Greek statues; while as for the eyes, my heart grew faint with trembling when I looked into them: they were so large, and starry, and limpid, and so richly warm in their golden-brown softness, like velvet pansies when the light did not strike upon them; then they grew like two deep pools of crystal waters over tawny sands, with a diamond sparkle on the surface.

Her complexion was richly clear and freshly coloured with the tinge of a maiden blush rose, excepting when she flushed up, as she did whenever I looked at her. A face it was where modesty and tenderness struggled to control merriment and healthy spirits.

The hair, which crowned all this loveliness, was a wonder to behold; it spread out massive and soft as spun silk, and was like a new guinea for colour, catching all the sunbeams until it glowed about her dark eyes like a glory, long and tangled in its waviness.

As for her dress, I never knew what it was like,—something soft and light, which just suited her in its simplicity.

Her voice also was silvery and musical, and of that reed-like, husky clearness which thrills upon the hearer in its low tones. It had gained the juicy quality which had always missed in the old Penelope; indeed, in its sweetness it resembled, in a way, the voice of Alsander when he spoke at his gentlest.

But what struck me as most peculiar about Quassatta was that she could no longer speak to me in my own native tongue. It was the strange language of Alsander that she used, and which many of the other pirates understood. Nor did she appear to remember my mother tongue either, for whenever I spoke to her she would only shake her head prettily, as if in doubt about my meaning, and turn to Alsander for an explanation.

He told me that she had quite forgotten her past for the present, and that this was the original language of mankind before the Tower of Babel had been built, so that it came natural to her as the original and universal gift of Nature to humanity; and explained, as the cause of this, that in her hurry to get away from the volcano she must have taken too large a dose of the elixir, woman-like. She was now fresh, as if she had been newly created, a grown-up and unsophisticated child.

If this was so, could she be considered any longer as being his wife, whose unruly desires I had to guard against? And in my love for her—for I felt that I loved her now—was I wronging my friend and adopted father?

I did not tell Alsander of my present perplexity and growing feelings of mutiny; but at the earliest opportunity I took Sir John aside and asked his opinion of the matter, telling him at the same time of my awakened feelings.

I was sorry that I had taken the knight into my confidence the moment I did so, for his black eyes suddenly blazed out with savage anger on me, while he bit his red lips till the blood came, and his face went deadly white.

"So you love Quassatta already, having only known her a single night?" he snarled in my ear, clutching me tightly by the arm.

"I cannot help myself, Sir John," I faltered nervously, frightened at his sudden rage and wicked look. "But if she still belongs to him I shall try to fight it down, for the sake of my oath."

"You had better fight it down, Humphrey, if you want to live," he whispered hoarsely; "for Quassatta belongs more to him than even Penelope did, and he is not the man to forgive a trust betrayed."

I shrank from Sir John after this, with an uneasy feeling on me that he was also in love with Quassatta, and likely to prove a formidable rival.

We stayed one day at the hut to recover ourselves, during which Alsander occupied himself mostly with Sir John and his two followers, Indian Jos and Sambo, leaving me at perfect liberty to amuse Quassatta as best I could with my utter ignorance of her language. Not altogether alone we were on that day, for the envious Pierre Denis followed us about everywhere and clung to us like our shadows, much to my discomfort, and I fancy also to hers, for she spoke to him angrily once or twice, at which, however, he only shook his big, pasty-looking head and laughed in a mocking way.

Next morning we were all in the saddle once more before daybreak, my horse, as before, double-laden, at Alsander's express desire. He seemed to take a special delight in putting us together; perhaps to show his utter faith in me. While I was both delighted and troubled at this misplaced confidence, for every hour I was getting more enthralled, in spite of all my good resolves.

However, boy-like, I managed to fling care to one side and enjoy to the full that gallop, with Quassatta's arm about me, through the forest and the fields, until we once more reached the city of Laverna.

XVIII

The Spartan Boy and His Hidden Fox

For the next week or two life went on at the palace of Laverna in much the same extravagant way that it had gone on before we left on that life-renewing expedition; only to me it had an added attraction in the constant presence of the beautiful and light-hearted Quassatta, even if the perfect sunshine of our pleasure was considerably marred by those shadow clouds, Sir John Fenton, in his new development of character, and Pierre Denis, *au nalurel*.

We could not get far away into the delicious grounds by ourselves without one or the other turning up at unexpected places to join our company, which, as all the world knows, is considered complete when it is composed of two, but sadly incomplete when another is added to it. I have often thought that this literary pirate would have made a splendid priest: he was so fond of making up a third.

However, we were both young, and not easily dampened or depressed; and not being able to converse much, excepting by our eyes, we did not give a spy much to catch hold of. For, being held as I was by my vows, and she by her natural shyness and ignorance, we never got past a look or a blush when our eyes or our hands accidentally met. The days were too bright and our hearts too much satisfied with the present for us to think of passing these bounds; so we ran about, gathering flowers, or picking fruit, or catching butterflies, or swinging in the hammocks until we were hungry, and then we turned to and eat from the plenty scattered around us, like two schoolboys; and learnt in time never to heed the cat-like entrances and watchful looks of our evil-minded and puffed-out tormentor, but to laugh and romp with each other as freely when he was present as when we knew he would be hiding, traitor-like, amongst the foliage.

With Sir John Fenton it was different. Somehow he chilled us both when he came near and cast upon us his angry glances, under frowning brows. Quassatta always grew silent and depressed when she saw him, and used to stop suddenly in her game and stand before him with downcast eyes and hands folded over her breast, as you see peasant girls standing before the lordly and arrogant rector of the village. For myself

I was quickly learning to abhor this young, evil-looking knight as much as I had formerly liked him in his doating simplicity—getting to abhor him as much as I had done the old witch Penelope, now transformed into the darling Quassatta.

My adopted father, Alsander, had never been so kind or free with me as he was now when we met, which was not often, for he was neck-deep in preparations for a great ocean raid, and so spent most of his days superintending the arming and provisioning of the ships in the harbour, or studying charts and holding war councils with his captains, while they waited upon the return of their messengers and scouts, getting ready to put to sea at a moment's notice when the word came.

I was eager to join him upon this expedition, for, much as I was getting to love Quassatta, I could not bear to miss the prospect of a fight. But he said, "No," in his kindest voice.

"Next voyage, Humphrey, my son, you shall join us; meantime I want you to stay at home and teach Quassatta to speak English. Only, since she has forgotten, do not let her know that she was once Penelope and my wife. I shall tell her that myself when I am ready; only never you forget it, remember."

How I writhed within myself at those words as I repeated my vows to him to watch over the girl and guard her safely for him,—writhed at my own helplessness to resist either her or him, and at the same time despised myself for the unspoken treason which lay at my heart. It is acute torture for an open-hearted and candid boy to have a secret which he must keep to himself and a charge committed to him that he feels unworthy of; and it needed not his present warning to make me remember the falseness and hopelessness of my position, for I could never quite forget that the innocent Quassatta had belonged to him in the past and must belong to him in the near future, in spite of her winning ignorance of her cruel fate. I could never forget all this while the watchful Pierre Denis was near, although when playing with her I very nearly approached to being happy and forgetful.

Yet that lightness only lasted when we were near to each other and laughing. Each night when she left me to go to bed the memory came on me again and stabbed me through the night, until with the sun she came out and lifted the half of my burden away with her sweetness, all the time that the poison sting was going deeper and spreading the poison wider.

It comforted me a little, however, to think of her ignorance and forgetfulness of the past, and that I was at present the principle object of her love and tenderness, although my heart grew hot and heavy when I saw how free and loving she was to Alsander, for she would spring into his arms and kiss him whenever she saw him, and that without any shyness of me being near. He was also always gentle and affectionate towards her, but never lover-like or effusive. It seemed to my gnawing jealousy as if he was going to work leisurely to make her love and trust him, before he told her her destiny and took her completely from me; and that felt like putting me upon a slow fire and roasting me to death, for he always kept me at hand when she was the most lavish with her caresses, and so I had to endure it without showing what I suffered, like the Spartan boy with his hidden fox. At such times Sir John Fenton used to sit watching me under his bent brows, with a sneering smile that maddened me. What a change had come over that old man since he had quaffed that life-renewing draught! All his kind instincts and good qualities seemed to have perished with his old body, and only the spirit of one of his evil and remorseless demons to have possession now of his handsome new frame.

"I know that I can trust you, Humphrey," observed Alsander pleasantly, while Quassatta sat on his knee with her arm about his neck and her head on his shoulder, looking into mine with her soft, lustrous eyes with all the tenderness of a finished coquette, yet, as I supposed, in utter ignorance of her awful cruelty. She knew he was speaking about her to me, although she could not tell what he said; and from hearing him speak pleasantly she naturally thought it must be good, so looked all the more fondly at us both.

"Denis tells me you are merry together and no more, and he is the first man to notice wrong if there be any; so I am satisfied with you, and shall feel easy in my mind when I am away to leave you with her as her guardian. So teach her English if you can, and don't let her feel lonely during my absence."

He looked at Sir John with his ruby coloured, lambent, but expressionless eyes while he spoke, and gently stroked the golden fleece of the fair young head on his shoulder while the knight looked down with flashing eyes and hands clenching and unclenching, as he gnawed with his white teeth at his blood-red lower lip, but saying nothing in reply.

As for me, I felt as if I had been plunged into hell, and only waited for my release from the presence of this gentle-voiced, chalky-faced pirate king in order to be able to rush out to the garden and the darkness, where no one might see me, and where I could roll on the ground in my despair and howl away some of the pain that was gnawing at my swollen heart.

XIX

A Twilight Sail

At last the scouts came in; and the pirate ships left the harbour, carrying away Alsander, Sir John, and all my other acquaintances, and leaving me behind with Quassatta and our shadow, Pierre Denis.

It was a brave sight, those gallant ships being towed out of the harbour with the cloud of row-boats in front of them; and Quassatta and I, with our shadow behind us, watched them from the front balcony, where beneath us we could view the city, with its single street and shores all crowded with the gay women and men who had been left behind, cheering and waving their waist-bands and mantillas to the farewell.

The *Vigo* went first, freshly painted dark blue, with the silver band and facings, and that skeleton and woman ensign floating at her stern; and on the lofty poop King Death, dressed in black, with silver bars across his chest and bone-like lines down his arms and legs, wrought so that he appeared like a gaunt skeleton, with his white hair streaming over the silver shoulder-blades and breast-bones, a weird and a gruesome sight. Sir John Fenton stood by his side, also dressed in tight-fitting sable-hued velvet; and near at hand, as mates, Indian Jos, and Gabrial Peas; while the gigantic bulk of Sambo stood prominently in the waist amongst our old *Vigo* lads, Jack Howard, William Giles, Peter Claybroke and the rest. They were amongst the ordinary seamen, for they had yet to prove their metal. Old Robbie Crooker wasn't amongst them, for he had fallen into the snares of that half-bred, but majestic Spanish beauty, and now made a good and easy living fiddling in the public-houses for the carousers ashore a billet and mistress which exactly suited him, for he had no love for bloodshed, excepting such as he could safely let out with his lancet, while he always lost his little head through overweening conceit and that oblique eye, unless under the control of a strongly developed woman. The Spanisher was considerably younger and better looking than the Mrs. Crooker whom he had left behind, but she was also deadlier and as domineering, so that Robbie had found his safe anchorage.

King Death took none but strong and able-bodied men with him on this trip. There were five large treasure galliases expected shortly, which they intended to intercept and capture on their way north, which meant stern fighting, so he had picked his crews carefully for this occasion.

None of the ships which sailed out were so large as the *Vigo*, but they were all swift sailors, which could be handled easily, and they were closely packed with the best boarders in the colony—eight carracks in all, with a couple of swift-sailing pinnaces to act as scouts; each freshly painted, according to the fancies of their captains, and with their own ensigns flying from their poops and mast-heads.

So we saw them slowly towed across the wide lake and disappear one by one behind the headlands; then we returned to our quiet life of ease and pleasure, while we waited upon their return.

I did not attempt to teach Quassatta English beyond a few words with which to help the intelligence of our signs. Why I did not do this was selfish and wrong policy, I will admit, as all selfish motives are in the long run; but to my jealous mind it appeared to be the best for my present happiness. That it wasn't so, I was not to be expected to know in my youthful simplicity.

I resolved that I would not disturb her confidence in me by teaching her to understand Alsander's words, when he returned and spoke to me in her hearing about my duty and charge. If he chose to tell her in her own language that I was only the sheep-dog, he could do so. As yet I knew he had not done this, from her behaviour towards me. I would snatch what guiltless pleasure I could from the present while it was ours. This is how I reasoned with and punished myself.

During that first day after they left us I was somewhat surprised to find that the spy, Pierre Denis, did not obtrude his unwelcome presence upon us. Yet I thought that this might be only a cunning trick of his to inspire us with false confidence and so trap me, and that, for all I knew, he might be watching us, as he sometimes did, under cover; so I was extra careful not to be too free with my guileless companion.

But my fears proved to be groundless, as the sequel showed me.

Pierre had been foresworn from his favourite drink—rum—for a long time; and so, much as he wished to keep temperate in order to watch us, his fatal solitary habits had overcome his spying propensities: the parting glass which he had taken with the captains had awakened the dormant thirst for more; so that we came upon him, instead of him finding us out, during the first afternoon, sitting beside an outside table, more than half intoxicated and resting his head on his crossed arms.

He was not sleeping, and by instinct guessed our proximity as we stood looking at him, with the glasses and rum decanters in front of him; and lifting his head, he fixed his watery, bloodshot eyes upon us, while he rolled his tongue over his swollen lips, and at last found his voice:—

"I am not well today—the sun perhaps, or internal grief, for my heart is broken."

As he sobbingly uttered the words the tears rushed from his eyes in copious streams and rolled down his flabby cheeks.

"Why are you brokenhearted?" I inquired curiously.

"You are the cause, with your infernal poetry. Shakespeare is the cause also, with his accursed plays. Say, sir, do you consider Shakespeare to be a great writer?" He looked at me savagely as he asked the question.

"He is considered to be so in England."

"Ah, yes, in England perhaps. Ha! ha! But here what is he compared to me?"

"I don't know," I replied, "as I haven't seen your work."

"Ah, you traitor! you'd like to see it, wouldn't you?"

"I should like to see it very much."

"Then you won't, accursed interloper that you are! I was the genius of Laverna before you came to break my heart with your verses. Now what am I? eh?"

As I did not reply to this question he poured out a large glass of the neat spirits and drank it off. Then continued:—

"A man with a mighty soul, without being understood by the pigs. That's what I am; the son of an Emperor, who ought to be wearing a crown; that's me; a broken-hearted genius and neglected by all."

And with these self-pitiful words the pumpkin-like head once more sank upon his crossed arms, while he blubbered and wept like a lubberly schoolboy.

I drew Quassatta away from this neglected genius, feeling satisfied that we need have no fear of his spying on us for that afternoon, at any rate.

Pierre Denis, the weeping pirate, was not very fond of going out to the fight at anytime, so that his indulgent king gave him the task he was most fitted for—that of over-looking others. And fairly well he did it, only for these lapses of his; he preferred to stay at home blubbering about his own misfortune, or speaking mightily, while his friends were out fighting for him.

He wasn't greatly loved in this community of dare-devil cut-throats. Not that they did not like poetry, for they mostly all had a weakness in that way themselves, verse-stringing and twanging of the guitar being one of their diversions when at leisure. But they liked a man who could take a man's place on deck when battle was the order, and strongly believed in the cutting of a man's head off first, or the stringing of him up yard high, before attempting to string a rhythm about the glorious action, and Pierre always fell decidedly short of the heroic in the estimation of these dauntless, if wicked rovers.

Quassatta and I left him to his solitary enjoyments, while we sought out ours, which, now that he had removed himself, were not difficult to find in that palace of delight.

There was no one else, either in the palace or the city, whom we were in the least degree afraid of watching our actions, now that Denis was off duty; so, unloosing Martin from his chain, we took him with us and together set off towards the shore.

Strange dog that was. For, as I had changed in my feelings towards Penelope now that she was Quassatta, so he had done also, and now regarded her, if not with over-much affection, still with passive and indifferent tolerance. He seemed to recognise in her something that was of importance in my estimation, so, dog-like, indulged me, yet with a dubious shake of his wise big head, as if it was beyond his comprehension.

He followed after us docilely enough, and served by his presence as a protection. Not that anyone, however, sought to molest us as we passed down the lanes and through the street. The revellers were still at it in the same mad and reckless fashion, only that they all appeared to know us, and respect us, for they doffed their hats or waved their cutlasses gallantly towards us as we went by; sometimes shouting out one of my little ditties, as a compliment to me and my companion, but with no rudeness or blush-raising remarks. In fact, to look at them this afternoon they might have been honest planters and mariners taking their ease ashore, instead of the notorious main-rangers that they were.

We went to the shore and got into a small skiff; and while she sat in the stern and Martin lay down in the bows, I took up the oars and set to rowing her over the lake,—so smooth and peaceful that it looked like a mirror reflecting all above it.

Quassatta watched me admiringly as I bent to my work; while, although I was just getting into my seventeenth year, I felt big enough and strong enough to protect any woman and take my part with any man, for I had never suffered a day of illness all my life, and there is something in these climates which makes a boy feel and grow like a man in a very short time. Also I was quite well aware, as every boy must be who is passably good-looking, although he may not own it when taxed, that I was a more suitable mate for a girl like her, as far as looks were concerned, and honesty also, than any of the others about the island; while, as for Alsander, it was a sacrifice of lovely innocence which I could not bear to contemplate.

The luminous twilight was once more settling down upon the lake as we sailed out from the shore,—the twilight caused by those high bluffs, which intercepted the afternoon sun and cast their shadows over the waters with that radiant lustre over head, and the outline of the distant forest ranges, so sharply, yet so velvety, standing out against the golden space.

There were no sun rays about to lighten up that luminous halo of golden hair, and yet it seemed able to absorb the light from above, so that it shone like sunshine before my amorous gaze.

Was this Penelope, before whose presence I had shuddered with loathing, who now thralled every emotion, so that it felt like a religion to worship her more than a breach of faith to my king and friend?

Yes, she was getting to be my divinity, and her love the bourne towards which all my aspirations tended. When one is drawn completely within the embraces of a torrent, from which there is no escape, and which is bearing him on with resistless velocity towards what he knows not, it is better to sit down quietly and struggle no longer; and this is the stage which I had reached now. I would do no active wrong to Alsander; but since he had flung me into the torrent, I would sit quietly and take what passive pleasure I could get,—without resistance, at least, so long as our watcher, Pierre Denis, was incapable of betraying us, or of marring our joy with his obnoxious presence.

I felt much easier after this, in my mind, now that I had packed conscience up like a cumbersome parcel, and left it behind me; nay, I felt a species of exultation and satisfaction to think that Pierre, the spy, was now sitting with the rum bottle before him, and my caged conscience beside him—both spy and monitor made useless and blinded; a savage pleasure that Alsander had not busted my fidelity so much but that he must also leave a watcher to tell him all that passed during his absence; a delight to think that the spy had already betrayed his master and given me my liberty. It felt like putting a prisoner upon parole, and then locking him in as well. I was the prisoner who had given his parole, and then been deprived of his liberty, and who, by the negligence of the jailer, finds himself free to do as he pleases.

If Alsander had trusted to my honour utterly, I think that I would have been faithful to it and him, even in trivial matters of observance. I do not know this, though, for first love is like naught else for making a perjurer of a man. But he had not trusted me, and now he was betrayed—not by me, but by this ignoble traitor, Denis.

Let him look after his master's rights when he was once more able to do so. Chance had yielded up the present to me, and so, with a wave of boyish joy and freedom from care, I made the drunken sot, Denis, the keeper of that package called conscience.

We floated well into the lake as I made these reflections with my head down and the oars in my hands, while that bewitching maiden reclined before me, all perfection and tenderness, and the light gradually stole out of the dome above, leaving the stars coming out one by one, like fairy lamps hung up in that green vault to show young love the road to heaven.

We were far from where the vessels lay at anchor; we were alone upon that liquid world, for the dog Martin did not count, as he lay sleeping in the bows and dreaming of old hunts,—alone upon a world of our own, with only those lustrous orbs above, repeating themselves in the liquid smoothness around, and in the distance only the lights from the streets, dripping down, and the faint sounds of singing and tenderly struck guitars.

We had not spoken, for we could not understand each other, but as long as the light had remained with us she had leaned back dabbling her little hands in the waters, and looking at me with her large and dewy eyes.

Now I softly drew in the oars, to rest my arms before we turned back; and as the skiff floated motionless my fresh love fell upon me like a great wave of curbless devotion, so that instinctively, and without knowing what I was doing, I knelt down before that divinity and held out my arms, speechless, and yet thrilled with holy prayer.

The maid could not see me, for it was too dark, and I had sunk down without a sound or a disturbance of the skiff; but the magic of the moment must have been upon her also, for even as I knelt I was aware that the indistinct haze of hair and light dress was gliding towards me slowly and silently; then, with a soft sigh, she fluttered against my breast, while our lips met together in that long first kiss, which made us one for ever.

XX

The Watchdog Betrays His Trust

That selfish orgie of the faithless jailor and spy, Pierre Denis, lasted nearly three weeks without ceasing, while Quassatta and I enjoyed such a heavenly holiday as falls to the lot of few of human mould.

Honestly I tried several times to rouse him out of his stupor, and set him right by removing from his reach the rum, and even forbidding the servants from supplying him with anymore, for I hated to see the lovely grounds where I and my love walked in desecrated by such a revolting sight as that howling and staggering figure, blinded with drink, unwashed and dishevelled, crossing our path and trampling down the flowers in all directions as he went, pursued by imaginary crawling things and devils, and shrieking out his imprecations and horrifying hatreds.

I was also fearful lest he might in his paroxysms do himself or someone else some hurt, or be discovered by his master to our injury.

But all my efforts were useless. He had the cunning of a maniac, and was always able to steal or get at the rum somehow; so that at last, like my tender scruples, I gave up all effort to control him, and went my own way, keeping out of his as much as it was possible to do, and taking the best that I could out of my present opportunity.

After that evening upon the lake the conditions of our friendship changed, or, rather, deepened, between Quassatta and myself. We had now a mutual secret, which, although unspoken between us, was perfectly understood, and with her stirred heart also awoke the womanly instinct of shyness and love of secrecy.

We met each morning as usual; but I noticed now that before people she was not so free towards me. It was only when together and no eye watching us that she unbent and became all clinging tenderness and devotion, yet so modest and gentle through it all that it ever seemed as if an angel stood between us, bidding me stand off and not hurt the delicacy of this pure and unblemished flower.

And was this Penelope the unruly and turbulent, who had scared me with her passion? or a new creature, made specially for me, when I could be worthy enough to hold her?

That was the thought which ever and anon flashed upon me and gave me such perplexity.

She did not romp now as she had done before that kiss, but walked sedately by my side, with a happy smile forever upon her rosy lips, and a dewy moistness in her velvety eyes. We walked soberly through the glades and avenues of vines, with the gorgeous butterflies swimming around us, while the large bunches of ripe grapes hung ready to our reach—walked along hand in hand, happy as children, and seldom touching the grapes which hung so ripe and ready for the gathering, for we felt no need of them yet. We were not at all thirsty, but contented to be near to all the loveliness and to look upon it, feeling satisfied that it was there when we were ready for it.

Sometimes we sailed again upon the lake, and waited until the stars came out before we left it; but we did not kiss again on that lake, and but seldom on the shore. I felt that the one kiss was enough, and that too many might make us forget the thrill of that first one; and I think that she understood what was in my mind, and felt the same.

No one hindered us in our going or coming, for the palace and grounds were deserted of all saving servants, and that dirty demoniac, who rushed about when he was not too far overcome, with the slavers hanging at his stubbly beard, and the echoes filled with his cursings. And as he always heralded his approach with wild cries, we had plenty of time to get out of his way.

At times we would sit together on a bank or by the side of the stream. Then timidly my arm would steal round her slender waist, and she would lay her fair young head upon my shoulder for a little space; then starting from me at some imaginary sound, she would turn and gather flowers, which she always gave to me when they were made up into a posy.

At nights, however, she would grow bolder with me, particularly at the moment of parting. It was bright moonlight now, and we stayed out together later than we did on the dark nights. When the moment of parting came, she would draw me within the black shadow of a bush, and, putting her arms round my neck, would kiss me on the lips, whispering in her broken, musical voice, "Gooda-night." After which, before I could recover from the trembling which was shaking me, she would dart away from me and quickly disappear.

I could not keep her from learning a little English, for she had set her mind upon this, and made me repeat names of things which she saw as we walked, and which she named first in her own language and then conned over and over in mine, until she had learnt them off by heart.

She could say "Gooda-morning" and "Gooda-night," also treasuring up what she heard me say about Pierre in his present condition. She would say in a contemptuous tone, as she pointed at him when he ran across us, "Drunkena sot!" or "Dirta hoga!" I felt that I could not guard my mother tongue long from this inquisitive child of Nature.

So the days and nights sped on, until Pierre Denis ran himself aground and was carried helplessly into a strong room, raving mad with the blue devils, where he lay shrieking and groaning, or weeping and flinging himself about, until the drink died out of him, and he became once more himself again, white and trembling as he walked about, but watchful as a cat over our actions, and with a crafty, half-witted leer upon his flabby mouth. Our hours of freedom and enjoyment were over.

XXI

Bringing Home the Treasure Galliases

O n the seventh week after they had left us our fleet came back, one carrack short, but bearing with them, instead, four of the largest galliases that I had ever seen in my life. Indeed, unless I had seen them and heard my father speak about the great castle-built ships of the Spanish Armada, I would not have believed it possible that men could handle such clumsy great hulks, for rich-looking although they were as far as gold work and ornament were concerned, and massively handsome as they looked upon the water, to capture them had been almost too easy a task for King Death and his captains in their little craft.

The fifth gallias had managed to escape from their clutches and run into Rio Janeiro, after sinking the pirate carrack sent in chase of her, having, for a Spaniard, a brave captain, and a wonderfully plucky crew. So, knowing full well that this gallias would not again leave port until they thought the sea would be clear, King Death had sailed homeward with his gold-laden prizes, leaving only the pinnaces to beat about and give timely warning when she next set sail.

"That will be your chance, Humphrey, my lad, if you wish to distinguish yourself," he said to me the night he landed. "We shall place two of the carracks under your command, and send you out to capture this shy gallias. In three days' time we shall have you all ready to take the seas."

My heart bounded at this prospect opening up of seeing active life, for the past two weeks had been very wearisome since Pierre Denis had recovered, and I was afraid of betraying my fond secret now that Alsander was once more back.

Both carracks and treasure ships were considerably crippled by the engagement, and appeared from the Straits one after the other, with broken masts and splintered sides, while some of the sails were riddled into holes until they looked like fluttering rags, which accounted for the slowness of their sailing, and proved that the treasure had not been captured without a contest.

A few of the pirates also were missing, without counting the captain and crew of the lost carrack, which had gone down with all hands aboard, in sight of the fleet, but too far off for them to save any of their unfortunate comrades, their own hands being over busy at the time to be able to do more than sympathize and promise to avenge.

Many of the survivors also were wounded and maimed. They were put ashore first, and taken to the hospital to be cured, and their lasting injuries reckoned up in the prize money, so many hundred pieces being placed to each sufferer's credit over his fellows against the loss or maimed limb or lost member, before the general distribution took place.

They were very fair toward each other, these subjects of King Death, and always set a fund apart for the wounded or killed, so that those who escaped this bout might not grudge risking their lives on another occasion. Thus for the loss of a right arm six hundred pieces of eight were allowed; and for the blinding of an eye, or the taking off of a finger, one hundred pieces; and so on. According to what was reckoned the greatest affliction got the highest compensation. If, however, the pirate was killed outright, and had no one belonging to him to stand for heir, then his prize and compensation money went into the standing fund of ordinary expenses.

They did not bring many prisoners back with them, for the Spaniards had resisted bravely, mostly preferring the sword to a life of slavery. Only about a score of poor fellows, and half a dozen young girls, daughters of Spanish grandees, going home to convents, were with them; but who would have been more fortunate had they plunged into the waves, than they were now alive. And, well treated though they were, I saw these poor captives led away to the common prison, to be kept until they were put up to auction—watched them with helpless compassion.

The *Vigo* was the least injured of all the ships, although she had been through the hottest of the engagement. Like the king, she seemed to bear a charmed life; a few splinters had been torn from her sides, but no damage of any importance elsewhere, save what could be quickly repaired—the foretopmast shot away and a spar-end or so missing. She lay now amongst that battered fleet almost as fresh as when she had started upon her voyage.

Sir John Fenton had been wounded in the side, and being still unable to move, was borne in a litter up to the palace; so also was Jack Howard, and our old first mate, William Giles. Jack only slightly, with a bullet through the arm and a slashed head; but Giles had lost his right leg, and was in a dangerous condition, owing to the want of proper attendance and the extreme heat of the season.

I went along with Jack to the hospital, and heard his yarn after they had made him comfortable:—

"They had sighted the five galliases at noon, not far from Cape Frio, and had hung about them harassing them all that day till night fell; then drawing off for an hour or two, during which the wind had freshened, and forced the great ships apart, so that when morning broke they could see them lying about five miles apart from each other.

"This was the chance which our Admiral, King Death, had waited for; so sending six of the carracks to annoy the four most distant ships, with our flagship, the *Vigo*, and the *Serpent*, thus we dashed forward to the nearest gallias, taking her both sides at once, and boarding her with a rush, before the dons had got the sleep out of their eyes.

"It wasn't hard work, the first capture, for although they might have taken warning from our badgering the day before, we found them all unready, and had them overboard in no time. Those who were able to move we forced to jump, and all who showed fight were soon corpses cumbering the decks. We did not spare a man-Jack amongst that first lot, for the king wanted to get at the others before they took fright.

"Then, leaving half a dozen boys on board to steer her, we trooped back to our boats and skurried off after the others, picking them up one after the other, and cutting down all who stood up against us; for the old hulks lay like floating wharfs waiting on us to take possession, while every deck that we cleared made our work all the easier, there being more of us to do it.

"I never saw such a captain as King Death is for coolness, nor one so like a tiger as Sir John Fenton has grown in his second youth. As for that Indian Jos, why, he is the devil with his cutlass and dirk for stabbing and cutting off heads.

"These three were everywhere where the Spaniards clustered closest, with Gabrial Peas stealing down below and finding out skulkers. That's the job he takes amongst the boarders, and very thoroughly he did his quiet work, as we found out afterwards. When we came to search the ship's cabin, helpless women and old men were to be seen lying about with their throats cut and their bodies mutilated horribly, all the handiwork of the hairless and whispering Gabrial, whom I hate now to think of, after the ghastly sights I helped to move afore I got my wound.

"Indian Jos is most devilishly cruel when he is on the job; but he does it above board, so that it don't seem quite so bad. As for the captain, he just went to work like a mower in a hayfield—cool and steady, giving his orders all the time in his clear voice, while he mowed on to left and right with that long sword of his in the one hand and a pistol in the other, cutting a lane through those nearest to him, while he kept his red eyes all about him, picking out the boldest with his bullets, when he could not get at them with his sword.

"He must have had thirty or forty pistols stuck about him, I think, for as soon as one was empty he pitched it in the face of someone coming on, and plucked out another without a pause; and after he had got rid of the right side lot of weapons he changed his sword into his left hand, and went on as easy as before, not a bit angry like, but just as if he was playing at a game of dice.

Sir John, on the other hand, was blazing and yelling with fury, like a raised cat, close beside the admiral, with a boarding axe in his hand, braining all that came in his road, and making a sickening mess both of himself and the decks. By the Lord! I wasn't sorry when at last I saw him struck down and fall backwards into the arms of Alsander, who at once carried him out of further danger.

"The sky was now getting foggy with the gunpowder smoke, so that we could hardly see friend from enemy, while the sharks were busy with those who had jumped overboard, by the time that the fourth gallias struck her colours and we could call a halt.

"It was in the midst of this confusion of smoke and fighting that the fifth ship sneaked away, after riddling the carrack which had gone after her. When the smoke cleared off, we could just make her out as she drove before a fresh breeze below the distant horizon, with the sinking carrack about four miles from us down to the maindeck in the water.

"Three of our vessels went off in chase of the vanishing prey, while another tried to get up to the wreck, but they were too late: the great ship had a good start and a strong wind, and so got safe into Rio before they could reach her; while, as for the pirate wreck, it went down like a stone in about three minutes after we had sighted her, with all aboard.

"Then they turned to look after the wounded and clear out the dead. Alsander, when he had seen to the comfort of Sir John in his own cabin, came up as cool as ever and set to judging the prisoners. And that is, to my mind, the ugliest part of a pirate life, for they made short work of the chiefs and wounded, making the first walk the plank without wasting anytime listening to them, and chucking the second lot after them to feed the sharks.

"Then the rest of the day was passed scrubbing down and sousing the decks and cabins; after which the working crew were told out to each craft. And so in company we all turned towards home.

"A weary voyage that was to us that lay wounded below, for we had contrary winds most of the road, and everyday had to keep a sharp look-out for strange sails ahead. Twice or thrice we fell across passing vessels, and then our least injured carracks would give them chase. The *Vigo* was the most successful at this running game. So that I think on the whole we managed to scuttle three of these poor merchantmen, sinking their crews without mercy, while only two managed to get out of our clutches. For our king served them out the same whether they ran, fought, or struck, taking what they had most useful from them, and sinking them afterwards, not considering them worth saving, as they were slow sailors, and only an encumbrance to our fleet."

"I suppose it is a pretty rich haul you have got now, Jack, and you will be a wealthy man if you get your share with the rest?" I said to the wounded man.

"Yes; Indian Jos says that we may reckon upon fifty thousand pieces of eight each man, after it is divided; so that I can buy my freedom, and start life as a planter, if I like."

"And will you do this, Jack?" I asked.

"Not if what I hear is true—that the king is going to send you after that other gallias. I must be in that game with you, Humphrey, my boy."

"So you shall, Jack, if I can manage it," returned I, shaking him by the hand and leaving him to get some rest.

XXII

Admiral Humphrey Bolin

No native of Plymouth could ever be made to think that the killing of a Spaniard should be called murder, or the taking of a Spanish treasure ship to be anything otherwise than a most meritorious action. Therefore I left Jack Howard with a pleased feeling about their success; although, like Jack, I wished that Alsander had shown a little more magnanimity over his captives. But this uneasiness I also pushed resolutely out of my mind, with the reflection that a man of Alsander's great experience knew best what to do with such enemies; and so I went up to the palace meditating upon my own approaching promotion to the leadership of two vessels, resolving that I would cover my name with glory or die in the attempt.

It was nightfall when I reached the palace, where I found a large gathering of pirates and their favourite sultanas assembled in the great hall, feasting right royally, with their king at the head of the table.

I would gladly have been excused from this feast when I saw that Quassatta was absent, and that Pierre Denis was sitting on the left side of my adopted father, for I thought that I might find her elsewhere; and I could see, from the evil but satisfied look on the informer's face that he had gained Alsander's ear by some crafty invention; but as I paused irresolute at the doorway the king observed me, and beckoned me over to a vacant seat at his right hand, in such a definite way that I felt escape to be impossible.

Then I went up to where he sat and took the place indicated to me, noticing as I did so the malignant smile on the lips and gleam of hatred in the eyes of Captain Pierre, who was opposite to me.

It was a magnificent hall, richly covered with oriental hangings, and brilliantly lighted up with countless altar candles, placed in huge silver holders, the gleanings of many Spanish churches.

From the lofty ceiling swung a deep, gold-fringed punkah, which the slaves pulled to and fro, causing a grateful air to play upon the flushed faces of the guests, and at the same time drive away the mosquitoes. Here and there stood broad-leaved palms in large vases, while from the open windows came the delicately blended perfume of exotics and ripe fruit borne on the night air, with the sound of lapping waves on the shore and plashing fountains from the gardens.

The tables were loaded with viands, placed in rare dishes of gold, silver, and porcelain, while richly cut decanters of wine stood within easy reach of the exquisitely cut glasses and goblets. All the world of art and luxury appeared to have contributed to this pirate feast.

Hordes of obsequious slaves moved about, bringing on or bearing away dishes and platters,—trembling slaves, who never knew the moment when a blow from one of those brawny fists or a smash from the butt-end of a pistol would not be delivered to them for some imaginary carelessness or lack of attention. These pirates were superb epicures in their eating and drinking, and merciless tyrants to their servants, although boisterous and jovial amongst themselves.

"Pierre tells me that you have been a faithful attendant upon Quassatta during our absence," observed Alsander gently, as he fixed his scarlet eyes upon me.

"I have tried my best to do my duty," I murmured, blushing up in my confusion.

"Have you taught her to speak good English yet?"

"She has learnt a little," I replied, still looking down at my plate.

"But not enough to say '*Goodbye*' to you yet, I suppose?"

"No; I don't think that she has learnt the word 'goodbye' yet."

"Ah, that is a pity. However, it does not matter greatly, as I can say it to her for you, Humphrey, my son, in the original language; besides, you are not likely to see her again before you go upon your expedition."

"Why so, king? I have still three days left, have I not? I might still have time to teach her that word."

My voice trembled, in spite of myself, as I uttered these words, for my heart was aching with despair. I understood what he meant, and knew to whom I was indebted for this new cruelty—that pasty-faced, watery-eyed, malignant drunkard opposite, who was watching me with his gloating smile. As I spoke, I lifted my burning lids and fixed my eyes upon the dead-white face of my tormentor, who did not frown or smile, but regarded me as he ever looked,—sightlessly and without emotion.

"Because for one thing, my son, you will be too busy with your preparations for sailing. An admiral has to look after every detail of his expedition if he wishes to succeed in his enterprise; and I wish you to manage this affair for yourself, although, of course, I will help you with my advice. Besides, Quassatta has a grave duty to perform, and will be engaged for a long time to come in nursing our wounded guest and friend, Sir John Fenton. So now you see why it will be impossible for *my future wife* to take anymore lessons in English from you for the present."

I felt choking as I heard these low words half whispered to me by this white-haired, pink-eyed master of my fate, and, reaching over, poured out a glass of wine and swallowed it hastily, without replying. Quassatta, the darling of my soul, his future wife, to be the constant attendant and nurse of that demon-possessed, handsome knight, who gloated on murder like a tiger, and drank down human blood like a cannibal, while I was separated from this innocent victim by rolling oceans, without even the poor consolation of a brief farewell!

"Captains and gentlemen," resumed Alsander, raising his voice to his quarter-deck tone, "I have a toast to propose, which is that you all drink to the success of our young friend here, Humphrey Bolin, the newly appointed commodore, in his expedition; and may he bring back the prize in safety, and distinguish himself as a member of our free order. To the young Admiral Humphrey Bolin!"

The toast was responded to boisterously by these free and daring pirates, who did not appear to be in the slightest degree jealous of my sudden promotion—that is, all excepting Pierre Denis, who neither charged his glass nor rose when the others drank, but gazed down upon his plate with covered eyes and trembling lips.

"You are not drinking, Captain Denis," observed Alsander, looking at him steadfastly.

"No," mumbled Pierre; "I am sworn against drink for the present."

"Then fill your glass with water, if you will not take wine," repeated my adopted father.

"No; when I don't take rum, I taste nothing else, as you all know," again replied Denis sullenly.

"As you like, captain," returned Alsander shortly, turning away his gaze from the boor, who continued sitting and drumming his fingernails against his plate, while I rose and uttered a few incoherent words of thanks, mingling my speech with a few high-flown, boyish sentiments about duty, glory, and honour, at which the pirates laughed and cheered boisterously, shouting out,—

"Never bother about the glory, if you bring safely back the gold; we will welcome you right heartily then, never be afraid, and without asking too many questions."

For the next two days I was kept hard at work with the two carracks placed at my disposal, while the newly returned crews were unloading the treasures and storing them: strong chests of gold and silver, pieces and ingots of solid metal, packages of unset pearls and jewels, besides other valuables, which were to be sent off to France for sale before the division could take place; for all was done amongst these pirates methodically.

Meanwhile a few of the chests were opened, and each man was paid five thousand pieces of eight on account; with which sum, after the whole was stored, they went off to spend in the public-houses, and with the hungry dames of fortune. I never could have imagined the wealth which was piled up carelessly, as if it had been bags of grain, inside this store.

Then the volunteers had to be sworn into my service, and capable captains and officers appointed for the two vessels; for I discovered that my position was more honourable than responsible on this expedition, as is that of so many other court-appointed admirals—that is, I was to have the glory if we succeeded, while the capable men were to have the responsibility and hard work. "Atleast," thought I, "they will not be able to prevent me from sharing in the fighting, even if I have not much to say in the steering."

The ship which was to carry me personally was named the *Turtle*, and my consort was called the *Harpy*; both fine, swift vessels, well manned and armed, as well as plentifully provisioned.

Much to my disgust, I found that my captain was to be Pierre Denis, with Indian Jos and Gabrial Peas for under officers, and Sambo for our cook. Indian Jos and Sambo I could have tolerated, but Denis and Gabrial Peas were not to my mind. However, these arrangements I could not alter or control; indeed, I soon discovered that in my position as admiral I had very little to do with any of the business, excepting to obey the orders of Alsander, and prepare to strut about the poop as an ornament, which hurt my foolish pride very deeply.

However, I had my way with regard to Jack Howard, who was able to come aboard before we sailed and take the post of third officer; also Peter Claybroke, who I appointed to be the fourth; while most of the old *Vigo* men who were unwounded volunteered for the *Turtle*, and were passed by Alsander.

The *Harpy* was manned and officered by casual acquaintances whom I had come to know during my sojourn on the island, and with whom, not knowing much about, I had no fault to find.

So on the third morning we were towed out of the lake, without my getting a glimpse or a farewell from my sweet, lost Quassatta. I leaned over the rail watching the distant palace windows, without getting a sign from her, while I could see King Death standing alone on the lower balcony, with folded arms and blue glasses over his red eyes, watching the sailing of the ships, and his long white tresses lying upon his black velvet doublet. His was the only and the last figure that my eyes could rest upon as we slid between the cliffs and lost sight of that gay city Laverna.

XXIII

Humphrey Asserts His Position

I wasn't permitted to indulge much in the way of heroics with that hateful and hating captain of mine forever jeering at my attempts at dignity, disputing each suggestion that I made, and wantonly contradicting my wishes every chance he had.

If this piratical stringer-together of empty words was a contemptible character on shore, while we were equal and he was on private duty only, his aggressiveness and sullenness, envy, ill-will, and bombast, all so equally blended, made my position as honorary commander almost unendurable; and, only for the timely interference of Indian Jos, I think I would have put his muscles to the test before we had been one day together, so obnoxious did he make himself to me from the instant that he put his foot aboard, in his attempting to turn me into ridicule before my men. Fortunately he was not much respected by his own acquaintances, while I was sure of the fidelity of my father's old crew. So that he did less damage than he might have done had the case been different.

We cleared the straits and reefs, while I still leaned sadly against the taffrail, thinking about the girl I had left behind me; and had gained the open sea, when he approached me with a palpable sneer on his blobby lips, and a hating gleam in his bleary grey eyes, and with a broad wink at Indian Jos, who stood at the wheel. He touched his hat with a mocking affectation of humility, and said,—

"Well, Admiral Bolin, we have reached open water. Will you kindly give me your orders for the day?"

I regarded the evil face before me for some minutes in silence, and after I had composed my feelings, replied,—

"Yes, Captain Denis; be so good as to call the officers and sailors together, so that I may speak to them."

"But why so, admiral? Am I not enough for the present to be ordered about?"

"No, Captain Denis. I command you to do as I desire, and at once."

"But suppose that it does not suit me to obey you in this present boyish fancy of yours?"

"Then, by St. George, I'll try which is the better man!" I cried hotly, rolling up my cuffs, preparatory to having a tussle. I had seen my father in a similar position as I was then placed, and how he settled any dispute before it got too far; and I felt that it wasn't Humphrey Bolin's son who was going to be mocked at and bullied for nothing.

"I think you had better do as the admiral bids you, Captain Denis," shouted out Indian Jos from the wheel, while my two mates, Jack Howard and Peter Claybroke, sauntered over to my side quietly, ready to see fair play.

Pierre Denis saw these signs, and, like the coward that he was, caved in with a bitter scowl.

"Call up the men, Claybroke," he snarled, as he turned away.

In a few moments I had them all under my eye on the maindeck, as I stood above them on the poop. Then I spoke up boldly and heartily,—

"My lads, you have taken service for this voyage of your own free will, to obey me and your officers. If any man amongst you feels at all discontented with the choice of your king, on account of my youth and lack of experience, I want him now to step forward and say so, while there is yet time to leave me and go back."

"No! no! We have taken service willingly, and we'll stick to you so long as you don't show the white feather."

"That is all I ask or expect. Now, what I want to say is, that if any man has a complaint to make at anytime, he will come to me direct with it, and to no one else on board. I know little about steering a ship, and nothing at all about the waters we are in; therefore I shall not attempt to interfere with the captains or officers in this department. Also, I have yet to prove my courage and fighting qualities to you all, which I hope to do to your satisfaction; but one thing you must never forget, and that is, I represent your chosen king, and that my word is law, when I give it, until we return to Laverna again; that I must have your obedience and respect, without any grumbling. You understand me?"

"Yes, admiral; and we give it freely and loyally."

"Right, lads. There stands your captain and officers, whom you must honour and obey, as I expect them to honour and obey me. In return, I shall strive my utmost to be your true friend, and right any wrong you may have, if you come to me with it; and also to knock down or pistol any man who disputes my authority on this or my consort ship, whether he is captain or ordinary seaman. Go to your duty, lads; and come, gentlemen, into the cabin and hold council together. Captain

Denis, give your orders for the captain and officers of the *Harpy* to be signalled on board."

As I finished speaking, and waved my hand, the crew cheered lustily, which told me that I had won their favour with my bold words; then, without another glance at the baffled Pierre Denis, I turned my back on them and went down to the cabin, to wait for the coming of the leaders, determined to show them once for all that I wasn't going to be a toy admiral.

"You've got it in you, my boy," said Indian Jos a few minutes afterwards, as he joined me at the table and began to spread out the charts. "Stick to your guns like a man, and you'll find we will all stand up for you."

"I mean to do that, Jos," I replied resolutely. "Has Captain Denis signalled?"

"Yes; I saw to that before I left him. You will have a struggle with him, I can see; but if you are stiff, he will cave in, for he is a regular cur at heart."

"Thanks, Jos, for your support. Now let us examine the charts."

Jos was busy posting me up as to the routes and markings of our voyage, when the captains and officers entered in a body and took their places according to position of grade,—all except Denis, who ignored my sign for him to sit at my right hand.

"I think we should choose our chairman for this council," he began, when I stopped him short.

"No, Captain Denis. I am your leader, and therefore your chairman. Sit down in your proper place or else leave the cabin."

He looked at me for a moment with a heavy scowl, and then, dropping his eyes before mine, took his place at the table, while a broad grin of satisfaction flitted over the faces of the others, proving to me that they did not resent my arrogance. It was now that I felt my own power, and that this was the only way to manage this lout, upon whom kindness and consideration would be equally thrown away.

As I looked round upon these swarthy, dare-devil faces, I felt a new sensation surging within me. My boyhood and bashfulness had dropped from me like a cast-off coat, and a stern spirit of command taken possession, and made me feel how easy it was to become a master of men, if one has only grip enough of himself.

I was tall for my age, and felt as strong as a young lion. Not one of the men present but had weakened themselves with drink and debauchery, so that I could have tackled the strongest with confidence in my own strength, if it came to a tussle; and this is a comforting thing to feel when one intends to assert himself over men.

I spoke to the council squarely, telling them that I wished to understand their movements clearly, while placing myself under their practical experience; and so, from one remark after another, before we separated I was able to grasp the meaning of their instructions and their own intentions, and therefore in a position to put in my word of advice without making myself ridiculous.

Pierre Denis showed his nature in his advice, which was to take with us three or four of the small craft then beating about us, sail towards Cape Frio, and while the pinnaces scouted, hang about and lie low, so as to take the enemy by surprise and with safety, a policy which was repugnant to me, thirsting as I was for distinction; so I up and uttered my hopes.

"Gentlemen, my idea is to sail boldly on to Rio Janeiro and seize the gallias in the docks, if we do not meet her on the way, challenge her to open fight, and take her by force, seeing that wo have men enough to do it."

"A good idea, that of the admiral's, boys," replied Jos, looking up from the chart; "that is, so far as Rio is concerned, although not quite feasible as he puts it; and I think I know as bold a plan, and one more likely to be successful."

"What is your plan, Jos?" I asked.

"Well, my opinion is that this treasure ship will stay where she is until some more galliases come from Spain, so that we may hang about for months without getting at her; while, as for facing the batteries of the town in open light, it isn't to be thought about. Now, my plan is, to sail for Cape Frio and land a few of us there—myself for one, say; and while the carracks keep out to sea so as to watch for her, we will steal over-land to Rio, and kidnap the ship as we may see our chance."

"How many will you require for this task?" I asked.

"A dozen volunteers at most. More would make it risky. I'll pick out the men that I can trust, and undertake to lead them through the forests, for I know that part well."

"Splendid!" I cried enthusiastically, forgetting my newly acquired dignity in my sudden pleasure; "and you will let me be one of the volunteers, won't you, Jos?"

"If you want to go, admiral, you can, for you are master; only you'd be safer aboard along with Captain Denis there, who, I swear, has no desire to see Rio from the land side. Have you, captain?"

"As much as you have, I dare say, if I hadn't my ship to look after," responded Denis snappishly; "particularly if the admiral here meditates upon leaving us at Cape Frio, there will be all the greater need for me to keep on board."

"Right you are, as usual, captain," cried Indian Jos loudly, looking at me to turn the conversation, which I did by dismissing the council.

"Are you all willing that we should try this plan of Indian Jos's?"

"Yes; if he is willing to take the risk of being caught and hung, and can find other volunteers besides yourself to go with him, we cannot well object."

"Then it is settled; we go straight on to Cape Frio, and anchor there until we land; after which the *Turtle* and *Harpy* will cruise about as near to Rio as possible, so as to pick us up if we are successful, or to tackle the gallias if we should miss her. That is enough, gentlemen. Now to your posts, and let us get on."

XXIV

The Capture of the Gallias

After this programme had been arranged, I managed, by avoiding all disputes with Pierre Denis, and only asserting myself at such times as were strictly necessary, to keep something like order on board, and pass the time fairly pleasantly until we arrived at Cape Frio, round which we sailed some fifty or sixty miles, bringing up at a sheltered cove about four days' journey from the city, into which we meant to get if possible unobserved.

We had good weather all the way, and a steady southerly wind, which took us along swiftly, and which, until it changed, would prevent northward-steering vessels from leaving that port.

Here we landed, as Jos said, a devil's dozen, I making the odd man; taking with us our weapons and ammunition, also provisions enough to last us five or six days. If caught, we intended to give ourselves out as shipwrecked seamen, and offer our services to the captain of the gallias. If undiscovered, each man was to go by himself, when near the town, and creep under cover of night into the ship, there to hide as best we might until we were all together, when we would look out for our opportunity.

"It will be easy for us to enter the town from the land side if we go in separately, dressed, as we are, like Spanish sailors," remarked Indian Jos; "as it is on the ocean side that they keep the sharpest look-out; and also to slip aboard one by one, for they don't keep much watch in harbour; and the best hiding-place will be the mast-heads, where we may lie for days unnoticed and see all that goes on below."

So, having arranged as to signals and other details, we set out on our perilous journey, Indian Jos taking the lead of our men, who were mostly half-breds, with a perfect mastery of the Spanish language, and all men that Jos could depend upon.

I was the only member of the party that could not speak the native tongue, but this Jos provided for by telling me to play dummy; while, with some dye, he made me in skin and hair as like a Spaniard as he could do.

I left the dog Martin behind me under the charge of Jack Howard, who promised to look well after him. Good old Jack! he let me go with great reluctance, and was much put out that he could not accompany us on our expedition; but this Jos would not have, as two dumb men would look suspicious and endanger our plot.

I need not tell you all the particulars of our journey through the forests and swamps of this Santa Cruz land. There were tracks which Jos knew, having once escaped from slavery here, and which took us direct to the city; otherwise it would have been a hopeless journey, with all the many dangers of reptiles and wild beasts and the chances of losing our road. Even as it was we had a weary journey, and endured much in the form of discomfort and dread.

On the third afternoon we began to see signs of humanity and cultivation, with open tracks; and then we walked more warily, and resolved to lie hidden until night, and walk the rest of the way under darkness.

Jos was very restless on this afternoon, and when I questioned him about his uneasiness, said that he had a suspicion that we had been followed for the past day and half.

"However, I will soon find out, if you lie low and make no sign," he said, after placing us under cover.

While we rested amongst the jungle, our guide crept back into the forest which we had left, so silently, that I no longer wondered at his title.

Two hours afterwards he returned with a grim smile of satisfaction on his yellow face. The sun was nearly down by this time, so that in a short space we could once more proceed.

"Yes, boys, we have been followed; and it is a lucky thing that I went back—lucky for us, although it may not turn out so for the foul traitor who has tried his best to trap us, as he will find out when I get aboard again."

"What do you mean, Jos?" I asked.

"This," answered Jos, holding up a piece of blood-stained paper, on which I recognised the handwriting of Pierre Denis.

"Listen, lads, and I'll tell you how I found it, and read it out afterwards. I was sure that it wasn't a beast which kept making the sounds I heard now and then this past two days, so I just crept back for a mile or so, until I came upon an Indian, who was sitting waiting, as I could see, for us to get ahead of him a bit and until the sun went down.

"I watched him closely for a while, thinking he might have friends behind him, until I saw him pull out this scrap of paper to see if it was safe; and then, after looking at it, put it back again into his waist-belt, and to pass the time, begin to toss up the gold pieces that he had got for his work. Then I was sure of my man, and went for him quietly.

"I left the skunk for the panthers to finish after I had taken his letter and wages; and now what do you think of my find?"

Jos read out the paper in Spanish, while the listeners showed by their flashing eyes and oaths that it concerned us closely.

"What is it about, Jos?" I asked after he had finished, looking at the excited faces round me.

"Just this, admiral: it is a short letter from Captain Denis to the governor of Rio Janeiro, giving a full description of us and our purpose, offering to sail in with the *Turtle*, and deliver it and all on board into his hands, and also to lead a fleet to the island safely. That's what it is; signed in his own name."

"The infamous traitor!"

"Yes; he also arranges a code of signals, which are to be given when he appears, so that he may know that the game is bagged and that his terms are agreed to."

"What are his terms?"

"A safe passage to Spain, and a fair share of the plunder. He wants to die a rich man, and has grown tired of pirating. But I think we have him at last,—the fool! to try to dodge Indian Jos."

It was a frightful shock to me to hear this perfidy revealed by Jos; and, like the rest, I swore an oath that I would do my best to outwit and punish this miserable Pierre.

"Is he likely to come into the harbour soon, Jos?" I asked anxiously.

"No; he will dodge the *Harpy* first, and hang about until he fancies we have been in and caught. Most likely he will wait for a boat to come out with the governor's message before he ventures near."

"Then let us meet him with the gallias and give him the signals he expects!" I cried, getting to my feet, for now the night had come. "When shall we reach Rio?"

"Before daylight, if we push on," replied Jos.

"Then let us push on, and fortune may favour us sooner than we expect."

As we went along under the starlight, with the large leaves drooping on either side of us, for we were still within the partly cleared forest, I asked Jos how he thought Denis could have secured the services of this Indian unperceived by the others, for we had left them all camped together on the shores of the cove.

"That part of the game would be easy enough to manage, if he had the will," replied Jos gratingly. "Pierre Denis knows this part of the country nigh as well as I do. Besides, the native was only a mongrel, who owned Spain as well as Santa Cruz for a fatherland. Say the traitor meant to do us from the first, and had prepared his letter; then a walk into the forest would show him the passing native, with whom he struck the bargain, telling him not to lose sight of us until we entered the town. I know the breed well: they are faithful to their employer, and as keen at following a trail as blood-hounds. And if I hadn't seen the paper and gold in his paws I might have only killed him, without searching him, thinking that he was doing a piece of trailing on his own account."

"Then you killed him, Jos?"

"What? Do you think, admiral, that I would let him have the chance of being able to tell his story to a passing friend?"

"No, I suppose not. But suppose that Denis has employed more than one?"

"I have thought of that also, and it does not seem likely. However, we are in for the game now, and will have to take our risk. If we get there before daybreak, we may find the town and the ship unguarded. I know a part of the wall where it did not use to be closely guarded, as it was considered unscaleable; but I got over that part of the wall when I made my last escape, and I can get up it also. If there is no *fête* on, the townsmen will be mostly all sound asleep. Then we need not separate, for I can take you through some of the lanes to the harbour without being disturbed. In five more hours we will be there."

Swiftly we sped through the forest and through some tobacco fields, until we came to the highway, along which we went without meeting a human being; then, about an hour after midnight, we came to the city, all dark and gloomy looking with the wall round it.

"We are fortunate," whispered Jos. "It is a fast day in Rio, and the folks have gone early to bed. Now follow me."

He crept along under the wall until he came to a portion where the ground sank to a valley, leaving the wall standing above us nearly forty feet.

"Wait till I get up and throw you down a rope," he whispered; and grasping a couple of daggers in his hands, he took off his boots and began to climb up like a cat, planting one dagger as far up as he could reach and drawing himself up to it, while with his toes he clung on to the rough edges of the stones until he had inserted the other dagger, and so on, until we saw him disappear over the parapet.

It was a slow and laborious climb, while we waited below for what seemed a long time before we saw his head appear over the wall, and next moment heard the flap of a rope against the masonry.

"All safe; come on," we heard him whisper; and then, one after the other, we went up hand over hand along that rope, until we stood beside him on the rampart; after which he drew up the rope, and once more coiled it round his waist.

"Are there no sentinels about?" I asked softly.

"There was one when I got up, but I settled him," he replied. "Now we can go on."

Through dark narrow side streets with high walls we all crept softly, for we had removed our boots, and held our knives in readiness, until I saw a glint of water in front: we had reached the harbour without being disturbed.

There the gallias lay, moored at about a hundred yards from the quay, with the open bay in front of us—a mass of bulky blackness and without a light.

"We must swim over to her," whispered Jos. "Strike for her bows, and don't make a noise."

Like thirteen water rats we slipped into the bay, and made silently towards the anchor chain—a short swim, which we all did easily. Then, while Jos climbed up the chain, we waited in the water, watching for his signal.

At last we saw it—a wave of his arm over the forecastle; and then we followed him, and soon stood upon the deserted decks. I did not think about the danger of sharks until we were safe; then I shuddered, as the thought all at once struck me.

What a careless set these Spaniards were!—not a man was on duty, although we could hear the sleepers snoring within the forecastle.

"Wait till I fasten them in, and then the ship is ours," breathed Jos; and while we waited, with the water dripping from us, he stole away.

"Now for the anchors," he said, when, after a short time, he returned to where we stood. "The ship is ours, and her captain and crew safely secured below. Gently does it, lads."

Together we worked with a will at the windlasses as gently as we could turn them, until, after about an hour, we had both anchors out of the water and hanging over the sides. After that was accomplished it did not take us long to cut the hawsers, and then we were free to drop the sails.

At last we had them down, and filling with the light morning land breeze. With a thrill I saw her beginning to move softly and silently while we stood beside Jos at the helm, which he was steering.

How had fortune favoured us, and what an easy capture it had been up to now! Past the houses we glided, under the bristling walls of the fortress; and still the captive sleepers snored on, all unconscious of their fate.

None of us spoke or moved from our positions as we glided out to the open sea in that heavy hour of darkness; and, as far as motion went, the vessel might have still been moored, for the ocean was smooth almost as a mill-pond. If all went well we should be beyond the cannon shots before daybreak, slowly as she was going.

Not a sound and hardly a light on shore, as we gradually left it behind. The sentinels must have kept a sorry watch on the fortress walls to let us get away so quietly, although it was so dark that we could hardly see each other.

"The wind blows right out in the open," murmured Jos, holding up his hand to feel it. "Go aloft, boys, and lower all the topsails, for we shall be up to it presently."

Another half-hour, and the gallias was in good sailing trim and already beginning to hasten on her tracks, with a light but steady breeze from the south filling out her sails. If the sleepers were not all drunk, they must wake up soon now, for she was beginning to plunge and swing, with the town a good four miles to our stern.

"Get the guns into position for raking the decks, lads, if they break out of their prison; we shall have daylight presently to help us."

Slowly the light began to break to seaward, while the land became enveloped in silver haze, as we ran to the deck guns and pointed them both ways, after we had seen that they were already loaded.

Day comes quickly when it once begins in these parts, so that after the first lingering warning it was on us with a rush, as from our position on the forecastle and poop we could hear that the heavy sleepers were waking up. But we were masters of the position, and the gallias was ours, as easy as if it had been given up to us.

XXV

A Game of Bluff

I do not think that the most conceited young sprig on earth could have flattered himself that his influence had anything more than that of the most ordinary sailor to do with the taking of this great ship. Indian Jos was our hero and leader, pure and simple, to whose superior craft and guile we now, for the moment, Were able to control the destinies of the Spaniards under the hatches or behind the securely fastened doors, unless they chose to blow her and us up in the air, or were numerous enough to break out and overcome us. It was Jos who promptly thought out matters, and without apology or excuse of any kind gave out his commands as he handed the wheel to one of the men:—

"Steer her east-nor'-east, so that we may all the sooner sight our carracks. Now, admiral and lads, they are waking up below, and we must dodge them until we know how many they muster. For they may be thirty, if the main body have slept ashore; and again, they may be two hundred strong. You, with the others, go to each side of the deck— half one side, half the other—and fire the outer guns one after the other as fast as you are able to shoot. There is my flint and steel, Mike Lemmon. Light this fuse as quick as you can. This will let our friends know where we are, and bring them up, besides covering us with smoke, so that the prisoners won't be able to tell how many we number. Now be off, and wake them up properly, while I hail the cabin lot first and order them to surrender."

The matches were quickly lighted and applied to the touch holes, as we ran from one deck gun to the other, sending off the charges as fast as we could. Bang! bang! bang! they went rolling along the ocean in thunderous reports and blotting out the rising sun and yards with the volumes of white smoke. We knew now that the Spaniards must be awake.

"Ahoy! down there," shouted out Jos in his loudest and most grating of voices, in Spanish, after silence was once more restored. "Is your captain aboard?"

"Yes," promptly replied a shrill voice from one of the windows. "What is the meaning of this, and who are you?"

"Pirates, and in possession of your ship; so that it means death to every mother's son who offers to dispute with us," answered Jos, in his most bullying tone.

After a moment of silence the voice again spoke:—

"And if we surrender, what will be our fate?"

"Your life and liberty granted; only your answer must be given quick. What is it to be?"

Another moment of suspense, and then the voice again spoke:—

"We surrender. Now let us out."

"Can you get out of the window, if we fling you a rope, one at a time?" asked Jos.

"Yes," replied the same voice, only nearer; "we are out, you robbers!"

As he spoke five or six figures vaulted over the taffrail amongst the smoke and made at us without a pause; and then, before I knew where I was, my hanger was drawn and I was in the thick of my first engagement, with a blind fury in my eyes, and striking out right and left as more figures jumped in upon us from the poop, forcing us backwards with their increasing numbers to the main-deck and on to the forecastle.

They must have had a passage right through the under decks to the cabin, for they were coming on by dozens at a time, although not so boldly as they would be presently when the smoke had cleared off.

The pirates were, as I have said, all picked men and fought like devils, as I could see from the bodies they were leaving behind them while they retreated.

Before we leapt from the poop Indian Jos caught up the fuse, and while he kept the enemy back with his cutlass he touched the poop guns and set them off. I heard the crashing of broken wood and the shrieking of the wounded in the forecastle, as I ran with the others after Jos, still holding the burning fuse in his hands, along the maindeck and up the ladders on to the bows, where we took our final stand.

The Spaniards, now masters of the poop, permitted us to reach this final stand without following us, for they were confused with the smoke hanging about, and had not yet realized our force; therefore, while they waited for their men to gather and the clouds to clear, so as to ascertain our number—while they paused irresolute—Jos prepared the guns to cover the upper deck, bidding us get behind cover as much as possible, so as to protect our bodies and keep them from guessing our number.

The ship was now sailing before the wind, with her helm left to chance, at a fair rate, so that from where we stood we were able to look clear over the ocean unimpeded by smoke.

"Our carracks are coming on, Jos," I cried, pointing to where the two vessels tacked towards us—one about a mile distant, and the other four or five miles.

"Yes, I see," replied Jos. "Now, lads, let us keep this stand for another quarter of an hour and we are right; here goes for one lesson to the dons and to keep the fog about them."

While speaking he had sighted one of the forecastle pieces and fired it at a low level. "Bang!" and once more the smoke rolled towards them.

Another cannon now went off, with the same result. We could not tell how many were killed and wounded on that poop, but, from the yells which broke from that fog, we all knew that Jos hadn't fired a blank shot.

At this moment I felt a shock against the ship which nearly threw me from my feet, and then, as the smoke blew abaft, I made out the flag of the *Harpy* fluttering alongside, while over the bulwarks swarmed the swarthy faces of the pirates as they leapt aboard, holding their cutlasses in their jaws.

"To the poop, Harpies! to the poop!" yelled Jos, gripping his hanger and plunging amongst his brother pirates. Then in a body we rushed along the maindeck and up to where the doomed Spaniards now stood clear of smoke, with a swarm of dead at their feet and with white faces, holding their swords points down, as a sign of submission—all excepting one old, small, withered man, who still, but vainly, tried, by words and energetic actions, to inspire them with courage.

"Hold, friends! they surrender!" I shouted, as I saw the captain at last desist in his efforts and pause, leaning on his sword.

As I shouted out this command the *Harpy* men stopped their rush; then the captain turned to me and said, "Well, admiral, go up to them and make your terms, as you are in command."

While my friends waited on the result of my interview on the maindeck, I took Jos with me as interpreter, and went up the steps, picking my way over the slain, to where the Spanish captain stood with the remnant of his crew. Jos had wrought rare havoc with the two guns, so that I numbered only about forty men able to stand upright.

"Who is your commander?" haughtily inquired the Spaniard, as he regarded us both, in our poor clothing, with undisguised contempt.

Ivo pointed to me, while he ordered the old man to give me up his sword.

"That whelp!" he replied scornfully, which words Jos interpreted literally to me, making my cheeks to burn with shame. However, I controlled my passion and stood in front of him, holding out my hand for his weapon.

I saw the proud old man look at me, while he lifted his sword as if he was going to stab me; then, with a deep curse, he snapped the blade across his knee and flung the pieces overboard, after which insult he folded his weakened arms across his thin chest and waited for my next move.

I was glad that I had enough of old England about me to keep my temper, and resist the openly expressed desire of Jos to be allowed to cut him down. We had won our prize fairly and easily, and so could well afford to be magnanimous.

"No, Jos; we must keep to our terms, even if they have broken their faith: we promised them life and liberty, and so I mean that they shall have both."

"Well, admiral, since we haven't lost any of our men, and you are inclined to be generous, we won't baulk you, so give your orders and we'll obey them."

"Then tell him that he may take the boats and go off without delay; he can easily reach Rio before nightfall."

"All right, governor; only you may live to repent this mercy to a revengeful don like him," grumbled Jos, as he translated my conditions, which were accepted as gracelessly as the grandee had surrendered.

In deep, sullen silence the Spanish crew got out the boats; and, taking their places, rowed away towards the land, while we prepared to clear off the dead and examine our prize.

She had not been emptied, as we feared, but evidently had been about to proceed upon her voyage, for we found the holds and stores plentifully supplied, so that shortly afterwards we had halved our men, and, loosing off, the two ships ran merrily towards the approaching *Turtle*.

I told Jos and my other companions, who knew of the treachery of Pierre Denis, to keep it to themselves for the present, as I intended to give him a fair judgment when we met. There was no mercy in my heart for him now, for he richly deserved death—not only according to the pirates, but by those laws which govern all honest men.

I also had intended to have lured him aboard by the signals which he had himself arranged, so that I might convict him the more thoroughly; but this was out of the question now, owing to the turn of events. He must have seen the taking of the gallias, and knew that his designs had failed.

So, before we were well settled upon our way, the *Turtle* was close to us; and then I had the pleasure of once more grasping the hand of Jack Howard, as he came aboard.

"Where is Captain Denis?" I asked my old friend, seeing that the traitor was not in the boat.

"Drunk as a hog in his cabin, where he has lain ever since we parted company," replied Jack.

Ah! Perhaps his conscience had once more driven him to these bestial indulgences, or his weak nature could not resist temptation when placed in a position of trust.

"Take me to him, Jack, for I must see him," I said; so together we left the gallias and went over to my own ship.

XXVI

PIERRE DENIS TAKES THE ONLY ROAD LEFT OPEN TO HIM

Captain Pierre Denis was not a wholesome object to look at upon that afternoon when we brought him to trial in the grand cabin of the gallias *St. Agnes*, after we had got rid of the Spanish owners, dead and alive.

We were on the high seas, and scudding northward toward our island, out of sight of the land, and well prepared for attack or defence, as the case might chance, when I called a court-martial of the officers and men. For in a matter like this all had to be consulted.

Personally, I had discovered Pierre Denis past all remonstrance. He had been drinking heavily for the past four or five days, with a free let and no impediment; and was now upon that fine margin of delirium when a man may see something humorous even in his own execution, and when he hasn't left the faintest perception of right or wrong.

So this treacherous drunkard appeared before us, unwashed, unshaven, and unabashed, flaunting his atrocious perfidy, as if it had been a bravery, in our faces, and demanding from us, instead of mercy, just a little longer time to finish his debauch before we gave him the yard-arm.

"Yes, I meant to hang him, and the whole boiling of you, if I had a chance. You worthless scum of the earth! not to recognise a nobleman and a genius, when you had him amongst you. Certainly, string me up if you like; and make those wind-bags, William Shakespeare and Ben Jonson, rejoice that their master has been wound up before he could finish his play. And bury my immortal drama with me. Do you hear, you dogs? For I wouldn't have anyone benefit by my work after I am gone—no, not a soul; and far less him who has broken my heart with his poetry."

I knew what the pitiful object meant, as he stood swaying before us, with his large head wagging and his bibulous lips trembling, and so did the others, for they laughed loudly at his foolish words. I felt a profound wonder and pity rise in me to think that any man could become so base for such a paltry cause. But perchance the baseness and meanness had been always there; and so, if it had not been me, it would have been someone else equally innocent who would have raised his inherent venom.

"Yes, that is my writing to the governor of Rio Janeiro, and if it had gone straight to its destination, I'd have cleared the nest of Laverna, and gone a rich and an *honoured* man home to my own country. As it has not gone right, I suppose you'll be after marooning me, which I don't care that for,"—he snapped his finger and thumb in our faces,—"so long as you leave me enough rum to kill myself with decently."

"Maroon the like of you, skunk!" cried Jos savagely.

"No! we don't maroon your sort. We skin them alive, or par-boil them in oil. Marooning and hanging are too good for a coward and a traitor."

"Coward?" repeated the drunkard, turning his blood-shot eye on Jos.

"Yes"; and Jos, reaching out his open hand, struck him on the mouth. "If you had a fight in you, I'd give you the chance. But, say mates, hast ever seen Pierre Denis stand up fairly to a man?"

"Never!" came in one unanimous voice from the crowd of judges. "He always liked better to play the spy."

"You have struck me, Indian Jos,—and I forgive you."

"Bah! yes, you always forgive until you get a chance to bite back again."

We were not long over the judging of the miserable wretch; his guilt was clear, so that he was condemned promptly to death. Most of the pirates were in favour of slow torture, which they were adepts at: but I threw in my authority, and therefore it was at length decided that he should have his choice between hanging and walking the plank.

On hearing his sentence, all the Dutch courage went out of the cur, and he flopped on his knees, howling and weeping for mercy.

"Maroon me, for the love of God! if you cannot pardon my *slight* offence!" he yelled. "Put me on a lonely shore, or on the borders of some sickly yellow mud swamp, with half a dozen bottles of rum, and I ask for nothing else."

"You're great on yellow swamps, ain't you?" sneered Jos. "But we haven't got any such handy to oblige you with, so you'll have to be content with blue sea, or a dance aloft; for these are the only roads left open now to you. Yet, if your taste turns to rum, I vote that we let you go up wet. Give him a couple of days' square drunk, lads, and then string him up."

"Yes! yes!" eagerly cried the drunkard. "Give me two full days with the rum free at my disposal, and then do with me as you like,"

The fancy tickled these erratic rovers; thus he was led away to his prison, with orders for a hogshead of rum to be placed handy beside him, so that he might drown his fears while he waited. And he went off ironed and chuckling inanely at his respite.

That night the *Turtle* echoed with his ravings. He had drunk diligently all day, and spent the evening in the company of more devils than ever Penelope had been able to call up.

On the third day they dragged to the deck a violent maniac, who gibbered and frothed at the mouth like a mad dog. They meant to hang him, and so had pinioned him firmly for the purpose.

As I looked on the horrible and drink-swollen monster, blaspheming and unconscious of his doom, I felt that we had been doubly cruel in allowing him to damn his soul, as well as dooming his body. But I could do nothing to avert it, so could only look on with great disgust.

Twice he broke from his jailers, thinking them to be devils, and ran shrieking round the decks, all heedless of their kicks and blows, fighting and writhing in their hands, until his ropes fell from him, and his face was dark purple and horrible to witness.

On the third time he made for the shrouds, and ran up them like a wild cat, with the sun blazing on his uncovered head and half a dozen of the men after him. He was giving them good sport, and they did not object to a little delay.

Up to the first yard, along which he scudded as if on solid ground, with arms waving wildly, and the short sharp yelps of a wild beast breaking from his lips. He ran without support along that rounded spar, with his head turned behind him, as to some invisible enemy, and the watchers expecting his fall every moment.

I knew how it would be, and I was not sorry to see the last of the revolting sight. He never paused when he reached the yard-end, but took the leap clear out, flashing through the air, and falling with a flat crash on the waters, which splashed up and closed on him instantly, thus blotting out as obnoxious a character as ever crossed my turbulent path.

We saw him no more, nor his great work either, which he must have taken with him to Davy Jones' locker. For the sharks are plentiful in these waters, and seldom allow a swimmer or his baggage to rise to the surface, unless he is one who, like Indian Jos, has practised the art of fishing for them. Neither were we troubled for the rest of our voyage by pursuers from Rio or strange vessels, but sailed on steadily until we once more entered the reefs and glided within the cliffs which walled in the pirates' isle.

XXVII

THAT VOICE AGAIN

With what a palpitating heart I waited for the first glimpse of that pirate city on the hill, as we glided through the narrow straits! and when at last we burst out upon it, all a glowing in its life and colour, what a glad bound my heart gave at the home-like sight!

It is so easy for one to make a home where they have found love, even although it be despairing love. As we glided within the lake, I thought instantly upon that evening when together we had sailed over it, Quassatta and I, and every furrow which we cast up seemed like the sweet embraces of old friends.

I looked up towards the balcony where last I had seen Alsander. He was still there, for our coming had been intimated to him; and beside him I saw two or three other figures,—captains,—the slender form of Sir John Fenton, and the floating robes and golden crown of Quassatta—all waving to us their welcome with handkerchiefs or cutlasses before the salvoes from the ships around us filled the air with smoke, and hid their further actions from us.

When at last we arrived at our landing-place, after what seemed to me an interminable time, I found fore-most of the crowd the king and Quassatta, who, in her eagerness to greet me, darted up the ship's side and flung herself into my arms; when, after kissing me fondly on both my cheeks and lips, she shied from me and stood regarding me with a glance of tender reproach, which I interpreted as being meant to express her joy at my return and sorrow that I should have left her without saying goodbye.

"Quassatta has missed her *brother* Humphrey during the short five weeks of his absence," observed Alsander, as he boarded and also embraced me, without displaying the slightest sign of displeasure at the warmth of her greeting. "So have we all missed you; but you have done wonders in the shape of despatch. Is the ship well loaded?"

"Yes, king; she carries a goodly store of gold and silver ingots from Peru, diamonds and other precious stones from Rio, and other goodly merchandise, which I think will give you pleasure."

"And you a good bounty, Humphrey, my son. You have done famously. But where is our friend Pierre Denis?"

There was no alteration in his impassive face as I produced the letter and told him about the doom of the writer—only two violet sparks seemed to light up his blue spectacles, and a firmer closing of his white hand over mine.

"You did wrong, Humphrey, to let him die so easily; you should have brought him back to us safely, so that we might have tortured him, as he deserved, and as you would have been, if that letter had been carried safely to its destination. However, that does not matter now; and I am glad that you have escaped his snares and returned so quickly with your prize, proving yourself such a man, for you are just in time to take part with us in a great enterprise, which we are now preparing for."

"What is it, king?"

"No less than the conquest of the Spanish Main. We are tired of taking solitary ships, and strong enough now to go north—to Terre Firma, Panama, and Mexico. We mean now to conquer the land from the Spanish robbers and found an empire for our heirs. You shall be a prince in reality soon, and Quassatta there an empress, while each captain who sails with us shall be made the governor of a province."

As we walked up the hill towards the palace Alsander explained his project more fully, and Quassabba clung to my arm, gazing with tender, moist eyes up to my face; while on all sides I could see extensive preparations going on for a long voyage—herds of cattle being driven along the roads from the inland country to the shambles, fresh meat hung up in the sun to dry, while the strand was covered with packages and casks of provisions and drink, wheeled down there in readiness to be embarked.

Many of the galleons and ships were also lying stranded, with hordes of carpenters, seamen, and slaves calking and painting them; and, what was most unusual, there were no idlers about the streets—all were hurrying to and fro, and working with a will; while the gay girls stood watching them, or helping where they could.

"It is ten years since we had our last big expedition through the Caribbean Sea and the Gulf of Mexico, so that they have almost forgotten King Death. Then we brought home fifty ships, laden to the water's edge nearly with riches. Now we are going to visit them with an Armada, worthy of Philip himself."

"I trust it will have better success than his Armada had, Alsander," I replied, feeling as if there was something ominous at the fatal word.

"Yes; for we serve different masters, Humphrey. King Philip sailed in the name of the Church, while we sail in the service of the devil, who always helps his own."

I shuddered at his wicked boast, but without replying.

"Death and the devil will be our watchword on this expedition, and every able-bodied man on the island has volunteered, so that we leave behind us only the women to guard our treasures."

"And the slaves?" I asked, thinking with dismay about them.

"Our women are Amazons, Humphrey, and are well able to look after the slaves. Only Quassatta goes with us, for I wish to make use of the Church before I demolish it. Quassabta will be married in the cathedral of Panama, and her wedding will be celebrated with a rare bonfire after the service, I can promise you: she shall have light to see her way to bed that night, I swear."

My heart sank heavy as lead in my breast as I listened to all this and looked at the glowing face of my innocent companion, leaning upon my left arm so fondly, and going to her awful doom with such blind confidence.

We met Sir John Fenton on the balcony, now almost recovered from his wounds, and who greeted me with a wan smile as he held out his hand. Then, seizing my opportunity, while they were all engaged in discussing matters, I stole out to the grounds with Quassatta, where together we spent the afternoon without being disturbed.

Her tardy education in English had been totally neglected during my absence; and, although I was able to make out a few words of the Indian-Spanish, which the pirates mostly used amongst themselves— that original language of mankind, as Alsander termed it—I was not far enough advanced to carry on a conversation with her, or question her about her life for the past five weeks; but this mattered little to us two, as we walked through the groves, happy in each other's proximity. She had pardoned me for leaving her so abruptly, now that I had come again, and made me, for the time, happy with her coy fondness and silently expressed pleasure.

Alsander, surely, had not told her yet of her destiny, or she could never have been so light-hearted or cruelly kind to me; for, as we walked together, she took that sort of possession of me which a woman only takes over the man she loves when she is satisfied that she is loved, and which is so difficult to define, although felt so utterly by the one who is covered by it as with an invisible garment.

"What will she do when the truth is revealed to her?" I thought, as I looked into her limpid eyes with a troubled regard. I had seen those eyes grow big and turgid with terror, beam with the sunlight of mirth, and grow deep and humid with the tenderness of affection, also once or twice flash with scorn on Pierre Denis; but I could only imagine what they might be like when filled with despair, or burning with rage. And either, or both of these expressions, I would be fated to witness within the next month or so, if Alsander kept his oath.

Could I not take her away, and make our escape in one of the many small pinnaces which stood in the harbour ready to put to sea? No! that thought had to be rejected as impossible when I considered those watch towers and the many cruisers outside. Before we could clear the reefs we should be caught and brought back to that implacable king, who was so gracious to his friends, so cruelly relentless to those who braved him. We were both helpless prisoners, with nothing but death or misery before us, unless she became reconciled to her fate, in which case there lay only death for me.

It was useless to struggle against this destiny; better for me to forget, and her to learn nothing of the future until the blow fell. I resolved to mix in the hottest of the fighting, and, if possible, die before she knew her fate. Then perhaps she would forget me, while I should be at peace.

With this resolve, I composed myself and grew wondrous calm, even going the length of joining in her mirth with a strangely light heart. She was mine for the present, and I would be hers always, for the arms of Death looked now to me like the outstretched arms of Love, waiting upon me to fall into them and be happy.

So we walked together happy and undisturbed until the evening came, with the full moon, bathing the earth and lake with silver lustre. Then, at the firing of the supper gun, she left me to go to her own apartments, for she never joined in the riotous festivities of the pirates.

The hall was crowded on this night, and all in great glee over the coming expedition; for if in the lands they were going to devastate there would be plenty of hard marches and heavy fighting, yet they knew that the gold and jewels were to be picked up as plentifully as shells on the sea-shore, and little they cared for hard knocks where rich plunder lay behind.

Sir John Fenton did not sit down to supper. He was nursing his strength, so as to join the fleet, and keeping early hours, with temperate diet.

It was past midnight when, at last, I was able to break from the orgie and get out to the balcony, where I could cool my fevered head with the night breezes and enjoy the pale glory of that tropic moon.

Over the lake the vessels floated that were ready for their cargo, with the loaded barges rowing toward them, lying round them, or coming back empty; while from the decks the cranes kept up a constant creaking, as the chains were hoisted from the barges to the hatches, for the men were working day and night at their willing tasks.

On shore, where the stranded ships leaned high and dry, the pitch-boiling fires were blazing, while the dark figures moved about with their buckets and tar-brushes—a cheering bustle, and enlivened by the chants and choruses which they sang as they rowed or worked.

Beneath me, and between all these preparations for rapine, and where I leaned over, hung the silent gardens, with their drooping leaves and dew-drenched meshes, wafting up delicious perfumes, and breathing only holy peace.

Over my head floated the great round white moon on a cloudless, but star-spangled dome, and trailing her light over the ornamented walls, and into the open casements, where my love now waited, or slept.

From the hall came the drunken shouts, loud blasphemies, or coarse laughter of the revellers and their women, with now and again the quiet, clear voice of Alsander, checking the riot for a moment.

She was resting—my strange charmer—on her soft couch, with the slaves squatting about her, fanning her, and keeping from her fair skin the tormenting mosquitoes. This they would do until morning, without remission. Poor slaves, who had no rest; and sweet love, who knew not, as yet, sorrow or discomfort, or any of those troubles which go to make noble and true women—a full-grown child, who had still to learn everything of life.

I grew melancholy as I thought upon all these things and the crimes which enveloped that innocence with these careless comforts—melancholy with the yearning, but hopeless passion, which thrilled me through and through.

Suddenly upon my ears fell another and a familiar sound, which brought all the wicked past flashingly before me, and filled me with fury and disgust.

The monotonous, musicless, shrill voice of the old and loathed Penelope, chanting out her hateful rhyme:—

And Jack lies 'neath the seaweed, in the deep and silent sea,
And I am waiting on the shore, with nothing left for me.

The awful dirge was coming through the open casement, within which I had pictured Quassatta. I listened for a few moments, appalled and thunderstruck, thinking of my father and Tom Blunt, feeling a madness gripping at my brains.

Was the old life coming back to my innocent? and was the adoration, which felt more to me than the love of life, to be changed into unutterable loathing? For, with that voice and that song, I could never again console myself with the new-born beauty of Quassatta; it would be always the lewd witch, Penelope, who turned my soul sick with self-hatred.

I could bear it no longer: with a howl, like a wild beast, I put my fingers into my ears and rushed from the balcony, and away to the far-off corners of the gardens, followed still by the echoing of that hopeless voice, and surrounded by jibing devils.

XXVIII

The Sailing of the Pirates' Fleet

The next fortnight passed in a wild tumult and uncertainty of my feelings respecting that poor victim, Quassatta.

When beside her, looking into the limpid purity and richness of her dark eyes, with her fresh loveliness and golden halo, I felt as if guilty of sacrilege to harbour such evil doubts about such pure perfection. Also her voice, so musical and low-sounding in its clear vibrations, made me ashamed that I could ever connect it with the musicless accents of the singer of that dirge—that is, such humbling thoughts filled me with misery at my own injustice. But the instant that she left me the sallow duskiness of the witch rose up and blotted out all the freshness of that young image, while the loud, soulless tones drowned the tender inflections which had lingered behind.

How can I define my present feelings? I hated Quassatta for the sake of her old self, Penelope, and adored Quassatta for her present self. When near her, I could not bear to part from her; when away, I had no wish to see her again.

So it fell that we came to see less of each other, and in the subtleness of her love she grew pensive and silent at the change in me, which she saw, without being able to understand. And as I heard less of her voice, the other voice echoed the more strongly in my heart; and as her fair face grew clouded with this unexplained sorrow, so I seemed to see, brooding over it, the shadow of that other face which she had cast behind her.

Sir John Fenton also noticed the alteration in my behaviour, and I think felt pleased at it, for he became more gracious towards me, and sought me out more when Alsander was absent in the town; getting wearied, I suppose, with his own company now that he was once more growing stronger.

But as for me, I liked his company about as little as I did my own now, and began to search for all sorts of pretexts to get amongst the seamen and buccaneers. Now it would be a cattle raid which drew me away early in the morning, and kept me employed until far on in the night; or I would accompany Alsander and the captains to the shore, where they were superintending the provisioning and sorting up of the ships, and staying with them until they returned to the nightly revels, in which I also joined heartily, in my vain attempts to drown dull care. I was miserable with bitter disgust at myself.

Quassatta and I walked no more alone in the gardens, and saw each other but seldom in the palace. She had her fair share of pride, and avoided me after the first day or so; not of her own free will, poor innocent, but because of what her eyes only too truthfully read. Thus, little by little, we two were drifting apart, and Alsander was beginning to reap the reward of his patience.

To him she had always shown affection and tenderness; and now that she had not me to lavish her heart upon, she clung the more to him, sitting on his knee at those leisure times when he rested, with her head on his breast, while he gently stroked her hair, but never now turning her face in my direction.

As I thought over this when I was alone, the sacrifice did not seem so great as it had done; she had been his in the past, and by right she was his still. As I imagined her nestling up to him, it was no longer Quassatta that sat there, but the evil witch whom I loathed. So I went about with a dead love weighing upon my heart, a dull load to carry, which nothing could lift off, and with the constant gnawing at my vitals, as if I had loved a bodiless vision which would never be forgotten, strive how I might.

Yes, that torturing vision of loveliness haunted me day and night, with the transparent witch-mask over it, through which only I could see the perfect dreams, yet kept ever driving me back, like a vain love within a real hatred.

Meantime the pirates were pushing on with their preparations: getting ship after ship painted, floated, and loaded; polishing up the guns and facings, until they burned under the hot sun; also getting their own pistols and hangers burnished, and sharpened up to the highest perfection, all the while singing with the glee of anticipation, as if they were going on a holiday, instead of to slaughter.

We had a hundred and forty vessels, of different sizes, all ready almost for starting, with an army of staunch volunteers, numbering close upon seven thousand, and three thousand slaves, who had volunteered, in order to work out their freedom. King Death could have had more, but he only took the best men, and had no wish to crowd his ships with maimed, useless, or spiritless numbers.

One day, when I was with Alsander on the lake, and finding him in an amiable mood, I asked him about my father and Tom Blunt. They had gone home to England, he told me, with a treasure ship as a present to King James; in return for which they were to ask a royal commission for him to be appointed vice-regent for England on the Spanish Main, after they had driven out the dons. Then they would no longer be pirates, but British subjects, and at liberty to go as they liked.

It seemed a good idea, and one which my father might well carry out successfully without any risk, so I felt satisfied, and more inclined than ever to help my adopted father in his designs. They were heroic; and if our king spread over them his legal protection, they would be both lawful and honourable.

"We shall have the English flag over Spanish America before your father brings out the sanction of the king; and then whoever likes may return to England as an honoured subject."

I had no wish left to get beyond Panama, or even to live up to that cathedral service. If a fortunate shot or cut could give me my release from pain, I would be satisfied; but this desperate resolve I kept to myself.

The slaves of the island were placed under the control of their half-bred taskmasters and overseers. Poor slaves! I know not why I always pitied them so profoundly whenever I thought of them, except it be that many of my own countrymen were amongst them. However, I consoled myself with the thought that if we were placed under British protection all English subjects would then have to be set free.

The women had been drilled to their new duties, and with such disabled pirates as were useless for active service, such as William Giles, placed over them as officers, were left to guard the fortresses, stores, and look-out posts. I did not envy Bill Giles or his brother officers their commission with such an army of wanton hussies to look after; but that was their concern.

At last we were ready, and one fine morning we left the harbour and lake almost empty, while we crept out of the straits like a flock of wild birds on the wing.

The old *Vigo* went first, with King Death, Sir John, Quassatta, and myself on board, and all the others who had been with me before. A host of captains and mates crowding the decks, and the long line of galliases, galleons, and carracks following behind, with the deserted females shrieking out their last farewells on the heights behind.

A gallant sight that was as we run out of the reefs and got into sailing order on the open sea, which appeared crowded with sails of all sizes and shapes, as the light vessels darted about like a cloud of swallows, and the majestic ships furrowed up the blue waves and bellied out their great canvases to the steady-blowing breeze. Pirates we were, going forth clean and span, like prosperous conquerors, with never a fear in our hearts, so brave and mighty did we look in our strength and multitude.

XXIX

Towards the Spanish Main

I had many opportunities given me to admire King Death during this voyage; for his rare qualities as a great commander,—indeed, he might well have been likened to some of the most celebrated captains in the world's history,—for his moveless calm and serenity of temper, also for his intimate knowledge of men. He had that ingratiating familiarity which made everyone he spoke with feel as if he had a special interest in his welfare, yet, at the same time, able to environ himself with such reserve that no one dared take a liberty with him. Perhaps it was his extraordinary appearance and lifeless pallor which set him apart from all other men. He was also a good listener, but seldom spoke except to issue his commands.

On the deck of his vessel he appeared to see everything that took place around him—even to a sail carelessly placed on the smallest and most distant ship, which he instantly pointed out and had set right; so that the captains felt that the master's eye was upon them, and took a pride in showing off their best seamanship.

In the council he had the art of drawing out all their opinions, and listening with rare patience until they were done; after which he delivered his judgment promptly and decisively.

In the battle, as they all knew, he seemed to bear a charmed life, for he exposed himself to the hottest fire, and stood under it like an iceberg until the moment to strike came. Then he was worthy of his weird name.

In the feast he could drink the hardest-headed soaker under the table, and rise up cold and placid, as if the spirits had been only water. It was this gentle coldness which made them believe in him so implicitly.

I saw him, before we were done with that campaign, put many poor captives to the most exquisite torture, in order to make them confess where treasure might be hidden. But, while I grew sick and faint with horror, I never saw a sign upon that white face of either emotion or fury, never a change in the clear music of his questions. I think Penelope was right when she said that he had lost his soul, and that the returning spark of life had only lit up his intellect. I think, if any human blood had stirred in his heart, that he must have suffered somewhat, or even taken a savage pleasure in the moans or shrieks of his tortured victims. But he seemed to feel neither revenge nor pity,—only a calm, scrutinizing desire to learn what he wished from suffering seemed to possess him, and urge him to carry his investigation out to the bitter end.

We had no grumblers or mutineers on board any of the Vessels, for every man had sailed with him before, and knew that, while they could trust to his justice, never one could hope to benefit by his mercy. He had made the laws which governed them, and would hearken attentively to the meanest, if he had a just cause of complaint, and right him, by those laws, if they were infringed, even by his strongest captain; but woe to the complainer if he had not justice on his side—Alsander at once became his executioner.

Yet he was gracious and smooth-spoken always. I never heard an oath fall from his lips, for the words he used needed no garnishing, and they were never repeated; so all who were under him became doubly attentive when he did speak, and treasured up the words as golden.

But no one can live altogether isolated from his fellows, and therefore thus it was that he chose me out to unbend to, and make a companion of, as being the youngest and the most unsophisticated. I sometimes fancied that he held me in his estimation as I held my dog, Martin, and no more.

I had no post of command on this expedition, excepting that of adopted son and confidant; and, as on shore, he gave over to my charge the amusement of Quassatta, despising me, as I thought, too utterly to be jealous of me. Indeed, I began to fancy that he was not so pleased at the coldness which had sprung up between us two, and took every means in his power to bring us to a better understanding.

"Why did you not teach Quassatta English when I gave you the chance, Humphrey? It might have relieved your mind."

I could only evade the question and promise to do my best on board, which, however, I neglected to do, for the reasons I have already named.

No one ever benefits by narrowness, as I found out afterwards; and this ice-cold man, who liked to investigate the feelings of men, left me calmly to my own punishment, without giving me a single hint to lift me out of myself-made despair.

Thus we sped on as the winds best favoured us, the swifter sailors suiting themselves to the slower and larger ships; so that we kept in company like a pack of wolves, allowing no ship who lay in our path to escape us. We spread over that ocean like a great net, catching all fish, and leaving burning wrecks behind.

It seemed almost monotonous and inglorious, the ease and surety of these solitary captures; for with our fleet, no ship, however large, ever thought about resisting; and with our swift pinnaces we allowed none to escape once they were sighted, for we wished to descend upon the mainland without warning, and take possession of the first strongholds before they could be prepared for us. After that we would take our risk with the other cities and strongholds.

So we went along, keeping as compactly as we could before a fair, if light wind, and, like a great company of merchants, absorbing every single adventurer that we met. There was no fighting at all with them; some attempted, for a little while, to depend upon their own dexterity, but as we had lightness as well as strength on our side, they ran a short space and then gave in with the best grace possible.

The *Vigo* took no part in these ignoble captures, so that I had no chance to see how the prisoners were treated afterwards; but I knew the laws of the pirates, and could guess fairly near as to how they would be served. Those who were willing to take the oath of allegiance to King Death were accepted, and divided amongst the other crews; those who remained obstinate, or were not reckoned to be of any use, were promptly despatched, for they kept no prisoners on this expedition. Also, if the ship was considered worthy of service, it was retained and added to the fleet; if condemned, they made a bonfire of it, using its flames to light us upon our road, and show the pirates the way to their mouths on the dark nights.

The men of the *Vigo*, and I believe those also on board the other ships, were not kept idle during the weeks which we spent sailing. For many hours each day they were drilled and made to practise their guns and swords; also at such times as the winds failed us we all had to take a turn in the boats, and exercise our muscles by towing our ships along. And in this and other employments did Alsander keep them too busy to weary, and at the same time prepared them for the privations and forced marches before them. Drink and meat were served out lavishly twice a day, so that no one had any cause for grumbling.

The *Vigo*, being a flagship, had the busiest time of any; for we were continually on the move, tacking and cruising about the fleet, as the admiral reviewed them, my own duties being various and many. Serving him as I did as *aide-de-camp*, I did not have many opportunities of being long beside Quassatta; yet I think, on the whole, during this voyage, the reserve between us became less than it had been that last fortnight ashore.

She enjoyed the journey vastly, finding something to amuse her every hour in the ocean changes and the constant prizes which we drew within our circle. To her it was a holiday and a pastime, for as yet she had not seen any close fighting, and this wholesale piracy being conducted so methodically looked matter-of-fact and common-place enough.

Sir John Fenton also did not disturb me much with his attentions,—either to her or myself,—as he passed most of his time over his scrolls and magical works. As I saw him thus engross himself in his old pursuits, without troubling himself about outside matters, I became more satisfied as regarded him.

Quassatta and my dog, Martin, had become great friends. I think the hound resented my coldness towards her; or, with some instinct which dogs have over human beings, was able to read both our hearts better than we were ourselves, and so did his best to bring us together again. He used to lie beside her on the poop, and receive her caresses with placid contentment, while I hung aloof in the company of Alsander and watched the pair askance, taking Martin round the neck when she had gone below, and kissing him on the part where I had last seen her lips resting on his downy head.

Sometimes, also, of a night, while the men were singing, or telling yarns, in the forepart, Alsander would bring out his guitar and teach her to sing those passionate Spanish serenades which go so well to that instrument. When I heard her sing with him, and after him, it made my doubts grow deeper as to whether that clear, soft voice could ever take on the jarring tones which I had heard under the balcony; it was so tremulous, and burdened with feeling, that I began to feel I must have dreamt it.

One night, to my surprise and flattering delight, I heard her sing a little ditty which I had made up for the men—one of the foolish things which had stirred up the gall of Pierre Denis so bitterly. Alsander had set it to music of his own, and taught her the words by ear; for do not suppose she knew the meaning of what she sang so thrillingly, and which I listened to so greedily:—

Serenade

"When our star gleams over the sea, love,
And the fire-sparks flash below,
Wilt thou think in that hour of me, love,
And the future none can know?

Wilt thou think there is no deceit, love,
In the heart that I gave; and oh!
Wilt thou pray that we yet may meet, love,
In the future none can know?"

As Quassatta finished singing, and turned to me with the expectant air of a child who has learnt its lesson well, and now expects approval, Alsander said, with a low laugh,—

"You see, Humphrey, that Quassatta has learnt more English in the short time she has been under my tuition than she did with you. She has learnt the word 'love,' as well as 'goodnight,' although I am not sure if she knows what it means yet."

But I was sure of that, as I looked my grateful thanks into those deep, clear eyes, now upturned to me.

Alsander rose soon after this, and went over to talk with his two chief mates, Indian Jos and Gabrial Peas, leaving us together with the mastiff between us, where both our hands met, as they found a resting-place upon his large soft head. It was the first time, for weeks, that we had been together all by ourselves, and tomorrow we expected to sight the land, which meant a long separation, if not eternal parting.

How, at that moment, I regretted my stupidity that I had not taught her to understand all I wished to say now, something of what the song meant which she had sung; how I cursed my own slowness in the language which she knew, for as I pressed her little hand I could not call up a sentence which might make my purpose clear, and bind her to me, at least, by words.

Above us the stars were burning brightly, behind us the ocean was filled with the fire-sparks, while away in the distance flared two condemned prizes, lighting up her sweet face and dark eyes ruddily with a warm blush, and our clasped hands and the dog Martin were buried in the deep shadow cast by the bulwarks.

"Quassatta," I murmured softly in her shell-like ear, as I reached my mouth over to it.

"Humphrey," she replied faintly, and, as I heard the whisper, the glowing face suddenly became lost to my view by a shadow cast over it, which, as I looked up, I saw was caused by Sir John Fenton, who, leaning against the rail with folded arms, shut out the burning ships, while his eyes seemed to pierce into mine with a baleful lustre.

My chance had gone by, and I might never again have another. As I looked up to that shadow face and felt the burning of those black eyes, my heart grew numb and cold, as if life was leaving me.

"CALL OFF YOUR DOG, BOY, or I shall stab it."

I looked up to find Quassatta vainly striving to hold back Martin, who stood, with bristling hair and bared teeth, growling deeply as he prepared to leap at the knight, who had drawn his sword, and was holding it back ready to strike.

"Down Martin, down, sir!" I cried sternly, seizing it by the collar and forcing it to its haunches.

"Yes, good dog, lie down and learn to know friends from foes," said the calm voice of Alsander, as he joined us, while the cowed hound suddenly collapsed, and crouched down abjectly, with his head between its paws.

XXX

A Successful Raid

Next morning we sighted land; and then, after a general council, King Death divided his army. The best seamen he left with the fleet, to guard the ships; cruise about the coast and pick up vessels coming and going, so that none might escape to carry the tidings to Spain, or to the inland cities which he meant to demolish.

Here I bade, for the time being, farewell to the *Vigo*, and Quassatta, who was left aboard, to go with the fleet towards Maracaybo Lake, there to wait outside on our coming overland.

We left the fleet somewhat short-handed, but of sufficient numbers to master any single ships that they might fall upon; and as their orders were to recruit, Alsander expected before we met again to find them strong enough.

For three days we were busy landing our men, with their provisions and ammunition. When we were ready to march on the fourth day, we numbered over three thousand free pirates and fifteen hundred slaves, who were conditionally free, and treated the same as the free men.

We landed on a deserted part of the shore, within a couple of days' march of the first Spanish settlement, and took with us only enough provisions to last the two days—some dried meat, which each man swung over his back, with his calabash of water.

So we waved our farewells to the fleet and plunged into the forest, each man, even to King Death and Sir John Fenton, carrying his own provisions and armour.

Many of our captains were most richly dressed and bejewelled according to their tastes. Alsander wore his strange silver and black skeleton costume, Sir John his usual sable velvets, for myself I had not been sparing in finery, although it was not long before I was glad to follow the wise example of Indian Jos, and many of the others, and get on in shirt and trunks only; for the weather was most sultry, particularly along the swamps and forest-fringed rivers, of which there was a very plentiful supply.

We did not make very rapid progress, for in some parts there were rafts to construct or dense brushwood to cut down; but in this, as in the carrying of our provisions, there was no favouring of individuals. So we tramped on, sending the alligators and poisonous reptiles scurrying out of our way, and bearing the stinging of the gnats and mosquitoes as best we could, while we crushed through virginal groves of verdure and blossoms surpassingly beautiful.

The first night we lay down in the centre of a dense forest, which appeared never to have been traversed before, and spent a night amidst the most unhallowed sounds of savage beasts on the prowl. Then the moment light came we were off once more, pressing forward with bloodthirsty eagerness, wilder and more ravenous beasts than any who had kept us from sleeping the night before.

Gold seemed to be the bait which lured all these rovers and buccaneers with such jocund courage through these malarious and fever-stricken swamps and forests, the same gambling spirit which makes honest merchants soil their purity in the marts, and heirs risk their patrimony amongst the money-lenders. Many who followed King Death in his quest after wealth had more than enough even for their appetites, and yet they could no more resist this dangerous enterprise than could the neediest amongst them.

Had I not been love-stricken and despairing, I should have gone for the glory of fighting, with the enterprise and adventure; less could not have satisfied my young blood. As affairs had chanced, I went now to find a quick release from my present troubles. For the youth in his teens can regard the King of Terrors with less repugnance than can the old worldling of seventy. As we see more of earth, I fancy, so we cling to it the harder. At least, so I have seen with those old pirates who in that campaign walked alongside of the Destroyer every hour.

And I had other golden opportunities of testing this theory in my march after Alsander, for the rack, the thumbscrew, and other exquisitely refined tortures invented by the grand inquisition for the disfiguring of God's image were everyday incidents in our lives; and so I invariably saw that the young men cared less for their lives than the old men. And it gave me a thought that perhaps the soul of man enters flesh under protest, and before it is too much covered by the incrustations of the world to be seen or felt, it makes its longing to be free obvious to outsiders. The art of torture and slaughter makes many a murderer believe in God, while the passively good may go on doubting.

I do not think that Alsander cared a jot for plunder, or for indiscriminate slaughter either. The desire for excitement and to conquer all difficulties alone possessed him and urged him onward to acts both heroic and infamous; and with the glamour of his matchless bravery over one, who would not have followed such a splendid leader even to perdition?

On the second day we broke from the forest and crossed a rugged mountain; and as we passed the ridge we saw the first city lying before us with its white buildings and signs of prosperity. Then we rushed down upon it like a cloud of locusts, and destroyed it root and branch. The governor was a brave Spaniard, who did not surrender without a struggle: for half a night they fought with us, laying many of our company low. But Alsander, like the white Angel of Death, swept over them, with that fury, Sir John, beside him, step by step, wading knee-deep in blood, and all regardless of themselves, until the castle and the town lay to our hands, to punish or to spare.

In the heat of the battle I loved my matchless commander; after it was over, when passion had cooled and the victims were brought up and tortured until they revealed where they had hidden their gold, who could think of it without a shudder?

For two days we stayed at this place, razing the walls and rioting as only pirates can. Then we left them, cowed and subjugated, taking with us sufficient prisoners to act as guides, and carry our treasures. After this we moved on, leaving our own and their dead to be buried as best the maimed and outraged survivors might be able to do it.

Onwards, over the mountains and through the plains, we rushed, resting each night in a ravished village or city. I kept close to King Death and his companion Sir John, scaling heights and slashing with my cutlass, which nightly required grinding, until it was worn to a stump, and had to be cast aside for fresh steel, until my arms ached; and, wearied out, I could sleep as soundly on a mound of corpses as upon a soft couch, following after King Death and vainly seeking to aggravate his spirit brother, who strode beside us with his dart, covering me as a shield and a protection. I had slain my hundreds, and yet never a wound came to show me that I was mortal.

So we reached the city of Merida, leaving a conquered country behind us and terrified fugitives flying in front. Some places they surrendered without a blow, paying their heavy ransom willingly to get rid of us, and treating the army handsomely to whatever they desired. Why the poor Spaniards cared at all to garner wealth for the pirates to reap I cannot tell, for they had been often before ravished and shorn;

but where gold is concerned no warning will serve. And as for their wives and daughters, I dare not speak of them or even think about the awful sights through which I passed.

I suppose all warfare is alike, and that it is best to draw the veil over it. Nightly Alsander, Sir John, and myself retired after our conquests, asking no questions and shutting our eyes and ears to what went on around us. They were demons which we were leading over the country, whom, until their lusts were sated, no man could control.

Before we left a town we laid it defenceless against our return. If they yielded easily, Alsander named their ransom, and waited until it was paid, giving to them such protection as he could with that horde behind him; but if they resisted, then they were put to the sword indiscriminately, and their property demolished utterly.

So we took Merida, Gibraltar, and Maracaybo, and were in time to see some of our ships sail into the lake, after destroying the watch tower on the watch isle at the entrance, we bringing with us eight hundred prisoners laden with treasure.

It took us five days to ship the gold and precious merchandise that we had gathered during these seventeen weeks of marching and fighting. And then we embarked once more, sending twelve of our vessels back to Laverna heavily laden, while we kept on our way towards Carthagena, having drained the province of Venezuela and the El Dorado of Sir Walter Raleigh. Our losses up to now had been nine hundred men, while over five hundred of our prisoners willingly took service in order to repair their fortunes, which we had ruined.

XXXI

The Fever of Battle

I had now become a full-fledged, blustering pirate by the time we boarded the *Vigo* at the subjugated port of Maracaybo—a youth who might at length shake hands with Indian Jos and Gabrial Peas, or with any other parded buccaneer amongst them.

Martin, my dog, also had fleshed his strong teeth in the battle, and could no longer be called the innocent that he had been when last he laid his broad head under the hand of Quassatta.

I found the sweet girl bored to death with her long isolation at sea, and glad to welcome anything for variety, even a young man clad in a blood-dyed ragged shirt, which had not been changed during the many weeks we had been playing our devils' game. Poor Quassatta! fresh and fair as when we left her, sprang into our crime-stained arms—Alsander's first, then mine, and next Sir John Fenton's—with the freedom of a happy child, finishing up by rolling on the deck with that reprobate Martin, who took her embraces as much his due as if he had never torn the windpipe out of a man.

We rested for a time at Maracaybo, in order to get our wounded men ready for shipping with the great treasures for home; and while we were waiting, Alsander sent messages to the different commanders along the coast, demanding their submission and fixing the ransom. Many of them agreed to our terms, and while they got the money and stores ready; Quassatta, Martin, and I spent the time ashore, seeing what was left of the city.

I do not think that Quassatta felt much for the vanquished; she had become used to queening it, and took their slavish adulation quite naturally. She had been so accustomed to slaves that they seemed to be the natural order of creation; and as for ruthless pirates, they were all the friends that she knew, and so seemed to be only in their proper place.

Alsander grew weary of the almost universal submission of the different cowardly Spaniards, for he was one who hated easy victories; therefore it was with a kind of icy mirth that he received the insolent messages of the commanders of St. Martos, Carthagena, Porto Bello, and the governor of Panama. They were determined to show fight to us, and that woke him up once more to action, for sitting still and counting out and dividing the ransoms was slow work.

So we sailed round to St. Martos, and after bombarding it for six hours, we took it with comparatively little loss, Quassatta watching the game from the distance, as she might have done a review.

Carthagena next fell into our hands, after a day and a night of hard fighting, with its rich booty. We carried out of that wealthy storehouse treasure enough to lade twelve of our largest ships, and for sixteen days rioted as the men felt inclined.

Then we came to Porto Bello, and took it after a fierce struggle, losing here over a thousand men and many more wounded. How hard a man may work when he is cutting off heads without feeling it, with the cannon rattling about him! Sometimes I was at it for twelve hours with hardly a pause, and yet never felt tired until the battle was over.

I cannot describe any of these fights very clearly, for I saw no more than a few feet about me—man after man jumping in front of me and disappearing, while I sawed on after Alsander and Sir John Fenton, too busy to look at them. With a tongue caked with thirst and the volumes of sulphurous smoke about me, I hewed my way up heights, up ladders, over walls, grappling sometimes with an enemy until his arms relaxed and I could rise again, and that brave dog beside me, taking his part like a brother, without even a thought that my hour might come.

Each battle was like the last: we gathered in force on the plain, and Alsander gave his orders to charge, leading the way always. I saw the heights over which we had to climb, with that blazing sun above, and from the walls the puffing out of smoke, while amongst it seemed black dots, which I knew were men. Then, as if someone had made me suddenly drunk, and all careless of the men who fell about me, I rushed after that silver skeleton who was leading me on, with his flashing sword and his sable companion who swung the boarding axe, for that was Sir John's favourite weapon. After this glimpse I knew and felt no more until we stood on the ramparts, with the black flag floating over us, and the standard of Spain lying under our feet amongst the dead and dying.

Then I would lean on my bloody sword and gasp for breath, while one of the conquered would humbly offer me wine to quench my burning thirst, while Alsander would look at me quietly, saying,—

"Well done, Humphrey, my son; we have gained another victory."

After that I would lay me down and sleep like a hog for hours wherever I could find a resting-place.

XXXII

The Taking of Porto Bello

Porto Bello was ours, and our next march was towards the capital of Panama, the place where I was to lose Quassatta, and still I was unwounded.

I do not think that I shall ever be able to forget this taking of Porto Bello, with its strong forts and dauntless defenders, with the atrocious cruelties which were committed afterwards on the poor inhabitants, no matter how long I may live. It took us five days' hard fighting before we finally spiked the last guns, and during that time we were like a host of blood-smeared, gunpowder-blackened demons, with our sword-handles glued to our wrists from the gore which spurted about us like fountains of water—five days and nights scaling walls, blowing up magazines, and hunting and harrying our enemies about the streets, or chasing them into the churches and convents, where they sought refuge in vain from our violence and mad rage.

During the fever of this time I was possessed of only one idea: that these were Spaniards, our natural enemies, who had tortured the natives of the land, and all vile heretics, who richly deserved their doom. Only the women and children I did my best to spare where I could do so, although my efforts and those of my Plymouth friends were not always successful.

We managed, however, to drive some of them into a large convent; and once there, I set Jack Howard and some of the others to mount guard over them, while I turned again to follow our pirate king.

Alsander fought like a cold and impassive devil, never shirking the hottest quarters, and showing no mercy. He strode on hour after hour unwearied, flashing his sword about and cutting down all who opposed him, as if he had been merely practising in a field of wheat. Never guarding his own body against shot, shell, or sword, he cut his way, with his white hair waving like a fleece, and his pink eyes burning like steadfast rubies; for he had laid his glasses aside, and on his dead white face never a flush of excitement. His appearance was so terrific, with those silver ribs and bones depicted on his habit, that many of the enemy shrieked with horror when they saw him, and, covering their eyes with their hands, either fled in a panic or waited on his coming like senseless sheep, and took his strokes blindfold.

Sir John Fenton was never far behind his friend, and seemed to be possessed by a sateless lust for blood and murder. He flew about with his battle-axe, filling the air with shrill shrieks like a mad fury, his black eyes blazing and rolling wildly,—to my mind a worse sight to witness than even the deadly activity of Alsander. I saw him many times dabble his free hand in the blood of a fallen enemy, but had no leisure to see whether he did what Jack Howard had told me of.

Alsander ever strove to be at his side to guard him, and often covered him when in his recklessness he wantonly exposed himself to the enemy; for Sir John was so mad that he saw nothing, while the king never ceased to watch all round.

Indian Jos, Gabrial Peas, and Sambo also seemed to have orders to follow and watch over the safety of the knight, who cared so little about himself, for they were always beside him and our leader, and often threw themselves in front and took cuts intended for him.

How they fought, these savage pirates, in their different ways, but all cool and easy! Jos naked to the waist, with his yellow ribs and old wounds showing up like embossed brass; in each hand a heavy cutlass, and caring no more for wounds than if they had been reed-flappings, but cutting down his men like nine-pins. Gabrial stealing on, light and stealthy, and stabbing as he crept. He was generally the first to find an entrance to the garrison, and open the gates without us missing him, until we found him inside, or on the roof, tearing down the standard, or firing the powder store. Sambo fought as if he enjoyed it thoroughly, laughing loudly while he pushed his bulky body through the enemy, pitching them over the walls, his body glistening with greasy perspiration.

At the first castle we drove the crowds inside; and then Gabrial found the magazine, and blew it up at one fell stroke, escaping himself just in time, while we hung back until the black shower of stones and severed limbs ceased to rain. Then we went on; firing houses, when daylight failed us, to get light enough for our deadly work at night.

Slowly we forced them up to the last castle, every inch of ground disputed as we went along. All the while our ships were playing their guns upon the outer walls, the air filled with cries and thunder, and the sky cloudy with smoke. Then into that we went also, rushing up the ladders, which we made the nuns and priests carry and plant for us, while the shots, fire-balls, and melted pitch poured down upon us from the besieged party above.

The governor, with three or four of his captains, fought to the last in their despair. Twice Alsander paused to offer this brave man quarter, while his wife and daughters clung to his knees; but his only reply was to stab them before our faces, and then his hour came.

Alsander waved us back from him, and took the Spanish commander alone, with the dead bodies all piled up between them, for he was the last survivor.

He was a brave man, but nothing in the hands of this demon king, who played with him skilfully for about ten minutes, as they stood face to face with that rampart of flesh between them.

"Take thy life, Spaniard, and with it thy liberty, for thou art a brave enemy," said Alsander, gently dropping the point of his sword, after they had fenced for a while. But the commander with a bitter smile pointed to the dead bodies of his wife and daughters.

"What is life without love or honour?"

"Then take thy death, brave man, and join those who are waiting on thee."

The weapons clashed and crossed twice again, then Alsander reached forward suddenly and ran him through the heart, catching the body as it fell still clutching his sword, and lowering it gently to the side of the fair corpses who lay weltering in their blood.

"We will bury them all together with honours," remarked our white king, as he wiped his weapon with the doublet of one of the dead captains and calmly sheathed it in his scabbard. "Now that Porto Bello is ours let us rest for the day; tomorrow we will look to the prisoners and settle about their ransom."

XXXIII

The Battle of the Plain

When the battle was over, I sought refuge on board the ship *Vigo* with Quassatta, for I had no wish to witness the sights that followed. Alsander gave way to my request for the protection of the captives I had shut inside the convent: they were mine to protect as I pleased, so long as they gave up their gold and jewels. This I promised, and went amongst them, collecting and telling them that they were safe with my men.

Poor wretches! they gave up only too gladly their treasures, calling down the blessings of all the saints on my head for saving them from the torture. And these were all that I dared to protect.

King Death and Sir John Fenton stayed with the rest of the pirates ashore, and what means they used to extort the wealth from the townsmen it behoves me not to say. What I did know was that hourly the boats brought heavy loads to the different vessels—our flagship with the others—until it was heavily laden. Alsander honoured the brave town of Porto Bello for their courage by taking as his own share as much of the treasures they found as the *Vigo* could carry; so that she was the first ship to be loaded.

We had lost heavily in this attack; for when he came to number up his capable men, he found that fifteen hundred was all he could spare from the ship to take with him to Panama leaving, even at that, the fleet short-handed; which had to wait in the roads for our return, and keep our flags flying on the different towns along the coast that we had taken, some of which had not paid up their full ransom.

Therefore, all arrangements being completed, our army set out on that overland journey, which we reckoned would take us five days at most; for the weather had been long dry, so that we expected to find an easy way over the mountains and through the swamps.

The distance was not great; but an army on the march goes slowly, and we had many natural difficulties to overcome.

Sir John Fenton did not take kindly to foot exercise, therefore he and Quassatta were carried in litters, by prisoners which we took from Porto Bello; but the rest of us walked, I keeping as closely as possible to the litter which bore my love.

Poor girl! she did not know why she was taken over this land, and was light-hearted that at last she had been allowed to accompany us; I, melancholy and depressed, keeping pace with the bearers as if I was attending a funeral, as indeed I was, for I was following the bier of all my hopes.

It is a glorious country, this Panama, for beauty of scenery, although unwholesome to those who stay long in it—that is, on the plains; yet it is fairly mountainous in parts, but in the valleys one has to be careful, for it is filled with dangerous swamps.

We marched along solidly, taking the paths mostly used by the traders; but as we drew nearer to the city, our guides made wide *détours* through the forests, as from our message we were expected.

We had to stop and fight our way often as we went along, for the Spaniards and Indians had thrown up banks to impede our progress; and these we had to scramble over and demolish, with an unseen enemy lying in ambush, retreating ever as we advanced and harassing us constantly, so that no one dared go to sleep by night. But, instead, we stood listening through the darkness and wearily watching for morning, so that we might push on again, It was a beautiful land over which we travelled, with rare blossoms hanging and clustering on every bend, while the monkeys haunted the tree-tops and flung down nuts and branches at us as we passed them, and thousands of bright plumaged birds fluttered about like animated flowers.

We went over ridges, getting wide views of the lagoons, jungle, and the winding river Chagres below us, picking our way through the rank, reed-woven marshes, where lurked the great pythons and the enormous alligators; yet looking fair and pleasant, with the lilies floating and the mosses dripping, and the vegetation lavish to excess; with those deadly reptiles amongst our feet and the watchful enemy throwing all sorts of impediments in front, so that we might be swamped and devoured.

Along the palmetto and cypress-fringed banks of that dark, yellow, sluggish river Chagres, where the fever-froth ay in patches, like the lilies on the marshes, so that it looked like some of our peat-stained streams after a heavy spate, only crowded with deadly things, and with steaming, sickly vapours rising from it, which, as we inhaled, made our blood to flow as sluggishly through our veins as the current crawled.

Through the jungle and forests, where wild beasts stalked, or home-like game broke through the cover—deer, wild turkeys, and many varieties of birds and insects—and as we marched and battled with our many difficulties, natural, and made by our watchful enemies, we were followed by dense clouds of ravenous mosquitoes, which would not be driven from our exposed parts, but crowded upon us with their irritating buzzing, stinging us frightfully.

Poor Quassatta, as she lay on her litter, grew languid and spiritless; yet, like the brave girl that she was, never uttered a complaint; while upon our leader, miasma, bites, arrows, and musket shots seemed to have no effect whatever; he stalked on calmly, encouraging his army with hopeful words, and inflaming their greed by drawing glowing pictures about the riches which were to be taken out of Panama.

When the river flowed towards Panama we launched the canoes which we had brought with us, and thus paddled the flagging ones along, while the strongest walked by the banks. At other times we carried them on our shoulders. Why these canoes had been brought I could not think until we reached our journey's end, and then I knew.

At last we climbed up to a hilltop, and beheld the city of our desires lying before us in all its beauty and stateliness, with its many churches, high walls, and strongly fortified castles: a city of spires and palaces, it looked, as it lined the shores of the open shallow bay.

Out in the roads lay several large ships, too far distant to defend the town, while behind us the land spread like a well-watered garden.

We could see that the Spaniards expected us, for over two thousand steel-clad cavalry and foot soldiers occupied the plains and cultivated fields between us and the earth walls, with their big guns placed ready for action.

Alsander called a halt, for the day, on the top of the hill, and while the tents were pitching observed the enemy attentively and the ships beyond.

"They are waiting for us to come this way," he remarked, "and have left their ships unguarded. Do you think, Jos, that you could take those ships for us tonight with a hundred men?"

"I'll do it with fifty," replied Jos coolly.

"Then take fifty picked men, after you have eaten, and twenty of the slaves, to carry the canoes, and make your way unseen through the woods to the shore. There embark as soon as night falls and capture those vessels. Fire each one as you capture them, for I want light for our work, and spare no prisoners; only save the last ship, in case we may want it afterwards."

Indian Jos nodded quietly on hearing his orders, and went over to pick his men and slaves. After this they sat down to the dried meat which they had brought and made a hearty meal.

"Gabrial Peas, you are the best man for getting into a town. Pick out what men you require, and go unseen to the north side of the city. From there get in as best you can, and give us light from within. While you are doing this, I shall amuse that crowd of steel-covered antelopes, who think to frighten us with their numbers and glitter. Go quickly; I'll give you two hours' start before we move down upon them."

As the two parties stole away in their different directions the king reviewed his small army and gave his orders to the leaders.

"Eat hearty, lads, and drink sparingly, for you will have some fighting tonight. You, Captain Ashplant, take three hundred men, and follow Gabrial Peas until you come opposite to that crowd. Then, as you hear their guns, rush in and take them from the right; only get between them and the walls, so as to cut off their retreat. You, Captain Lavogue, do the same from the left, while my company takes them from the front. I shall show myself to them before dark, so that they may be confident in their numbers, and get close enough to them before they can re-load to scatter them towards you. Take no prisoners."

After the six hundred men left us we waited for over an hour, showing ourselves as much as possible on the heights. Then, at the word of command, the seven hundred pirates prepared to go down upon that army of two thousand; while the slaves followed, bearing the litter with Quassatta at a safe distance, for Sir John Fenton, now once more active at the approach of war, took his usual place alongside of Alsander.

We went on in full sight of them steadily until we were just beyond range of their cannon, while the short twilight was falling upon us. Then we made preparations as if we were about to camp for the night, our enemies shouting at us derisively for our small numbers, and promising us all sorts of torture on the morrow.

When they saw us light our fires, their rage got the better of their discretion, and what Alsander had been expecting occurred—a large body of the cavalry suddenly dashed past the guns and made for us at a gallop.

"Go back, men, quickly, and fire low at the horses; when they are near enough, pretend to retreat, but spread out as you run, and make sure of each shot."

As the pirates ran backwards and over the fields, the Spaniards thought they were frightened, and spurred the harder after them, the foot soldiers following at a quick run, and foolishly leaving their barricade of cannon in their rear. Then, as the cavalry came to close quarters, our men suddenly dropped upon their knees, each one picking out the horse nearest to him, and discharged their muskets.

Next moment we were all engaged despatching the heavily ironed, unhorsed riders before they could get their feet from the stirrups; while the main body of foot came on through the semi-darkness, firing as they ran wildly and aimlessly, and killing more of their own party than they did damage to ours.

However, they soon discovered their fatal mistake, for after that first volley they came to a halt and turned to make their way back to their guns; then we saw that our six hundred friends had come to our aid in good time, for as we finished our grim work of slaughter, with a thunderous roar, the cannon were discharged full in the faces of that retreating army, cutting wide lanes of them down. Then, with hoarse yells, we made at them from all sides, while in their panic they hardly resisted, but turned about to run in all directions, while we hemmed them in and swarmed at them, our small camp fires only guiding us on, for it had been dark for sometime.

Suddenly from behind the walls leapt up several lurid flames, which, as they rapidly increased in strength, gave us light enough to distinguish friends from enemies. Gabrial Peas and his party had succeeded in their enterprise. So we fought hand to hand, no one giving or thinking about quarter; for now that the trapped Spaniards could see us they resisted bravely and desperately, not one amongst them attempting to fly. They were fighting for their wives and children, and we for the gold which they had hoarded.

Not a man escaped us on that plain, while in the city the fires continued to burn and spread, and away to the bay we could see that Indian Jos was doing his share with his customary methodical dexterity—ship after ship flared up, until the whole landscape lay ruddy and clear before us.

XXXIV

Death of Alsander

W e did not pause to rest after we had finished those brave defenders, but rushed in a body upon the city now almost delivered into our hands.

We found the gate open, for the inhabitants, in their panic, had taken shelter within the castles and churches; so that Gabrial Peas and his company had found an easy task as they ran through the almost deserted streets and flung the gate open, meeting us as we entered, and joining in our raid as we swarmed in, taking possession of the empty houses, and rifling them at our pleasure, leaving the forts and their defenders to be dealt with the next day.

"We shall celebrate that wedding tomorrow, Humphrey, my son," said Alsander to me, as we flung ourselves down inside one of the best houses, where Quassatta had been conveyed. "We shall get the marriage over first, before we finish our conquest. So go to sleep; and when you wake, deck yourself out in the bravest you can find, for I mean you to be the best man. You deserve this honour for your courage. Doesn't he, Sir John?"

Sir John was lying, panting after his exertions, on a couch, with his wearied lids almost closing; but at the question he looked up at his friend with a hollow glare, and answered,—

"Surely my punishment has been enough to satisfy even you, Alsander."

"All will be condoned tomorrow, my friend," said King Death softly. "After the priest has done his work, I shall be satisfied and let the past sleep."

The knight said no more, but turned his back to the wall, and lay quiet, and, as I supposed, asleep.

What offence had he committed which was to be forgiven tomorrow, after this hateful wedding with that pink-eyed, white-haired, cold monster, and that perfect image of youth? I thought, as I watched the pair, I had sought for my release many times, and might have had it often, had Alsander not thrown himself between me and the descending blades. He had always been beside me, like a guardian angel, as he was to this strange knight in moments of danger, for we both owed our lives a dozen times to his watchful care, as I well knew.

As he sat now in that carved chair sipping his wine, while round us lay the sleeping forms of the pirates, I marvelled at his freshness and coolness: no trace of weariness did he show in that chalk-white face or those steady white hands, only marred with the blood splashes, for none of us had as yet thought about washing; and yet no one had worked so hard. Truly he was the only man in the camp who was worthy to lord it over these demons.

My dog Martin had gone with poor Quassatta to her chamber, for he had followed her litter all the journey, and now appointed himself to be her guard. I was wearied so that I could hardly hold up my head, with the hard fighting and the numbness of despair.

"Have you told the maid yet about her destiny, king?"

"No; what use would it be? I like surprises, and have arranged this one carefully. You do not suppose that Quassabta will object to my choice, do you, Humphrey?"

He fixed his lurid but steadfast eyes upon me inquiringly, while I paused awhile, and then said drearily,—

"I don't know, King Death."

Next moment, in spite of the bitterness that was in me, I fell asleep, dreaming that I was once more with my love on the lake of Laverna, with the clear stars shining down upon us, and her sweet lips reaching forward to mine and thrilling me over.

I awoke late, to find beside me Alsander, still sitting in his chair, but with the gore stains washed from him, and by my side a richly ornamented Spanish dress of white satin and gold trimmings, with silken hose to match. He was in his ordinary war attire of black velvet and silver bone bars.

"You sleep soundly on this festive morning, Humphrey. Go to one of the rooms and deck yourself, for the bride is almost ready, and my men have been preparing the priest and the cathedral."

There was that in his gentle tones and steady glance which no one who knew him would think of disobeying. So I lifted up the dainty costume, and going into an empty chamber, quickly washed and arrayed myself in this costly gift of war. Possibly, I thought, some young don had brought this from Spain to conquer the inflammable feminine hearts of Panama; and while the vain owner lay dead on the plains outside, I was sorrowfully drawing them on, in order to see the last of Quassatta as an artless child.

Would she faint, or go mad at that altar, or, as I was doing, bear her misery like a patient slave?

I found them all assembled when I went into the reception room: Alsander calm and cold; Sir John sullen and silent; Quassatta, like a joyous angel of light in her radiant attire, trembling and blushing like a rose, as she watched me with star-like eyes; while a party of pirates, amongst whom was Indian Jos and Sambo, waited to accompany us to church, all decked out in stolen garments, and making a noble show, as they grinned with anticipation at the treat before them, for a sailor is sailor all the world over, whether he be a wicked pirate or a simple merchant-man, and can no more resist the pleasures of a show than can a country wench.

"You look like a prince, Humphrey, my son; and, by the powers below! I'll make you one straight away. Kneel down, boy."

As I knelt before him he struck me with the flat of his sword, as real kings are in the habit of doing when they wish to honour a subject.

"Rise up the Prince of Panama."

"The Prince of Panama!" yelled out the boisterous pirates, while I tried to bear my new dignity as easily as I could.

"Now, Captain Jos, have the bridesmaids been gathered?"

"Yes, King Death; they are waiting outside," replied Jos.

"Then let us proceed, Humphrey. Give your arm to Quassatta, for that is the duty of a best man, you know."

Quassatta took my arm with such a dewy upward glance that my heart nearly stopped beating. She did not know yet. Oh, what would she do when the truth burst upon her!

Outside we found a shivering group of twelve Spanish ladies, who had been captured by the pirates, forced to dress themselves in their best, and driven to meet us here. However, they fell instinctively into the train, having been informed about the part they were expected to play; so we went through the sunlit streets, passing many houses still burning, and followed by most of our men, all as gleesome as if they had never done anything wrong in their lives.

The day was excessively sultry and close, with low-lying, brass-tinted clouds creeping up from the horizon, and not a breath of air stirring; it seemed to me as if Nature had paused with horror at the sacrilege about to be committed.

At the cathedral we were met by the rest of our men, who led the way in through the open doors with loud shouts and laughter—not a spark of reverence amongst them.

Inside we saw a crowd of fearful nuns and monks, all clustered together close to the altar, and before it the bishop standing alone in lenten robes, but not a candle lighted. It was a rich and dimly lighted scene, with the stained glass windows, rich carvings, gold and silver vessels, statues, paintings, and marble floor; but depressing with those ghostly candles, which stood up in unlighted rows.

He was an old man, this bishop, with hair as white as Alsander's, and aristocratic features, which now wore a stern air as he paused facing us, drawn up to the full height of his tall thin figure,—a haughty and resentful Spanish face, which looked down upon us from the top of the altar steps, as he laid one hand on the communion rail, and raised with the other his silver crook in a threatening attitude.

"What is the meaning of this, Sir Priest?" asked Alsander in his clear, sharp voice, as he strode in front of us up the aisle, we following, while the pirates crowded after us into the church, until it was nearly filled. "Did I not command you to have all the candles lighted for this ceremony, and that you should dress yourself in your sacerdotal robes? How is it that I find a darkened church and you in your oldest cast-offs?—eh?"

Alsander paused at the foot of the altar steps as he uttered these arrogant words with one foot advancing, when the bishop waved him back.

"No further, heretic and blood-thirsty pirate, for you are in the presence of God."

"Well, old man, what care I for that? I have come to do the Lord a service by celebrating the most holy of your communions. Light up the church without delay, and dress thyself respectably."

"I will not commit sacrilege or desecrate this holy place. You have conquered us. Do with our lives as you will; but take the crime on your own shoulders, nor expect me to bear it with you."

While the bishop spoke, the church seemed to be growing dark, as if night was coming on, while the space grew so strangely sultry that I gasped for breath. Quassatta was trembling violently upon my arm, although I could hardly see her, while the pirates behind us were lost in the gloom.

"What!" cried Alsander, drawing his sword. "Are we to be defied by a womanly priest, and cheated out of our pleasure after travelling hundreds of leagues to have it. Take care, old man, how you tempt me to torture you into submission."

"Take you care, O pirate, how you defy your long-suffering God."

"God I have defied long ago, as the devil, my master, did."

"He will punish you, as He punished your master, the devil," thundered the bishop, with his crook raised, as if to ward off the blow of that uplifted sword.

"Then let Him, if He has the power!" shouted King Death loudly, while we shuddered at the awful blasphemy.

There was a moment's pause as Alsander lifted his face towards the roof, as if addressing the Almighty. Then I saw a vivid flash leap straight down towards the upraised sword, which shrivelled in the hand that held it like a strip of melted lead, while he fell prone to the feet of the bishop, more like a charred log than the corpse of a man.

XXXV

The Escape From the Church

That sudden blaze of light was followed by a moment of intense darkness, while the cathedral echoed with a startling peal of thunder; then again the lightning came, followed by quick flashes which hardly had a second between them, while the thunder pealed clap after clap, as if an army was cannonading us outside. It was a storm such as we might have expected from the hot stillness of the morning.

As I still stood, holding up my trembling companion, I saw Sir John Fenton dart over to the charred and featureless remains of our king, and bend over him, turning him about eagerly; then, as if satisfied with his examination, he started up with a shrill burst of horrid laughter, spreading out his arms to the air.

"At last! at last I am free! and he is dead—my master! my tyrant!" he shrieked out, with his black eyes blazing like a maniac's.

As I watched him, horrified, Quassatta dropped my arm and also ran over to the altar steps, flinging herself upon the blackened form and clasping it in her beautiful arms. So she lay motionless; while from the lower part of the church I heard the voices of the pirates mingling with the thunder.

I paid no attention to this uproar, but followed Quassatta, and tried to lift her senseless body, for she had fainted for the first time since I knew her.

"Leave that girl alone, Humphrey Bolin, for you now belong to me."

I started up at these words from Sir John, and found the knight clutching me savagely by the arm.

"What do you mean, Sir John Fenton?"

"Sir John Fenton?—ha! ha! I was Sir John Fenton while he lived to chain my every thought, but now I am myself once more—Penelope Ancrum, the Queen of Laverna, and your owner, my pretty slave."

"And who is Quassatta?"

"His daughter and mine, whom I hate as I did her father."

It was all revealed now, and my perplexity settled forever: the innocent had been designed for me from the first by her father, who only kept me in ignorance to punish me and his wife for that night in the cabin; and this was to be the day of his pardon and my surprise, which he had so cruelly and craftily prepared. As this came to me in a joyful rush, and I looked at my darling clasping that poor dead wreck, I forgave him all the torture he had caused me, and thought only upon his many kindnesses, and the maiden whom I could now love without a doubt. I had no room to think about the cruel Witch of Canterbury, or her words, for I no longer feared her.

"Look at me, I command you, Humphrey!"

I heard the old imperious words and looked into those glaring eyes without a tremor. Her evil power had gone from her as far as I was concerned, for love had made me strong; nay, as I gazed at her sternly, I saw with savage pride that her eyes fell before mine.

"So, so! is he beyond me, I wonder?" she murmured, fumbling with her hands about her belt where she kept her axe.

"Yes," I answered boldly; "beyond your spells, Penelope—I also am free."

"Not so, for your body is mine—you are my property by the laws of the land."

"We shall see about that," I answered, thinking on my prize money. I could purchase my freedom from that store easily.

At this moment the outcry from the body of the church became louder: something had taken place there more than the death of Alsander. What was it?

I stooped over Quassatta and raised her up; and as I did so Indian Jos came up in hot haste.

"We are in a cage, Humphrey; while we have been fooling ourselves, the Spaniards have gathered together and surrounded us. I told King Death to sack the castles before the wedding took place, but he would not listen to me; and now we are in for it."

I looked round the church. The bishop, nuns, and monks had disappeared, and we were mewed up with a furious mob of citizens and soldiers outside.

"Do you know their number, Jos?"

"Not to a thousand or so," replied Jos. "But the streets are crowded, while we barely number eight hundred, and half of our men have left their cutlasses behind."

"Where have the priests gone?"

"I don't know; they didn't come our way, better luck for them."

"Then they have made their escape from the back, perhaps some underground passage or vault; we must find that way out also. Are the doors barricaded?"

"Yes."

"Then let us hunt round and find this passage while we have time."

"I have found it, Prince of Panama," observed Gabrial Peas, vaulting over the communion rails, "and avenged our king's death at the same time. Follow me, lads, with as many trinkets as you can carry, and I'll show you the way out."

He set the example by lifting up the communion cups and platters, and stood with them in his arms; while the pirates thronged up in a body, taking what first they could lay their hands upon, and all regardless of the lightning which had slain their leader, and the thunder peals which mingled with the hammering in of the outer doors. I bore with me my dear love, still lying in that death-like swoon; while Indian Jos stooped and picked up the unrecognisable carcase of his commander.

"I cannot leave my master behind," he muttered hoarsely, as if apologising for this unwonted display of humanity.

"There is nothing to catch alight here—all stone-work," said Gabrial, with a heavy sigh, as he took his farewell glance round the church. Then he turned in behind the high altar, with us all following after him.

For finding his way out of a trap, or into an enemy's camp, there was no one amongst the pirates who held a higher reputation than the bald-headed Gabrial Peas; so that when he said that he had discovered the way out of our present dilemma none of us ever had the least doubt but what he would lead us out safely. Therefore we all followed him blindly, as he plunged into a dark passage and led the way down a number of stone steps into the cold vaults below the church.

I saw many strange sights as we went along, and in some of the chambers instruments of torture so barbarous and refined in their cruelty that I marvelled how men could be so devilish, all under the garb of religion. Indeed, as I took notice of these fiendish inventions, I thought better of my ruthless comrades, who were so rude in their modes of extorting secrets from their prisoners. A prisoner of the holy Church at Panama could be made to live weeks of hellish torment, whereas their troubles when they fell amongst us were ended in a day at most. Even the wild savages were simpletons in the art of torture compared to these holy fathers.

I felt glad that I saw these intricate machines before we came to the victims of Gabrial Peas, for I might have been shocked otherwise; as it was, I only hurried past the dead bodies of the bishop and his flock with a slight shudder. They had met their fate quickly, which was more than they would have served out to us, had we fallen into their remorseless clutches.

Yes, Gabrial Peas had done his work thoroughly while he was about it; he must have crept after his victims noiselessly and slain them one by one in the semi-darkness, for the vaults were lighted dimly with oil lamps. We stumbled over a nun or a monk as we passed along at irregular stages, until at last, after traversing nearly a mile of caverns, we saw the body of the bishop, who had gone first, lying across the doorway, which led us out to freedom.

We were outside the city walls, and emerged from a vegetation-covered cavern in the heart of the woods.

The tempest was still raging about us as we blocked up this passage with stones, and crept away as quietly as we could towards the hill from which we had first seen the city.

It was a wild storm, which tossed the foliage about and broke down trees, drenching us to the skin as we wandered along, disorganized and miserable; for Quassatta had recovered her senses now, and clung to my arm, while her mother, in her male disguise, kept sullenly beside us.

Thus we gained the hill as night fell, and all lay down on the wet soil to wait for morning, so that we might continue our retreat.

XXXVI

The Return to Porto Bello

I know not how I came to forget poor old Martin during this retreat, but so I did, until he joined our party during the night, making his escape from the city and tracking us out to the heights, where we lay all shivering together, for the rain continued to pour heavily upon us until long after midnight.

Next morning we held a consultation and buried that blackened body, which looked more like a half-consumed tree-trunk than a mortal man. Features and form were marred and obliterated, so that one might well have passed it for a decayed log, for all moisture had been scorched out of it, and it was light as cork as we lifted it up and placed it in the hole we had dug.

Penelope watched the corpse as long as it was uncovered with a half-doubtful, half-gloating regard.

"Art sure that this thing is King Death, Humphrey Bolin?" she asked me, touching it with her boot as it lay on the ground. "Art sure that the demon has not left something to deceive us, while he has only gone away in order to delude us into a false security, so that he may surprise us when least expecting him?"

"I wish I could think this, queen," replied Jos gruffly.

"Did you see him fall, Jos?—did you, Humphrey? did you, Gabrial, and you, Sambo? For it was so quick that it might have been a trick."

"Alas! there was no trick about that annihilation; we saw him struck and fall while still the lightning blazed."

"I wish I could be quite certain," said Penelope, with a deep sigh, as she turned away after another close scrutiny of the shapeless object. "Hide it from me forever! cover it up, and stamp the earth down upon it firmly, so that it may not rise again to torment me!"

She might have known that it was Alsander had she looked at Martin, who would not go near it, but crouched with his wet head hidden amid Quassatta's drenched skirts, all of a tremble, with his old horror, as if he could see more than we could hovering about the remains."

After we had buried our king, the men set to voting who should be appointed as our leader. I cast in my vote for Indian Jos as the most capable man, but they fixed upon me to fill Alsander's place, with Jos as the next in command. Penelope they recognised as the queen, whose rights would be acknowledged as soon as we reached the island; but until then I was to be responsible for their guidance.

Then we all discussed what we should do. Jos and a few of the others were for making another descent upon the city, and providing ourselves with provisions for the journey; but the majority set their faces against this. They were dispirited and tired of fighting, and wanted to get home again as quickly as possible; so that they carried the day. And after making a couple of litters for Penelope and Quassatta, we turned our backs on Panama and made off towards Porto Bello.

Penelope did not speak to her daughter, but showed her unnatural hatred in her silence—a condition of affairs which poor Quassatta seemed accustomed to, for she took her place quietly, and lay down on her litter to mourn for her father, who, with all his faults, had been tender always to her. Poor girl! I could not console her for her loss, except by looks and attentions, so I left her alone to battle with her own grief.

It took us eight days to get over that neck of land—eight days of horrible privations which I cannot even now think about without a shudder; through those awful swamps, ten times more dangerous than before, from the rains which had fallen, with hardly a bite to eat, and only poisonous water to drink; for few of us had firearms, and the game was difficult to catch; while all along we were harried by the Indians, who sent showers of arrows amongst us from the covers, thinning us out hourly, without even giving us a chance to retaliate.

Sometimes we killed a python or an unwary alligator, the flesh of which we divided amongst us, the pangs of hunger overcoming our disgust.

At last we sighted our fleet, and staggered down to the shores— scarcely three hundred famishing and fever-stricken men, leaving over five hundred unburied men lining the way which we had come so wearily.

What a drag those last few miles were to us, as we tightened our belts round our empty stomachs, each one feeling as if he were heavily ironed on arms and legs. Many had fallen with that frightful swamp vomit, and expired even as we crawled past them. Indian Jos and Gabrial Peas held out the best, but even they were feeble and pluckless; so that had the Spaniards overtaken us, they might have done with us as they liked.

Penelope and Quassatta were carried on board the *Vigo*, powerless to stand upright. Brave Quassatta! how patiently she had lain enduring that hunger and those pestilent exhalations! She now looked old and worn, with great hollow eyes and pale cheeks, over which hung the matted golden hair, all uncared-for.

When our companions saw us again in our sorry plight, and heard of our disasters, they at once hailed me as chief, and agreed with us to up anchors and away as soon as possible.

Having too many ships for the number of men left, they at once fixed upon the best sailors, and fired the others, after emptying them of their cargoes, the great but ponderous galleons being the first condemned. Therefore, after gathering together our small fleet of twenty laden vessels, the rest were set ablaze outside the harbour.

A glorious sight these great ships made as they swiftly caught fire and burned down to the water's edge,—a pleasant sight to the hating citizens, who knew that the expedition to Panama had failed, and that we were leaving them at last; thus they went about cursing us under their breaths, but helping us officiously, so as to hasten our departure.

We divided our company over the fleet: I, with Jos, Peas, Sambo, Penelope and Quassatta, also about a dozen of the sick pirates, were carried on board our old ship *Vigo*, Martin coming with us, a very dejected and lanky animal. Where Jack Howard and the other Plymouth lads had been taken I was too sickly at the time to inquire, as all I wanted was to lie down and rest.

So we sailed from Porto Bello, with treasure enough to satisfy the wildest dreams of the survivors, should they ever reach home.

XXXVII

Humphrey Ends His Journal

The first day we made little progress, for the wind was light, and before the morning of the second day, failed us altogether, leaving us sweltering upon that Caribbean Ocean for six or eight hours. Then all at once the calm was broken up by a sudden and furious gale, which gave us no time to prepare, but tore our flapping sails from the yards, along with the topmasts, and sent us driving over a boiling ocean nearly dismantled.

Several of our vessels ran foul of each other and went down with all hands on board, and as darkness fell upon us we could see the others beating away with their broken masts and the white waves lashing over them, while we tried our best to give them plenty of sea room, as we ran with the wind.

That boisterous hurricane did those who were sick and languid good, for it woke us out of our lethargy, and sent the blood coursing once more swiftly through our veins. Indian Jos, after gulping down some raw spirits, once again took command of the vessel, and with his cool head and sharp eyes kept us clear of our consorts.

All night long the storm raged with unabated fury, driving us seawards and towards the south; and when morning broke we were still tossing up and down those great seething mountains, with that savage blast behind, and not a sight of the other ships to be seen. They had either sunk or fallen far behind, for, as I have said, the *Vigo* was one of the swiftest, and heavily laden as she was, she could still walk through the waters.

Towards evening the gale left us as suddenly as it had come; and then, with a scarlet sun going down amidst torn-up clouds of orange, purple, and gold, with grass-green patches of clear sky behind, we rocked once again upon the tumbling ocean.

Next day was blazing hot and calm, and our fever came back with tenfold force. They brought us up to the deck, and spread awnings over us; and so we lay, without the power to lift a hand to our mouths, or able hardly to speak.

I had Quassatta beside me and the dog Martin, who fondly licked our clasped hands and faces as we lay on our backs speechless and helpless. It did not feel so hard a matter to die as I thought it would be, since I knew her to be destined for me, now that I had this fever. Her mother, Penelope, lay a little way off, but without looking at us or moving.

Another day, and the wind freshened, and we felt a little better and more hopeful. Then again it would die away, and we would be laid prostrate again; and so on we floated, getting better and bad again, with never a sign of the ships whom we had parted from.

Our trouble also was infectious and spread rapidly amongst our brother pirates, until no healthy man was left amongst them to help us or to guide the ship on her course. There we all lay about, eating when we could crawl towards the stores, and fasting when we were not able to move, an accursed and a doomed crew.

Day after day passed, while the *Vigo* drifted about as the wind blew, or lay rotting on the still ocean when it fell calm.

As the sickness advanced in its different stages, some died through pure exhaustion and lay amongst the hardly living, livid and decomposing, and filling our nostrils with deadly fumes, so that those who had not lost their senses, longed with disgust for death.

Others went raving mad and relieved us of their company by jumping overboard. Sambo went that road on the fourth day.

Indian Jos and Gabrial Peas died hard, as might be expected, muttering and cursing to the last, during the intervals that they were not raving about old murders or counting up their gains. However Penelope, Quassatta, and myself bore up in this lazaret I know not. Perhaps our youth was in our favour, while her story was true, and she could not die by natural means. My poor love lay quiet and passive beside me, slowly wasting away, while the dog tried, in his own dumb fashion, to comfort us.

Through the hot days and the cool nights we existed somehow. It was during the nights sometimes that I was able, with hard exertions, to crawl down to the cabin and bring up some provisions, and draw away the putrid corpses as far from us as possible to the fore part of the deck, where, when the wind blew, we were able to get rid of the smells. I knew not where we were drifting to, or if we would ever see land, and I hardly cared; for now we three were the only ones who drew breath, with that awful company of dead men in front of us, from whose bodies at nights blue burning gases issued and hung like their ghosts over them.

One night Penelope went raving mad, and, after several efforts, got up to her feet, imagining that she was in a fight, swinging her arms about weakly and breaking out with faint screams of subdued fury. After that paroxysm she sank backwards again, and began to rave about her evil past.

"Spare my father? Why should I spare him who gave me no name? who deserted my mother, and left us to starve, with all his riches? No, Alsander; I shall fool him out of every penny, make an outcast of him, as he made my mother, and kill him as I would my other enemies— me, Penelope Ancrum, who should have been Penelope Fenton, and an aristocrat. Ah! quick, Jos, with your knife, for the volcano is rising, and we shall be late. Quick! quick! help me to dress, Alsander. Now, now, I am what you have ordered me to be—Sir John, and the old fool, my father, has finished up his magic.

I listened languidly to these ravings, reading the meaning of them easily, and recalling that mountain where I had first seen Quassatta. I listened without any horror, for I was past all that now.

"I am wearied of this folly, Alsander; you have punished me enough for what you saw. Do with your daughter and the boy as you please, only let me go away. No; I must stay and see it out, playing the character of the man I hate next to my tyrant. Ah! Alsander, you will suffer for this yet. My daughter, too, how I hate her, for coming between me and the only sweetness which I have had for years! If he would but take his eye from me for an hour, I could kill her; but he holds me firm, and I must wait."

As she raved the yellow moon rose over the taffrail and lighted up the deck, with its ghastly company. It shone on my dear love, so thin and white, and on the wasted features and glaring black eyes of the witch.

"He is not dead; nothing could kill him, not even God's lightning. It is a trick of the vampires to deceive me. He will come again and hold me as he did before, making all my wishes vain. Ah! I shall never be free! never be free! never be free!"

*"For Jack lies 'mongst the seaweed in the deep and silent sea,
And I am waiting on the shore, with nothing left for me.'"*

She raised herself up to her knees and rocked herself to and fro as she began wailing out that awful dirge under the pale moonlight, while

I listened to it over and over again, without surcease, for hours, lacking the power to rise; until I seemed to see the spirits of countless victims crowding up and filling the deck—spirits of gentlemen and dames, and ordinary seamen, who swarmed up the shrouds and took possession of the ship, working it silently and guiding it upon its course.

My brain throbbed with fury and my heart grew faint as I listened to that dirge and watched these ghostly mariners. Then Quassatta faded from my eyes, with the witch and Martin, and I remembered no more.

EPILOGUE

De House of one William Shakespeare, Stratford-on-Abon.
Time, April 22nd, 1616.

I

Sir Humphrey Bolin's Adventures

Fill your pipes and glasses, friends all; and you, Sir Humphrey Bolin, now that we have a quiet night before us, let us hear the rest of that strange history of adventures, the rich fulfilment of which made you a worshipful knight, whereas I still remain plain Will Shakespeare; yes, friend, you are the greater man, after all, for while I have been able only to amuse our wise king, you have enriched his treasury."

It was a sober company of middle-aged men who had gathered on this evening before the last birthday of their host—neighbours all, with the exception of the guest, Sir Humphrey Bolin, the newly made knight, who, for his great services of bringing rich treasure to the King, had been so highly honoured.

There were present under this roof-tree three old schoolfellows of the bard, now prosperous burghers, to whom his plays were of little account, yet who liked him for himself, and respected him for his income; solid-faced yeomen, who occupied their accustomed seats as an institution not to be set aside, good listeners all of them, who spake little, looked wise, and smoked prodigiously.

William Shakespeare, world-worn and listless, with heavy lines on his brow and grey hairs in his beard, he has come home to Anne to be nursed up, for he has long felt weary of the Town, and his heart troubles him. The doctor tells him that he has lived too hard, and that he must be very careful now of any undue excitement, for it might stop at any moment, even while he sits in his chair. Therefore he does not smoke, although he encourages it in his friends.

Anne Hathaway has gone to her bed, after clearing away the supper dishes and washing up. She is of a homely turn, and does not like the smell of this new weed; but she is indulgent to her successful husband, and makes him as comfortable as she can.

Sir Humphrey Bolin, our old Armada hero, looks nearly as aged and haggard as his friend and host the poet. He has come to see him after an absence from England of eleven years, and having spent the day with him relating his own and his son's adventures abroad, now sits down to complete his story:—

"Yes, his wise and prudent majesty King James has honoured me with a title and a comfortable pension to support it; but I have had to work and suffer hard enough for it, as you shall hear.

"I told you how we took the ship *Vigo* into the pirate harbour of Laverna. Well, my son and the rest of the men had gone into the town to enjoy themselves, while my boatswain and I stayed in the cabin, to talk over matters and consider how best we were to get out of the scrape in which we were run.

"We were still considering things over a glass of rum, when suddenly we were surrounded by a score or so of pirates and hurried ashore; where, after spending a night in prison, we were chained to a gang of other prisoners and driven up the country to a plantation, where we were set to work in the fields with the other slaves. I' faith that was a life which, although his gracious majesty promised me a dukedom, I would not go through again willingly, not for six months at most.

"From the pirate city of Laverna to the plantation was long distance and through many dangers; indeed, our destination lay at the other side of the island, where, from the fields cultivated on the tops of the cliffs, we could look at times over the ocean which fretted itself against the jagged edges of reefs, at the foot of lofty and unscaleable, wall-like precipices, where one might watch the pirate skirmishers dashing about outside, with never a chance of getting to them.

"Tom Blunt and I consoled each other as well as we could under these servile circumstances. We were both old comrades and true sailors, therefore not easily daunted by misfortune. My son I often thought upon, and prayed that the Lord would give him and the other lads easier lines than those which had fallen to their captain and boatswain. So, while we laboured with the other starved, half-naked wretches, and bore our stripes with patience, we looked warily out for a chance to escape.

"Once we got into trouble through taking the part of some broken-down women against our half-caste overseers. Then we knew that they had worse punishments for slaves than field labour, for they set us to work under the ground, in a mine where they had discovered gold. Here we burrowed for over four months, without seeing the blessed light of day, or having a chance together in order to plan out our escape.

"At last, with the confinement, close air, and hard usage, Tom Blunt fell so sick that, fearing to lose our services, they let us both up once again to the surface, when we appeared more like earth-stained skeletons than human beings. So gaunt and ramshackey was my poor friend Tom that I could have wept to see so fine a fellow reduced to such straits, only that I saw he was weeping over my own state. Then I knew that to his eyes I looked as bad as he did to me. It is strange how a fat or a thin man never can be made to know his own fatness or leaness, Master Shakespeare."

"Unless he becomes as I am at present—somewhat dropsical; then he feels his own superfluous fat like someone else's luggage on him—a decided burden," replied William Shakespeare from his armchair. "Go on with your tale, worthy knight."

"They, our coloured slave-drivers, had no great desire to bury us too soon, so they left us alone for a day or two to recover our wasted strength; and in that idleness we hatched our plot, which was to keep up this illness as long as possible and then slip back to Laverna, and from there steal a boat and put to sea. For where we were then situated we had no chance at all of getting down to the sea, the precipices were so overhanging and smooth.

"One night a passing ship went on the reefs during a storm, and we could only watch her breaking up and her crew drown without a chance of saving them, as we stood above. That decided Tom Blunt and myself to try the overland route.

"Another thing also decided us on this course. Amongst the slaves were three Englishmen, who, like ourselves, had been trapped from their ships by the pirates. They informed us that while we had been in the mines they had heard a great expedition had taken place amongst the pirates, and that they had left the island almost unprotected. This was a lucky opportunity, which we all resolved to take advantage of.

"Therefore, after waiting patiently and feigning to be worse than we were, we found a chance to liberate the three Englishmen, and together we five made off one dark night, provided with such weapons as we could steal from our drivers, who were at the time holding a feast in honour of some of their saints, for mighty rigid Catholics these half-breds were when the memory of a saint had to be honoured by getting drunk. And now that their employers were absent, it was astonishing how many saints' days they managed to remember. Not that we ever objected to these holy feast days, for while they were carousing they did not trouble themselves to beat us too much. It was the fast days that we poor slaves dreaded the most.

"Well, one dark night we slipped out from the plantation sheds, free men, with our chains lying filed through behind us, and so lost ourselves in the woods and mountains which lay between us and the city by the lake.

"A long and a dismal march that was before we reached our destination. They followed us with blood-hounds, and many an hour we had to lie in swamps, amongst the reeds, up to the neck in mire, with our souls quaking for fear of the bloodthirsty beasts and the alligators, in whose lairs we were.

"At last we traversed the thousand dangers and discomforts in our way and reached the plains behind the city, with that cliff highway which was so carefully guarded day and night, yet up which we must pass.

"This was the most difficult portion of our undertaking; and as we lay concealed amongst the young maize, watching these parapets with their sentinels, many were the plans discussed and rejected as idle with us. So day after day passed, while we lived on that green maize and waited on the chance which at last came.

"One morning I saw a man come from the lower tunnel and walk along the road towards where we lay concealed. As he drew nearer I saw that he had a wooden leg, and in a little time made out the well-known features of my old friend and mate, William Giles.

"When I saw who it was, I no longer hesitated to reveal myself, but only waited until he was near enough. Then I stepped over to the road and hailed him.

"'Ahoy! Bill Giles; whither away?'

"'Captain Humphrey Bolin, as I am a badgered Christian!'

"He was very soon amongst us, hearing our story and telling his own troubles as captain of the female guardians.

"It ain't life for any man, far less one with a wooden leg, up there with the she devils, Humphrey, old friend; so if ye are going to sea, I'll join ye right heartily."

"From all he told me I reckon that he had as hard a fate as commander of the fortress as we had down the mines, for the pirates had been away over ten months, and the deserted females were getting rampageous, so that no man, however old or maimed, was safe amongst them.

"'I'll bring you down a razor and some female toggery, for you will never get past them as men. Lord, help us! they are ten thousand times worse nor a convent or seminary for young ladies. The sight of a stranger man would drive them stark mad in their present condition.'

"Thus it was arranged; and that night we were smuggled into the city as five old negress witches, come to tell the jades their fortune.

"This device took wonderfully well; for they were all superstitious, and as we gave them good fortunes, which William translated for us, we were treated with great respect and hospitality.

"At last we managed, through the help of William Giles, to gather provisions enough together and store a small pinnace; then one night we gave the wanton hussies leg-bail, and before morning dawned, we were out of sight of the island, making tracks for England.

"For three days we sailed without interruption; but on the fourth day we sighted the wreck of a galleon lying directly in our way, with only the stumps of her masts standing up, but otherwise looking right enough.

"When we got up to it, we discovered a melancholy company aboard, of spectres rather than men,—our old friends and shipmates, some of them, with about a dozen of the pirates.

"They had all been stricken with fever; and although now over that, were too weak to resist us when we boarded. So that we took possession of the treasure-ship, and finding some spare spars aboard, set to work rigging her up, using our pinnace also for that purpose; so that in a day or two we had her shipshape once more, and the pirates in chains as our prisoners. Jack Howard, whom we found alive, with Peter Claybroke, Roland Pring, and most of my other men, I doctored up, after I had heard the story of their adventures, until they were able to go about their duties. Then we set fire to the pinnace, and made for England.

"That was the *St. Catherine*, the first treasure-ship that I made a free gift of to his gracious majesty, and who, for the gift, made me admiral of the fleet with which I sailed again to Laverna, and after my son, as you have heard already. For the sake of the Plymouth boys who had been forced into piracy, I gave my prisoners their liberty before we reached England, with a boat and sufficient money to carry them to France; for our king is inquisitive, and I wanted no witnesses to implicate the Devon boys. Whether these pirates reached the shore or were picked up at sea and made slaves of I know not, as I heard no more of them."

II

The Last

The survivors of the *St. Catherine* could tell me nothing about my son Humphrey or the ship in which he sailed—the *Vigo*—so that, after some months' delay, I sailed once more from England, with my little fleet of volunteers, on a double mission: to discover, if possible, the fate of my son, and to exterminate the nest of pirates.

"As you know, Providence aided me in both these efforts beyond my expectations, for on the tenth week, being driven out of our course by a storm, we picked up the bamboo tube which contained the diary of young Humphrey's strange adventures, which was addressed to you, Master William, and which lies now before you; and the same Providence led us to the island, after many weeks, whereon the boy and his sweetheart had lived for months, without hardly a hope of ever seeing home again.

"That was a joyful meeting, I can tell you, between us so long parted; and I was rarely pleased with the daughter and grandson which he presented to me, for they had married according to the laws of the savages amongst whom they lived. So that I was too late to object, even if I had felt inclined, which I did not.

"The old *Vigo* we found could be made seaworthy with a little work, so we docked her and sorted her up, and brought her away with us.

"The taking of Laverna was not a hard matter, for the women were heartily sick of living so long by themselves, and gladly welcomed us; but it was a harder matter to keep my lads in order afterwards. However, I settled the matter by reading the church service over as many of them as were single men, and promising the others to bring out husbands for them as soon as I could. So we sailed again for England, laden with gold and jewels, every man-Jack of them who could do so taking home a foreign wife.

"King James was not over-generous with the bounty money; however, he gave each of the lads enough to live on comfortably, and all who liked to serve, honourable posts ashore.

"My next voyage out I redeemed my promise to the ladies by taking out a colony of lusty young men, many of whom settled with their wives on the island, which now belongs to England; and for the treasures that I brought back after three more voyages I was created a knight with enough to support the dignity.

"As for Humphrey and his pretty wife, Quassatta, they keep house for me at Plymouth, and are busy filling it with young Bolins as fast as they reasonably can. The dog Martin also is there, as sedate as his father was before him. We are not over-rich, as you may suppose, but we need none of us fear the wolf, for, between us all, having good experience of the Scotch king's generosity on the receipt of my first gift, I took good care to smuggle a trifle from the other ventures before I reported them to his officers, for myself and friends. You see, Plymouth lies on the way from Laverna to London."

As Sir Humphrey Bolin finished his narration, with a roguish twinkle in his keen blue eyes, the clock struck midnight: Shakespeare's fifty-second birthday had arrived.

"Your good health, old friend William, and many happy birthdays may you live to see, and I to join you in."

"Thank ye, friends all. I trust that I may have better health when next St. George's Day comes round," returned Shakespeare. "Excuse me rising from my chair this morning, and Sir Humphrey Bolin, my old friend, thank you again for your story, which has interested and excited me greatly. If I live, I must make a play of your adventures, with the doings of that most glorious defeat of the Spanish Armada, and call it after your son's wife—'The daughter of death'—ah!——"

As the poet reached this part of his speech, he suddenly stopped with the exclamation, and fell forward upon the scroll in front of him.

> *"Thole hands, which you lo clapt, go now and wring,*
> *You* Britaines *braue; for done are* Shakespeare's *dayes."*

The End

A Note About the Author

Hume Nisbet (1849–1923) was a Scottish-Australian novelist and painter. Born James Hume Nisbet in Stirling, Scotland, he was educated by Rev. Dr. Culross and received artistic training from a young age. At 16, he traveled to Australia and spent the next seven years painting, writing, and sketching in such places as Tasmania, New Zealand, and the islands of the South Sea. After studying theatre under acclaimed actor Richard Stewart in Melbourne, Nisbet returned to London in 1872 to pursue a career in painting. Although he found some success as art master of Edinburgh's Watt Institution and School of Art, producing such well-regarded paintings as "The Flying Dutchman" and "The Battle of Dunbar," Nisbet was more widely known for his extensive literary output. Nisbet published around two dozen novels and several poetry collections in his career, many of which were set in Australia. He is mostly remembered for his collections of ghost stories, including *Stories Weird and Wonderful* (1900) and *The Haunted Station and Other Stories* (1894).

A Note from the Publisher

Spanning many genres, from non-fiction essays to literature classics to children's books and lyric poetry, Mint Edition books showcase the master works of our time in a modern new package. The text is freshly typeset, is clean and easy to read, and features a new note about the author in each volume. Many books also include exclusive new introductory material. Every book boasts a striking new cover, which makes it as appropriate for collecting as it is for gift giving. Mint Edition books are only printed when a reader orders them, so natural resources are not wasted. We're proud that our books are never manufactured in excess and exist only in the exact quantity they need to be read and enjoyed.

bookfinity™

Discover more of your favorite classics with Bookfinity™.

- Track your reading with custom book lists.
- Get great book recommendations for your personalized Reader Type.
- Add reviews for your favorite books.
- AND MUCH MORE!

Visit **bookfinity.com** and take the fun Reader Type quiz to get started.

Enjoy our classic and modern companion pairings!

Printed in the USA
CPSIA information can be obtained
at www.ICGtesting.com
JSHW022325140824
68134JS00019B/1298